DEAN ING

FIREFIGHT 2000

BAEN
BOOKS

FIREFIGHT 2000

A Baen Books Original

Baen Publishing Enterprises
260 Fifth Avenue
New York, N.Y. 10001

First printing, June 1987
  Second printing, November 1987

ISBN: 0-671-65650-3

Cover art by Larry Elmore

ACKNOWLEDGMENTS

The following stories and articles originally appeared and are copyright as follows: "Fleas," *Destinies,* copyright 1979 by Dean Ing; "Manaspill," *The Magic May Return,* copyright 1981 by Dean Ing; "Malf," *Analog Annual,* copyright 1976 by the Conde Nast Publications Inc.; "Comes the Revolution," *The Future of Flight,* copyright 1985 by Leik Myrabo and Dean Ing; "Liquid Assets," *Destinies,* copyright 1979 by Dean Ing; "Lost in Translation," *Far Frontiers,* copyright 1985 by Dean Ing; "Evileye," *Far Frontiers,* copyright 1985 by Dean Ing; "Vehicles for Future Wars," *Destinies* copyright 1979 by Dean Ing; "Vital Signs," *Destinies* copyright 1980 by Dean Ing.

Printed in the United States of America

Distributed by
SIMON & SCHUSTER
1230 Avenue of the Americas
New York, N.Y. 10020

For Steve, David, Fran and Mark,
for all those possible tomorrows

CONTENTS

PREFACE 1
FLEAS 5
FIREFIGHT 2000 11
MANASPILL 23
MALF 69
COMES THE REVOLUTION 99
LIQUID ASSETS 109
LOST IN TRANSLATION 129
EVILEYE 155
VEHICLES FOR FUTURE WARS 167
VITAL SIGNS 199

PREFACE

When historians of the 22nd century are cudgeling their brains (and each other; God, I hope I can sit in!) to characterize the 20th century, their problem won't be lack of data. It will be the very diversity of that data. But what will they conclude from the structures of Gropius and Wright; the popularity of punk rock and Stravinsky; armies supplied with bayonets and ballistic missiles; citizens enjoying Volkswagens and Ferraris, fantasy fiction and epic nonfiction; cities drawing power from coal and nuclear plants?

I'm betting they will note the bewildering change of pace in each arena and will then ignore it, looking for something more arcane. But it's that change of pace, that variety of choice, that separates us most profoundly from earlier cultures! Look: people everywhere have *always* sought variety—not this *or* that, but this *and* that. There may be no better way to differentiate the free West from competing systems than to note the changes of pace available to the citizens of each.

Not that everybody likes to have the pace changed: I know some folks who like only the foxtrot, white bread, and Ford V-8's. Well, those things are all reliable, and tomorrow isn't. I understand and sympathize, but tomorrow is where we're headed, and all indications are

1

that it's going to be more full of variety, changes of pace, than today.

That goes for fiction as well as fact. Even the most hardbitten of hard-science fiction scribblers can opt for a change of pace to fantasy. It's a different set of mental gymnastics, and it keeps our sense of wonder from getting flabby.

On the other hand, a consultant helped me flesh out the background for one of the most far-out tales in this collection, then asked me why I considered it science fiction. "It wouldn't surprise me if it really happened," she said; "some marine invertebrates aren't too shabby in the brains department." It was her view that, if it's likely to happen, it ain't sci-fi. So then we got into an argument about the difference between SF and fantasy, and I cried, and she hit me. . . . Oh all right, so I added a bit of fantasy to our exchange. The point is, sometimes we reach into a sea of fiction and grasp a tentacle of what feels like fact. It can be unsettling. So why does it elate me? Maybe I *like* to be unsettled a bit. I suspect my readers like it too. God knows, anybody who likes being unsettled can have loads of whoopee in times like these!

But some of it is very serious whoopee. Take the title piece, for instance, which reports on the findings of a recent thinktank session on future weapons. I'd be disingenuous if I denied we had fun, but the purpose of that seminar was ultimately to figure out what an infantryman will mean by "small arms" in the next century. The diversity among members of that seminar was marvelous to behold. Well, of course: the thinktank people wanted it that way, knowing that variety is the spice of life, the source of strife, and a great provocation toward new ideas. Our conclusions weren't intended as fiction, but you never know. Tune in twenty years from now.

For better or worse, the collection you're holding may be a metaphor of tomorrow: terror and hope, right guesses and wrong ones, high tech and thatched cottages. Nothing wrong with a thatched cottage if you want one; the nice thing about tomorrow is, we can bring the best parts of yesterday along with us. Bearing that in mind, we can get useful tips not only from hard engineering looks at our near future, but also from playful peeks into our distant past. Just don't start complaining when you find that each piece in this book is a change of pace from the piece ahead of it, yet you keep finding echoes of previous scenarios in the next ones. That's the way the book works.

That's the way the *world* works. May as well enjoy it. . . .

FLEAS

The quarry swam more for show than efficiency because he knew that Maels was quietly watching. Down the "Y" pool, then back, seeming to ignore the bearded older man as Maels, in turn, seemed to ignore the young swimmer.

Maels reviewed each datum: brachycephalic; under thirty years old; body mass well over the forty kilo minimum; skin tone excellent; plenty of hair. And unless Maels was deceived—he rarely was—the quarry offered subtle homosexual nuances which might simplify his isolation.

Maels smiled to himself and delivered an enormous body-stretching yawn that advertised his formidable biceps, triceps, laterals. The quarry approached swimming; symbolically, thought Maels, a breast stroke. Great.

Maels made a pedal gesture. A joke, really, since the gay world had developed the language of the foot for venues more crowded than this. The quarry bared small even teeth in his innocent approval. Better.

"I could watch you all evening," Maels rumbled, and added the necessary lie: "You swim exquisitely."

"But I can't go on forever," the youth replied in tones that were, as Maels had expected, distinctly unbutchy. "I feel like relaxing." Treading water, he smiled a plea for precise communication. Perfect.

"You can with me," Maels said, and swept himself up with an ageless grace. He towered, masculine and commanding, above the suppliant swimmer. A strong grin split his beard as Maels turned toward the dressing room. He left the building quickly, then waited.

Invisible in a shop alcove, Maels enjoyed the quarry's anxious glances from the elevated platform of the "Y" steps. Maels strolled out then into the pale light of the streetlamp and the quarry, seeing him, danced down the steps toward his small destiny.

Later, kneeling beneath tree shadows as his fingers probed the dying throat-pulse. Maels thought: *All according to formula, to the old books*. Really no problem when you have the physical strength of a mature anaconda. Hell, it wasn't even much fun for an adult predator. At this introspection Maels chuckled. Adult for several normal life spans, once he had discovered he was a feeder. With such long practice, self-assurance in the hunt took spice from the kill. Still probing the carotid artery, Maels thought: *Uncertainty is the oregano of pursuit*. He might work that into a scholarly paper one day.

Then Maels fed.

It was a simple matter for Maels to feed in a context that police could classify as psychosexual. Inaccurate, but—perhaps not wholly. Survival and sexuality: his gloved hands guiding scalpel and bone saw almost by rote, Maels composed the sort of trivia his sophomores would love.

Research confirms the grimoires'
Ancient sanity;
Predation brings unending lust—
An old causality.

The hypothalamus, behind armoring bone, was crucial. Maels took it all. Adrenal medulla, a strip of mucous membrane, smear of marrow. Chewing reflectively, Maels thought: *Eye of newt, toe of frog. A long way from the real guts of immortality*.

He had known a feeder, an academic like himself, who read so much Huxley he tried to substitute carp viscera for the only true prescription. Silly bastard had nearly died before Maels, soft-hearted Karl Maels, brought him the bloody requisites in a baggie. At some personal sacrifice, too: the girl had been Maels' best graduate student in a century.

Sacrifice, he reflected, was one criterion largely ignored by the Darwinists. They prattled so easily of a species as though the single individual mattered little. But if you are one of a rare subspecies, feeders whose members were few and camouflaged? A back-burner question, he decided. He could let it simmer. With admirable economy of motion Maels further vandalized the kill to disguise his motive. Minutes later he was in his rented sedan, en route back to his small college town. Maels felt virile, coruscating, efficient. The seasonal special feeding, in its way, had been a thing of beauty.

Ninety-three days later, Maels drove his own coupe to another city and left it, before dusk, in a parking lot. He was overdue to feed but thought it prudent to avoid patterns. The city, the time of day, even the moon phase should be different. If the feeding itself no longer gave joy, at least he might savor its planning.

He adjusted his turtleneck and inspected the result in a storefront reflection. Maybe he would shave the beard soon. It was a damned nuisance anyhow when he fed.

Maels recalled a student's sly criticism the day before: when was a beard a symbiote, and when parasitic? Maels had turned the question to good classroom use, sparking a lively debate on the definitions of parasite and predator. Maels cited the German Brown trout, predator on its own kind yet not a parasite. The flea was judged parasitic; for the hundredth time Maels was forced to smile through his irritation at misquotation of elegant Dean Swift:

> So, naturalists observe, a flea
> Hath smaller fleas that on him prey.
> And these have smaller fleas to bite 'em,
> And so proceed, *ad infinitum*.

Which only prompted the class to define parasites in terms of size. Maels accepted their judgment; trout and feeder preyed on smaller fry, predators by spurious definition.

Comfortably chewing on the trout analogy, Maels cruised the singles bars through their happy hour. He nurtured his image carefully, a massive gentle bear of a man with graceful hands and self-deprecating wit. At the third spa he maneuvered, on his right, a pliable file clerk with adenoids and lovely skin. She pronounced herself simply thrilled to meet a real, self-admitted traveling salesman. Maels found her rather too plump for ideal quarry, but no matter: she would do. He felt pale stirrings of excitement and honed them, titillated them. Perhaps he would grant her a sexual encounter before he fed. Perhaps.

Then Karl Maels glanced into the mirror behind the bar, and the pliant clerk was instantly and brutally forgotten. He sipped bourbon and his mouth was drier than before as he focused on the girl who had captured the seat to his left.

It was not merely that she was lovely. By all criteria she was also flawless quarry. Maels fought down his excitement and smiled his best smile. "I kept your place," he said with just enough pretended gruffness.

"Am I all that predictable?" Her voice seemed to vibrate in his belly. He estimated her age at twenty-two but, sharing her frank gaze, elevated that estimate a bit.

Maels wisely denied her predictability, asked where she found earrings of beaten gold aspen leaves, and learned that she was from Pueblo, Colorado. To obtain a small commitment he presently said, "The body is a duty, and duty calls. Will you keep my place?"

The long natural lashes barely flickered, the chin rose and dropped a minute fraction. Maels made his needless round-trip to the men's room, but hesitated on his return. He saw the girl speak a bit crossly to a tall young man who would otherwise have taken Mael's seat. Maels assessed her fine strong calves, the fashionable wedge heels cupping voluptuous high insteps. His palms were sweating.

Maels waited until the younger man had turned away, then reclaimed his seat. After two more drinks he had her name, Barbara, and her weakness, seafood; and knew that he could claim his quarry as well.

He did not need to feign his easy laugh in saying, "Well, now you've made me ravenous. I believe there's a legendary crab cocktail at a restaurant near the wharf. Feel like exploring?"

She did. It was only a short walk, he explained, silently adding that a taxi was risky. Barbara happily took his arm. The subtle elbow pressures, her matching of his stride, the increasing frequency of hip contact were clear messages of desire. When Maels drew her toward the fortuitous schoolyard, Barbara purred in pleasure. Moments later, their coats an improvised couch, they knelt in mutual exploration, then lay together in the silent mottled shadows.

He entered her cautiously, then profoundly, gazing down at his quarry with commingled lust and hunger. Smiling, she undid her blouse to reveal perfect breasts. She moved against him gently and, with great deliberation, thrust his sweater up from the broad striated ribcage. Then she pressed erect nipples against his body. Maels cried out once.

When European gentlemen still wore rapiers, Maels had taken a blade in the shoulder. The memory flickered past him as her nipples, hypodermic-sharp, incredibly elongated, pierced him on lances of agony.

Skewered above her, Maels could not move. Indeed, he did not lose his functional virility, as the creature completed her own pleasure and then, grasping his arms, rolled him over without uncoupling. He felt tendons snap in his forearms but oddly the pain was distant. He could think clearly at first. Maels thought: *How easily she rends me*. She manipulated him as one might handle a brittle doll.

Maels felt a warm softening in his guts with a growing anaesthesia. Maels thought: *The creature is consuming me as I watch*.

Maels thought: *A new subspecies?* He wondered how often her kind must feed. *A very old subspecies?* He saw her smile.

Maels thought: *Is it possible that she feeds only on feeders? Does she read my thoughts?*

"Of course," she whispered, almost lovingly.

Some yards away, a tiny animal scrabbled in the leaves.

He thought at her: *". . .and so on,* ad infinitum. *I wonder what feeds on you . . ."*

FIREFIGHT 2000:

A REPORT ON ADVANCED SMALL ARMS CONCEPTS

Anyone who attends a future armament brainstorming session can expect some surprises. For me, the conference held at Battelle's Seattle center in January 1986 was no exception. One of my major surprises came when they said I could write about it. After all, an advanced concepts workshop is where you sow the seeds of preliminary designs. Odd as it may seem, these concepts aren't yet classified. You can expect that to change when some of these wild and woolly small arms systems germinate into the development stage.

Once upon a time it would've been a bit hifalutin' to talk about small arms as "systems." No more! To begin with, we have to expand our notions of what becomes part of a small arm. Is an infantryman's fighting suit a small arms system? If in doubt, we said "yes." We began by accepting an advanced combat rifle with caseless cartridges as a fact, no longer of special concern. Some of tomorrow's small arms will have innards as complicated as, say, today's cruise missile. A lot of that complication will be backup emergency subsystems; the armed services can't afford battle gear that works only part of the time. They also know that a man can only lug so much

11

hardware around, and that's why the U.S. ability to miniaturize its systems gives us a big advantage over the Eastern Bloc. Would you believe jet engines fired as rounds from a combat rifle? I'll get to those presently.

Our goal was to thrash out advanced concepts for the Army's Joint Services Small Arms Program (JSSAP). Battelle chose men from a variety of fields: its own labs, Army R & D centers, Texas University's railgun program, Los Alamos, Aberdeen, several other centers, and a few science fiction authors. Why science fiction? Because we spend lots of time peering at high-tech horizons. Some of us began as engineers and physicists; in my case, in preliminary design of rocket systems.

The steering committee wisely avoided holding a checkrein on our thinking. Once the ground rules were clear, they sprinkled us into three groups and hauled us back into plenary sessions for awhile every day to compare notes. By the end of this three-day skull-bump we had zeroed in on some small arms weapon systems that looked very likely—one in particular that embodied several subsystems proposed by each group. Just for fun, I'll tag some of those subsystems after first mentioning them, with "TAKE NOTE," and outline the full system last.

Each concept group focused on one of three broad fields: Target Acquisition, Energy Transmission/Storage, and Effects. By the end of the first day, each group was pumping out concepts that were hard to swallow on first bite. And yet, recent researches in very unlikely areas made some of the oddest notions seem more palatable. The Target Acquisition group was typical, beginning straightforwardly and adding some very advanced ideas.

How can targets—enemy troops and their assets—be identified quickly and differentiated from your own so that you know what to zap? Well, we can force the enemy's characteristics to give him away. We already use infrared (IR) and image enhancement scopes. We already have radar. How long before we combine IR, radar, and visual light into images that are displayed on a combat infantryman's helmet visor? The Air Force is already well on the way with its "Heads-Up Display" for fire control and navigation. We adapted the HUD to the battlefield. If it's stifling, we can air-condition it. If our man wants a zoom display, he can bloody well ask for it because his helmet computer will understand his spoken commands. TAKE NOTE.

Among our biggest problems in Vietnam were the mazes of tunnels dug by the enemy. With luck, skill, and deep-penetration bombs we cleared out some of those tunnels at great expense. Surely there must be some way to develop a more subtle weapon that will find the tunnels and then go inside after live targets. What, then; a robot?

Someone put previous researches together. After the work of Von Frisch with bees, scientists learned how to "talk" to them by using a dummy bee. Evidently, a worker bee's "language" is literally built in to its nervous system. In other labs, gene-splicing and restructured DNA show promise of modifying a bee's nervous system. Insects already have the best chemical detectors in the world, for mating and food-gathering. And bees have made hives in caves for a long, long time. Well?

The panel proposed an insect like a killer bee, bred for lethal sting and aggressiveness, and programmed to seek certain chemicals common to the enemy, but not to our own troops. It might avoid the smell of U.S. fatigues, while zeroing in on someone who smells of enemy rations. The bee would have a life span of a couple of weeks, perhaps less (workers have short life spans as it is). Drop a few packages of those sterile workers into a region honeycombed with enemy tunnels, and wait for your little live weapons to acquire targets in the tunnels. If you have pheromone sensors to track the bees from a distance, you can even locate the tunnel entrances—a great advantage in itself.

This "tailored hornet" concept seems less and less weird, the more we study it. We're not really making the insects do anything that they don't *already* do.

We're just nudging them to do it exclusively against the enemy.

A firefight can overwhelm the footsoldier with too much sound, light, odor, and touch. But if we encase him in full body armor (TAKE NOTE), he will need some way to use information he gets through his various sensors. For some years now, experimenters have been improving gadgetry that translates images into patterns across an area, like finger-taps. Sightless people wearing this equipment can walk down a street as if sighted, feeling painless taps in special patterns across their backs to warn of cars, curbs, and other people. It should be possible to improve this equipment so that a soldier could wear it as part of his battle dress. Will the information it adds be worth the trouble? It's still too early to tell.

Energy Transmission and Storage concepts ranged all the way from tiny rotary engines to beamed microwave power. Early in the next century, men may have to fight on the surface of the moon. They will need electrical power to run some of their systems. If our man is in deep shadow, he can't use solar power. Could he actually use an oxygen-breathing Wankel rotary engine to power a tiny generator on an airless planet? Sure he could; engine-driven torpedoes have carried their own oxygen supplies for many years, and Lord knows there's less back-pressure in a vacuum!

Other energy storage candidates include batteries, ultracapacitors, and even very small particle-bed nuclear power generators. The main problem is to devise a safe power of very high energy density and reasonable cost. Whatever you use, you don't want an enemy bullet to turn it into a bomb. A particle-bed reactor won't need refueling for a long time—but if it fails catastrophically, you won't care. A capacitor delivers a wallop of power, but must then be recharged. Small flywheels can store tremendous amounts of energy inside three-axis gimbaled mounts—but when that flywheel reaches the limit of its tensile strength, it is a frag grenade on your back. Superfilament materials are under development so that we can spin those flywheels a lot faster with safety, using them to run generators.

Smokeless powder and explosives are old-fashioned energy storage systems, though we seem to have reached a plateau there. But we may reach higher plateaus. The wizards of propellant chemistry say there are ways to make very dense propellant molecules. If we can cram twice as much energy into a small bazooka round, we might penetrate thicker armor or carry more rounds. We could also power very compact turbines capable of running small high-output generators, or of lifting heavy loads. TAKE NOTE.

The far-out chemical storage systems include metastable helium and antimatter. Metastable helium is a material that only exists in theory, proposed by Zmuidzinas of CalTech. If it can be processed and safely kept, we'll have an energy source that can be squirted into a chamber in very small amounts, yielding tremendous amounts of heat. It could power turbines, rockets, or projectile launchers, though nowhere near as powerful as antimatter.

Antimatter is the ultimate energy source. The stuff is out of the science-fiction bag and into the lab. Switzerland's CERN facility has kept antiprotons circulating in a huge storage ring for over three days. That's the first step toward creating and storing antihydrogen. The energy of antimatter, when it touches "normal" matter, is simply staggering. It doesn't just give up some tiny fraction of its mass of energy; it is *totally* converted to energy. Ounce for ounce it is thousands of times more powerful than an atomic weapon, but we should be able to control it like a tiny reactor. No, it won't be available within the next few years. Yes, they're working on it at Fermilab near Chicago. The soldier who carried an antimatter-powered beam weapon might have only a tenth of a gram of the stuff in its magnetic bottle, but if struck by an enemy bullet, that bottle would blow a very large crater. Solution: keep it inside your armor. That's the drawback of very high energy density: if your energy source fails catastrophically, you might not survive.

Power can be transmitted by laser or microwave; in fact, a small helicopter has already flown using electrical power beamed from a ground-based microwave source. TAKE NOTE. If we carry this concept to the infantry-man, we must design very compact receiving equipment and see that each man gets power on demand.

We studied too many devices to detail here: the turbine-driven "compulsator" which would power futuristic rail guns; devices that would literally burn battlefield trash (cut powder charges would make high-energy fuel!) to generate power; and fuel cells. We even studied a cold-gas launch system, in which compressed gas could mix with a small initial propellant charge. The result might have *no* IR emission, no flash, little dust signature and no net recoil. The projectile would contain a bazooka-like second stage, firing after the projectile was well on its way to the target. This launch system wouldn't be as compact as a big powder charge, but it might not give away the launcher position.

The Effects people focused on what small weapons can do to an enemy. A rifle-fired projectile carrying a bundle of tungsten wire can penetrate light armor to increase the lethality of a combat rifle round. The strobed vertigo munition, on the other hand, might not kill anyone. It wouldn't have to; it would emit a series of dazzling flashes pulsed at a frequency that is known to create temporary chaos in the human nervous system. We're talking about flashes of light so intense that, with eyes closed and hands across his face, the enemy would *clearly see the bones of his fingers*. Vertigo was our weasel-word for something like a grand mal seizure, and this weapon's effects might recur spontaneously in a victim. It's obvious that we would need to protect our own troops from its effects. TAKE NOTE.

The ramjet round is a simpler matter. A ramjet is a tube that gulps air and burns fuel like a blowtorch, exhausting it as other jet engines do. It has no moving

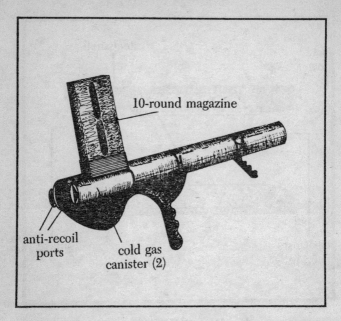

10-round magazine

anti-recoil
ports

cold gas
canister (2)

COLDGAS LAUNCHER, 40 mm. RECOILLESS,
AUTOMATIC FIRE.
(Note ambidextrous sights set for lefthand user.)

parts, but it must be moving nearly as fast as a .45 slug
before it develops much thrust. Its shape is very important. Now, instead of spraying kerosene into that
tube, we can line part of the tube with solid fuel. The
liner fuel needs very little oxidizer because air provides
oxygen. Some sort of tiny sabot will probably be needed
to force the ramjet tube down the rifled barrel. We
might build ramjets of, say, .35 caliber or less. Its sabot
would fall away as the round left the muzzle, allowing
the tube to swallow air, burning the liner fuel which
might be ignited by the air itself. The ramjet round boasts
two advantages: it lets us use oxygen from the air instead
of carrying all of it in the propellant; and it gives a flatter
trajectory, maintaining high velocity to the target.

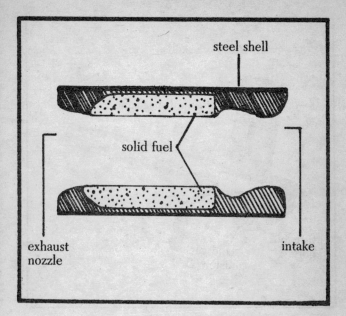

RAMJET ROUND, 8mm.

The lump gun would carry its own processor, slicing metal trash into needles to be fired. Turbine powered, it could fire clouds of flechettes by pressurized gas. This is a way to become almost independent of your fuel and ammo supplies!

Fire coordination sounds simple, but it will require that several dispersed weapons be coordinated to converge on a given target. TAKE NOTE. For this, we may have to develop very reliable burst-transmissions by laser or microwave during a firefight.

Personnel seekers include the "gnat" concept, a tiny guided missile no bigger than a hornet which seeks a source of motion, heat, or noise. The gnat might fly no faster than a sparrowhawk, but could carry and fire a slug at point of contact. The gnat would probably be a submunition, carried by the hundreds in a mortar round for dispersion by air. They'd also play hell with enemy helicopter blades. . . .

Finally, nuclear magnetic resonance (NMR) is a field of study that might help us detect any given substance, such as Russian gun-oil. Or NMR just might let us destroy very specific molecules using a maser beam. Hemoglobin, which carries oxygen in the blood, is a specific chemical. The maser might even be tuneable so that the victim develops mild cyanosis without lethal effects. Sometimes we want casualties, not kills. Think of a hostage situation. Enough said.

After chewing on schemes for acquisition, energy transmission, and effects for a few days, we put them together in various ways. A favorite systems concept from all this was the fighting pod, an outgrowth of today's experimental flying platform. It might be scarcely larger than a motorcycle sidecar. Our podman learns where the enemy is on his heads-up display from sensors, perhaps the laser IFF we mentioned. From the safety of this flyable, molded carbon-filament-and-kapton fighting pod that doubles as battle armor and is powered by a turbine or laser beam, he guides unmanned munition pods to picked spots by voice command and uses his heads-up display to find targets. He can range across and above the battlefield, calling for more munitions as necessary and serving as fire coordinator of several dedicated munition pods as he chooses, then turn to fresh targets.

This may seem like heresy to anyone who thinks of today's combat rifleman as a romantic figure, but a dozen men in fighting pods, controlling two hundred dispersed munition pods, could stand off a regiment of ordinary troops. If wounded, our podman could be carried to safety on an emergency zigzag course by his pod's automatic pilot.

The pod might be the ultimate fighting suit. The podman can move miles in minutes; he can remain invulnerable to strobe munitions or other sensory overloads by using outside sensors; his armor should stop most small-arms fire and nerve gas as well; and the pod

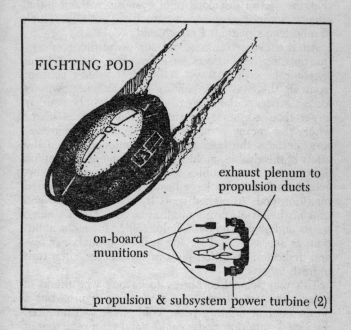

FIGHTING POD

exhaust plenum to propulsion ducts

on-board munitions

propulsion & subsystem power turbine (2)

can take him out of the zone fast. We can envision seafaring and spacefaring versions of the pod, which could just as easily be called a life-support system.

I left Battelle with some heady visions of future small arms systems, not knowing which ones will see a production line. But one panelist kept us from feeling too cocky. He reminded us that writer Robert Heinlein described many of those concepts years ago in *Starship Trooper*—but then, Heinlein himself is an Annapolis-trained engineer. That's fitting.

MANASPILL

"Keep your head down, Oroles," Thyssa muttered, her face hidden by a fall of chestnut hair. Cross-legged on the moored raft, his lap full of fishnet, little Oroles had forgot his mending in favor of the nearby commotion.

Though the lake was a day's ride end-to-end, it was narrow and shallow. Fisher folk of Lyris traversed it with poled rafts and exchanged rude jokes over the canoe, hewn from an enormous beech, which brought the Moessian dignitary to Lyrian shores. The boy did not answer his sister until the great dugout bumped into place at the nearby wharf, made fast by many hands. "Poo," said Oroles, "foreigners are more fun than mending old Panon's nets. Anyhow, King Bardel doesn't mind me looking."

Thyssa knew that this was so; Lyrians had always regarded their kings with more warmth than awe. Nor would Boerab, the staunch old war minister who stood at the king's left, mind a boy's curiosity. The canoe was very fast, but skittish enough to pitch dignity overboard when dignitaries tried to stand. And what lad could fail to take joy in the sight? Not Oroles!

Yet Thyssa knew also that Minister Dirrach, the shaman standing alert at the young king's right elbow, would interpret a commoner's grin as dumb insolence.

"The shaman minds," she hissed. "Do you want to lose favor at the castle?"

Grumbling, six-year-old Oroles did as he was told. Thus the boy missed the glance of feral hunger that Dirrach flicked toward the nubile Thyssa before attending to his perquisites as minister to King Bardel of Lyris.

Dirrach seemed barely to sway nearer as he spoke behind young Bardel's ear: "The outlander must not hear you chuckling at his clumsiness, sire," he suggested in a well-oiled baritone.

Bardel, without moving: "But when I can't laugh, it seems funnier."

"Averae of Moess is devious," the shaman replied easily, while others rushed to help the outlander. "If you think him clumsy, you may falsely think yourself secure."

Bardel gave a grunt of irritation, a sound more mature than his speaking voice. "Dirrach, don't you trust *any*body?"

"I have seen duplicity in that one before," Dirrach murmured, and swayed back to prevent further interchange. Truly enough, he had known Averae before, and had been uneasy when he recognized the Moessian. Dirrach breathed more easily now that he had slandered the man in advance. Who knew what crimes the outlander might recall? Then Averae stood on the wharf, and Bardel stepped forward.

Thyssa had not noted the shaman's glance because her attention was on the king. In the two years since his accession to the Lyrian throne, Bardel had grown into his royal role—indeed, into his father's broad leather breastplate—without entirely losing the panache of spirited youth. Tanned by summer hunts, forearms scarred by combat training with the veteran Boerab, the young Lyrian king fluttered girlish hearts like a warm breeze among beech leaves. And while Bardel watched the Moessian's unsteady advance with calm peregrine eyes, Thyssa saw a twinkle in them. Flanked by Boerab and Dirrach, arms and enchantment, Bardel of Lyris was a beloved figure. It did not matter to most Lyrians that his two ministers loathed each other, and that Bardel was just not awfully bright.

Thyssa, fingers flying among the tattered nets, seemed not to hear the royal amenities. Yet she heard a query from Averae: ". . . Shandorian minister?" And heard Boerab's rumbled, ". . . Escorted from the Northern heights . . . tomorrow." Then Thyssa knew why the castle staff and the fat merchants in Tihan had been atwitter for the past day or so. It could mean nothing less than protracted feasting in Bardel's castle!

To an Achaean of the distant past, or even to Phoenicians who plied the Adriatic coast to the far Southwest, this prospect would have inspired little awe. No Lyrian commoner could afford woven garments for everyday use; only the king and Boerab carried iron blades at their sides, each weapon purchased from Ostran ironmongers with packtrains of excellent Lyrian wine.

Nor would the royal castle in Tihan have excited much admiration from those legendary outlanders. Some hundreds of families lived in Tihan, thatched walls and roofs protected by stout oak palisades surrounding town and castle on the lake's one peninsula. Bardel's castle was the only two-story structure capacious enough to house king, staff, and a small garrison mostly employed for day-labor.

The pomp that accompanied Bardel's retinue back to nearby Tihan would have brought smiles to Phoenician lips but as Thyssa viewed the procession, her eyes were bright with pride. "Remind me to brush your leather apron, Oroles," she smiled; "if you are chosen to serve during feast-time, there may be red meat for our stew." Unsaid was her corollary: *and since I must play both father and mother to you, perhaps I too will make an impression on someone.*

*   *   *   *

Old Panon was less than ecstatic over the job on his nets. "Your repairs are adequate, Thyssa," he admitted, then held an offending tangle between thumb and forefinger; "but Oroles must learn that a knot needn't be the size and shape of a clenched fist. Teach him as I taught you, girl; nothing magic about it."

"Nothing?" Oroles frowned at this heresy. "But Shaman Dirrach enchants the nets every year."

"Pah," said the old man. "Dirrach! The man couldn't —ah, there are those who say the man couldn't enchant a bee with honey. Some say it's all folderol to keep us in line. *Some* say," he qualified it.

"Please, Panon," said Thyssa, voice cloudy with concern. "Big-eared little pitchers," she ruffled the ragged hair of Oroles, "spill on everyone. Besides, if it's folderol how do you explain my father's slingstone?"

"Well,—" The old man smiled, "maybe some small magics. It doesn't take much enchantment to fool a fish, or a rabbit. And Urkut *was* an uncanny marksman with a sling."

At this, Oroles beamed. The boy had no memory of the mother who had died bearing him, and chiefly second-hand knowledge of his emigrant father, Urkut. But the lad had spent many an evening scrunched next to the fireplace, hugging his knees and wheedling stories from Thyssa as she stirred chestnuts from the coals. To the girl, a father who had seen the Atlantic and Crete had traveled all the world. One raised across the mountains beyond Lyris was an emigrant. And one whose slingstone was so unerring that the missile was kept separate in Urkut's waistpouch, was definitely magical. Indeed, the day before his death Urkut had bested Dirrach by twice proving the incredible efficacy of his sling. It had come about during an aurochs hunt in which Bardel, still an impressionable youth, and Boerab, an admirer of Urkut, had been spectators.

As Thyssa heard it from the laconic Boerab, her father's tracking skill had prompted young Bardel to proclaim him "almost magical." Dirrach, affronted, had caused a grass fire to appear behind them; though Boerab left little doubt that he suspected nothing more miraculous in the shaman's ploy than a wisp of firewick from Dirrach's pack. Challenged to match the grass fire,

Urkut had demurred until goaded by Bardel's amusement.

Slowly (as Thyssa would embroider it, matching her account with remembered pantomime while gooseflesh crawled on Oroles's body), the hunter Urkut had withdrawn a rough stone pellet from his wallet. Carefully, standing in wooden stirrups while his pony danced in uncertainty, Urkut had placed pellet in slingpouch. Deliberately, staring into Dirrach's face as he whirled the sling, Urkut had made an odd gesture with his free hand. And then the stone had soared off, not in a flat arrowcourse but in a high trajectory to thud far off behind a shrub.

Dirrach's booming laughter had stopped abruptly when, dismounting at the shrub, Urkut groped and then held his arms aloft. In one hand he'd held his slingstone. In the other had been a rabbit.

Outraged by Dirrach's claims of charlatanry, Urkut had done it again; this time eyes closed, suggesting that Boerab retrieve stone and quarry.

And this time Boerab had found a magnificent cock pheasant quivering beside the slingstone, and Urkut had sagaciously denied any miraculous powers while putting his slingstone away. It was merely a trick, he'd averred; the magic of hand and eye (this with a meaningful gaze toward Dirrach). And young Bardel had bidden Urkut sup at the castle that night. And Urkut had complied.

And Urkut had died in his cottage during the night, in agony, clutching his belly as Thyssa wept over him. To this day, even Dirrach would admit that the emigrant Urkut had been in some small way a shaman. *Especially* Dirrach; for he could also point out that mana was lethal to those who could not control it properly.

Now, with a sigh for memories of a time when she was not an orphan, Thyssa said to the aged Panon: "Father always said the mana was in the slingstone, not in him. And it must have been true, for the pellet vanished like smoke after his death."

"Or so the shaman says," Panon growled. "He who

took charge of Urkut's body and waistpouch as well. I heard, Thyssa. And I watch Dirrach—almost as carefully as *he* watches *you*." The fisherman chose two specimens from his catch; one suitable for a stew, the other large enough to fillet. "Here: an Oroles'-worth, and a Thyssa-worth."

The girl thanked him with a hug, gathered the fish in her leather shift, leapt from raft to shore with a flash of lithe limbs. "May you one day catch a Panonworth," she called gaily, and took the hand of Oroles.

"He watches you, girl," old Panon's voice followed her toward the palisades of Tihan. "Take care." She waved and continued. Dirrach watched everybody, she told herself. What special interest could the shaman possibly have in an orphaned peasant girl?

* * * *

There were some who could have answered Thyssa's riddle. One such was the gaunt emissary Averae, whose dignity had been in such peril as he stood up in his Moessian canoe. Not until evening, after an aurochs haunch had been devoured and a third flagon of Lyrian wine was in his vitals, did Averae unburden himself to Boerab. "You could've knocked me into the lake when I spied your friend, the shaman," Averae muttered.

"Or a falling leaf could've," Boerab replied with a wink. "You're a landlubber like me. But be cautious in naming my friends," he added with a sideways look across the table where Dirrach was tongue-lashing a servant.

"You've no liking for him either?"

"I respect his shrewdness. We serve the same king," Boerab said with a lift of the heavy shoulders. "You know Dirrach, then?"

"When your king was only a pup—I mean no disrespect for him, Boerab, but this marvelous wine conjures truth as it will—his father sent Dirrach to us in Moess to discuss fishing rights near our shore."

"I was building an outpost and only heard rumors."

"Here are facts. Dirrach had full immunity, royal

pardons, the usual," Averae went on softly, pausing to drain his flagon. "And he abused them terribly among our servant girls."

"You mean the kind of abuse he's giving now?" An ashen-faced winebearer was backing away from Dirrach.

A weighed pause: "I mean the kind that leaves bite scars, and causes young women to despise all men."

Boerab, a heavy womanizer in his time, saw no harm in a tussle with a willing wench. But bite scars? The old warrior recalled the disappearance of several girls from farms near Tihan over the past years, and hoped he could thrust a new suspicion from his mind. "Well, that explains why we never arranged that fishing treaty," he said, trying to smile. "Perhaps this time Lyris and Moess can do better."

"Trade from Obuda to the Phoenician coast is more important than punishment for a deviate," Averae agreed. "Do you suppose we'll find Shandor's folk amenable?"

"Likely; they have little to lose and much to gain."

"Even as you and I," Averae purred the implication.

"Even as your king and mine," Boerab corrected. "Just so we'll understand one another, Averae: I'm happy as I am. Wouldn't know what to do with presents from Moess or Shandor, even without strings attached. If Lyris and the lad—ah, King Bardel—prosper, I'm content."

"Fair enough," Averae laughed. "I'm beginning to be glad your mana was strong during our border clash."

Boerab, startled, spilled his brimming flagon. "My *what*? Save that for commoners, Averae."

"If you insist. But it's common knowledge in Moess that our shaman spent the better part of his mana trying to sap your strength in that last battle. Practically ruined the poor fellow."

Boerab studied the lees in his wine. "If anybody put a wardspell on me, he's kept it secret." The barrel chest shook with mirth. "Fact is, I had high-ground advantage and grew too tired to move. If you want to believe, then believe in a safespot. For myself, I believe in my shield."

Boerab could hardly be blamed for denying the old legends. The entire region was rich in relics of forgotten battles where mighty shamans had pitted spell against spell, mana against mana, irresistible ax versus immovable shield. The mound that Boerab had chosen for his stand was a natural choice for a combat veteran; other warriors had chosen that spot before him. On that spot, magical murder had been accomplished. On that spot no magic would work again, ever. Boerab had indeed defended a safespot upon which all but the most stupendous mana was wasted.

All Boerab's life had been spent in regions nearly exhausted of mana. Of course there had been little things like Urkut's tricks, but—. Boerab did not commit the usual mistake of allowing magic to explain the commonplace. Instead he erred in using the commonplace to explain magic. Thus far, Boerab was immeasurably far ahead.

"I'd drink to your shield, then," Averae mumbled, "if that confounded winebearer were in sight."

Boerab's eyes roamed through the smog of the lignite fire as he roared for more wine. By now the king and Dirrach were too far in their flagons to notice the poor service. Boerab promised himself that for the main feast, he'd insist on a winebearer too young to crave the stuff he toted. *Ah; Urkut's boy,* he thought. *Too innocent to cause aggravation.*

As to the innocence of Oroles, the grizzled warrior was right. As to the consequences of innocence he could scarcely have gone farther wrong.

*   *   *   *

Thyssa, late to rise, was coaxing a glow from hardwood embers when she heard a rap on her door. "Welcome," she called, drawing her shift about her as the runner, Dasio, entered.

"In the royal service," said Dasio formally. The youth was lightly built but tall, extraordinary in musculature of calf and thigh; and Thyssa noted the heaving breast of her childhood friend with frank concern.

"Are you ill, Dasio? You cannot be winded by a mere sprint across Tihan."

"Nor am I. I'm lathered from a two-hour run. Spent the night with the Shandorians; they'll be here soon— with a surprise, I'll warrant," Dasio said cryptically, taking his eyes from Thyssa with reluctance. Seeing Oroles curled in a tangle of furs: "Ah, there's the cub I'm to fetch; and then I can rest!"

Choosing a motherly view, Thyssa set a stoneware pot near the coals. "Tell them Oroles was breaking his fast," she said. "You don't have to tell them you shared his gruel. Meanwhile, Dasio, take your ease." She shook her small brother with rough affection. "Rise, little man-of-the-house," she smiled. "You're wanted—" and glanced at Dasio as she ended, "—at the castle?"

The runner nodded, stirred the gruel as it began to heat, tasted and grimaced. "Wugh; it could use salt."

"Could it indeed," Thyssa retorted. "Then you might have brought some. Our palates aren't so jaded with rich palace food as some I might name."

A flush crept up the neck of the diffident youth. Silently he chided himself; though Thyssa and Oroles still lived in Urkut's cottage, they did so with few amenities. Without even the slenderest dowry, Dasio knew, the girl was overlooked by the sons of most Tihaners.

Presently, Oroles found his sandals and apron, then joined Dasio over the gruel. "What have I done now," he yawned.

It was as Thyssa hoped. After one dutiful mouthful that courtesy required, Dasio set her at ease. "The palace cook will brief you, runt. Big doings tonight; bigger than last night. If you can keep your feet untangled, maybe you can ask for a slab of salt—to jade your palates," he added with a sidelong grin at Thyssa.

Moments later, the girl ushered them outside. "Watch over him, Dasio," she pleaded. "And thanks for his employ."

"Thank old Boerab for that," said the youth. "But I'll try to keep the cub out of the wine he'll pour tonight."

Then, while Oroles tried to match his stride, Dasio
trotted slowly up the dirt road toward high ground and
the castle.

*   *   *   *

The Shandorians arrived in midafternoon, and all
Tihan buzzed with the surprise Dasio had promised.
Everybody knew Shandor had funny ideas about women,
but conservative Tihaners grumbled to see that the
emissary from Shandor was a handsome female wearing
crimson garments of the almost mythical fabric, silk;
and her eyes were insolent with assurance. Thyssa,
contracting a day's labor for a parcel of a merchant's
grain, knew it first as rumor.

Dirrach learned of it while powdering a lump of
lightest-tinted lignite coal in his private chamber. It
was the shaman's good fortune that such stuff was available, since when powdered it was unlikely to be as
visible when sprinkled from shadow into fire as was
charcoal or the sulphur which he used for other effects.
It was the region's good fortune that Dirrach's "magics"
had never yet tapped genuine mana.

Dirrach heard his door creak open; turned to hide his
work even as he opened his mouth to blast the in-
truder. Only one man in all Lyris had the right to burst
in thus. "Who dares to—oh. Ah, welcome, Bardel," he
ended lamely; for it was that one man.

"Can you believe, Dirrach?" The king's face was awash
with something between delight and consternation as
he toed the door shut. "Boerab and I just did the
welcomes—and where were you anyhow—oh, here I
guess; and the Shandorian has a girl for a servant.
Which is fine I suppose, because she's a woman. The
emissary, I mean. Is a *woman!*"

Dirrach drew a long breath, moving away from his
work to draw Bardel's attention. Too long had he suf-
fered the prattle, the presumption, the caprice of this
royal oaf. Perhaps tonight, all that could be remedied.
"Shandor puts undue value on its females, as I have

told you." He hadn't, but Bardel's shortsword outspanned his memory.

"The Shandorian's a bit long in the tooth for me," Bardel went on, "but firm-fleshed and—uh—manly, sort of. But where do we seat a woman at a state feast? You take care of it, Dirrach; Boerab's rounded up the kitchen staff. I'm off to the practice range; that crazy Gethae—the Shandorian—would pit her skill with a bow against mine. A woman, Dirrach," he laughed, shaking his head as he ducked out the door. His parting question was his favorite phrase: "Can you *believe*?"

Dirrach sighed and returned to his work. No believer in the arts he surrogated, the shaman warmed to his own beliefs. He could believe in careful preparation in the feast hall, and in mistrust for outlanders who could be blamed for any tragedy. Most of all, Dirrach could believe in poison. The stuff had served him well in the past.

*   *   *   *

Dirrach's seating arrangements were clever, the hanging oil lamps placed so that he would be partly in shadow near the fireplace. The special flagstone rested atop the bladder where Dirrach's foot could reach it, and specially decorated flagons bore symbols that clearly implied who would sit where. The shaman's duties included tasting every course and flagon before it reached the royal lips, though poison was little used in Lyris. Dirrach congratulated himself on placing the woman across from him, for Dirrach's place was at the king's side, and anything the woman said to Bardel could be noted by the shaman as well. A second advantage was that women were widely known to have scant capacity for wine; Gethae would sit at the place most likely to permit unmasking of a shaman's little tricks; and if Gethae denounced him it could be chalked up to bleary vision of an inebriate who could also be accused of hostile aims. Especially on the morrow.

Yet Gethae showed herself to good advantage as she swept into the castle with her new acquaintances. "I claim a rematch," she said, laying a companionable hand on Boerab's shoulder gorget. "Bardel's eye is a trifle too good today." Her laugh was throaty, her carriage erect and, Dirrach admitted, almost kingly. Already she spoke Bardel's name with ease.

Bardel started to enter the hall, stumbled as he considered letting the stately Gethae precede him but reconsidered in the same instant that such courtesy was reserved for the mothers of kings. "I was lucky, Gethae—ooop, damn flagstones anyhow; ahh, smells good in here; oh, *there* you are, Dirrach," Bardel rattled on with a wave. Actually the hall stank of smoke and sweat—but then, so did the king.

Boerab introduced Dirrach to the Shandorian whom he treated as an equal. "Sorry you were busy here, Dirrach," the old soldier lied manfully. "This sturdy wench pulls a stronger bow than I thought possible."

"Put it down to enthusiasm," said Gethae, exchanging handclasps with Dirrach. Her glance was both calculating and warm.

"Huh; put it down to good pectorals," Boerab rejoined, then raised his eyes to heaven: "Ulp; ghaaaa . . ."

"I accept that as a compliment," said Gethae, smiling.

Dirrach saw that such compliments were justified; the Shandorian's physical impact could not be denied, and a man like Boerab might find his judgment colored with lust. But Dirrach's tastes were narrow and, "I fear we have prepared but rough entertainment for a lady," said the shaman in cool formality.

"I can accept that too," she said, still smiling as she peered at the feast table. "Ho, Averae: I see we're to be kept apart."

Averae of Moess found his own place with a good-natured gibe to the effect that a small plot with Shandor would have been a pleasure. Plainly, the shaman saw, this woman enjoyed the company of men without considering herself one. Had he only imagined an invitation in her smile of greeting?

Dirrach found that it had not been mere imagination. All through the courses of chestnut bread, beef and

fowl, beer and honeycake, the shaman shifted his feet
to avoid the questing instep of the long-legged Gethae.
At one point Dirrach felt his false-bottomed flagstone
sink as he hastily moved his foot, saw reflection in
Gethae's frank dark eyes of a sudden flare in the fireplace. But Gethae was stoking a fire of another sort and
noticed nothing but Dirrach himself. The shaman took
it philosophically; he could not help it if Gethae had an
appetite for men in their middle years. But he would
not whet that appetite either, and pointedly guided
Bardel into dialogue with the woman.

Eventually the beer was replaced by a tow-headed
lad bearing the most famed product of Lyris: the heady
wine of the north lakeshore. Gethae sipped, smacked,
grinned; sipped again. Very soon she pronounced her
flagon empty and beamed at the boy who filled it. "The
lad," she said to one and all, "has unlocked Lyris's
wealth!"

All took this as a toast and Gethae winked at the boy,
who winked back. "I predict you'll go far,—ah, what's
your name, lad?"

"Oroles, ma'am," said the boy, growing restive as
others turned toward the interchange. "I've already
gone as far as the end of the lake."

"You'll go farther," Gethae chuckled.

"Here's to travel," said the king. "Keep traveling
around the table, Orolandes."

Dutiful laughter faded as the boy replied; servants did
not correct kings. "Oroles, please sir—but you're almost right."

Boerab, in quick jocularity: "In honor of the great
Orolandes, no doubt."

"Aw, you knew that, Boerab," said the boy in gentle
accusation, and again filled Gethae's flagon, his tongue
between his teeth as he poured. The boy's innocent
directness, his ignorance of protocol, his serious mien
struck warm response first from Averae, himself a grand-
father. Averae began to chuckle, then to laugh outright
as others joined in.

Little Oroles did not fathom this levity and continued

in his rounds until, perceiving that his own king was
laughing at him, he stopped, hugging the wine pitcher
to him. The small features clouded; a single tear ran
down his cheek.

Boerab was near enough to draw Oroles to him, to
offer his flagon for filling, to mutter in the boy's ear.
"No fear, lad; they're laughing for you, not at you."

Gethae could not tell whether Boerab was praising or
scolding the boy and resolved to generate a diversion.
With a by-your-leave to Bardel she stood. "At such a
merry moment, a guest might choose to pay tribute."

"Ill-said," from Averae, "because I wish I'd said it
first." More merriment, fueled by alcohol.

"I yield," Gethae mimed a fetching swoon, "to Moess—
for once."

Bardel understood enough of this byplay to lead the
guffaws. Averae bowed to the king, to the woman, then
performed quick syncopated handclaps before turning
expectantly toward the door.

A blocky Moessian—it was poor form to seat one's
bodyguard at a state feast—entered, arms outstretched
with obvious effort to hold their burden. At Averae's
gesture, the man knelt before the beaming young king.

"May you never need to use it, sire," from Averae.

Bardel took the wicked handax, licked its cold iron
head to assure himself of its composition. It was a heavy
cast Ostran head, hafted with care, and as Bardel swung
it experimentally the applause was general.

Except for Dirrach. The shaman muttered something
unintelligible and Bardel's face fell. "This pleased me
so," said the king, "that I forgot. Trust Dirrach to
remind me: no weapons in the feast hall. No, no,
Averae," he said quickly; "you gave no offense. Boy,"
he offered the ax to Oroles, "have a guard put this in
my chamber. I'll sleep with it tonight."

So it shall be mine tomorrow, thought Dirrach.

Oroles, cradling the wine pitcher in one arm, took
the ax with his free hand. Its weight caused him nearly
to topple, a splash of golden liquid cascading onto the
flagstones. Dirrach was not agile enough and, wine-

splattered to his knees, would have struck the boy who
bolted from the hall with wine and weapon.

But: "A boy for a man's job," Boerab tutted. "At least
we have wine to waste."

Dirrach quenched his outward anger, resumed his
seat and said innocently, "I fear we have given offense
to Moess." He knew the suggestion would be remembered on the morrow, despite Averae's denial which
was immediate and cordial.

Then it was Gethae's turn. The Shandorian reached
into her scarlet silken sleeve, produced a sueded pouch,
offered it to Bardel with a small obeisance.

"What else might Shandorians have up their sleeves,"
murmured Dirrach with false bonhomie.

"A body search might reward you," Gethae replied in
open invitation. Dirrach did not need to respond for at
that moment Bardel emptied the pouch into his hand.
There was total silence.

"Oh damn," Gethae breathed, and chuckled; "I'd
hoped to keep them damp." Bardel, perplexed, held
several opaque porous stones. One, by far the largest,
was the size of a goose egg, set into a horn bezel hung
from a finely braided leather loop. The others were
unset and all had been smoothed to the texture of
eggshell.

Dirrach almost guessed they were gallstones, for which
magical properties were sometimes claimed. Instead he
kept a wise look, and his silence.

Gethae retrieved the great stone. "Here; a bit of
magic from the northern barbarians, if you'll stretch a
point." She extended her tongue, licked the stone which
actually adhered to the moist flesh until she plucked it
away, held it aloft. Even Dirrach gasped.

The properties of hydrophane opal were unknown
even in Shandor; Gethae had been jesting about magic.
The Shandorians had imported the stones from the
north at tremendous expense; knew only that this most
porous of opals was dull when dry but became a glittering pool of cloudy luminescence when dampened. As
the moisture evaporated, the stone would again become

lackluster. Thus the Shandorians did not suspect the
enormous concentration of mana which was unlocked
by moistening a hydrophane.

Had Gethae known the proper spell, she could have
carved away the Tihan peninsula or turned it all to
metal with the power she held. Even her fervent prayer
for strength to pull a Lyrian bow had been enough
earlier, before the opals in her pouch had dried. Yet
none of this was suspected by Gethae. Her fluid gesture in returning the huge gem to Bardel was half of a
stormspell. She, with the others present, interpreted
the sudden skin-prickling electricity in the air as the
product of awe.

Bardel took the gift in wonderment. "Spit is magic?"

"Or water, wine, perspiration," Gethae chuckled. "I
have heard it argued that oil scum on water creates the
same illusion of magical beauty. And has the same
natural explanation," she shrugged. "Don't ask me to
explain it; merely accept it as Shandor's gift."

This called for another toast. "Where the devil is that
winebearer?" Bardel asked.

Oroles scurried back from his errand to pour. Even
Bardel could see the boy trembling in anticipation of
punishment, saw too that the outlanders had taken a
liking to the slender child. With wisdom rare in him,
Bardel suddenly picked up the smallest of the opals,
still opaque and dry. The king ostentatiously dipped the
pebble into his wine, held it up before Oroles who
marveled silently at the transformation. "For your services," said Bardel, "and for entertainment." With that
he dropped the opal, the size of a babe's thumbnail,
into the hand of Oroles.

Bardel acknowledged the applause, hung the great
hydrophane amulet around his own sweaty neck, pledged
packtrains of Lyrian wine as gifts for Moess and Shandor.
"And what say you of outlander magics," he asked of the
glum Dirrach. It was as near as Bardel would come to
commanding a performance from his shaman. He knew
some doubted Dirrach's miracles, but Bardel was cred-
ulous as any bumpkin.

Dirrach grasped his talisman of office, a carved wand with compartmented secrets of its own, and waved it in the air. "Iron strikes fire on stone," he intoned; "stone holds inner fire with water. But true mana can bring fire to fire itself." It only sounded silly, he told himself, if you thought about it. But the powdered lignite in the wand would keep anybody else from thinking about it.

Dirrach knew where the fireplace was, did not need to look over his shoulder as he manipulated the wand and trod on the false flagstone, feeding pungent oil to the blaze. He felt the heat, saw astonishment in the eyes of his audience, smiled to see Oroles cringe against the wall. He did not realize that the flames behind him had, for a moment only, blazed *black*. The gleaming hydrophanes of Bardel and Oroles were near enough that Dirrach's wandpass had called forth infinitesimal mana in obedience to a reversal gesture-spell. It did not matter that Dirrach was wholly incompetent to command mana. All that mattered was the mana and the many means for its discharge as magic. Knowingly or not. The jewel at Bardel's throat glimmered with unspent lightnings.

Unaware of the extent of his success, and of the enormous forces near him, Dirrach mixed blind luck with his sleight-of-hand and his hidden-lever tricks. The shaman was a bit flummoxed when two white doves fluttered up from the false bottom of his carven chair; he'd only put one bird in there. He was similarly pensive when the coin he "found" in Averae's beard turned out to be, not the local bronze celt Dirrach had palmed beforehand, but a silvery roundish thing which Averae claimed before either of them got a good look at the picture stamped on it. Inspection would have told them little in any case: the Thracian portrait of Alexander was not due to be reproduced for centuries to come.

And when a spatter of rain fell inside, all assumed that it was also raining *out*side; even royal roofs leaked a bit. At last Gethae sighed, "My compliments, Dirrach.

But tell me: how did you breed mice to elk? That was subtly done."

Indeed it was; so subtly that only Gethae had noticed the tiny antlered creatures that scampered across hearthstones and into the fire during one of Dirrach's accidental spells. Dirrach did not know if his leg was being pulled, and only smiled.

Bardel called for more wine when the shaman claimed his mana was waning. Oroles was pouring when Averae asked what credence might be placed in the tales of ancient shamans.

"Much of it is true," replied Dirrach, taking an obligatory sip from Bardel's flagon, thinking he lied even as he gazed at the truth gleaming darkly on Bardel's breast. "Yet few of us know the secrets today. You'd be surprised what silly frauds I've seen; and as for the nonsense I hear from afar: well—" Aping a lunatic's expression, hands fluttering like his doves, Dirrach began a ludicrous capering that brought on gales of mirth. And while his audience watched the wand he tossed into the air, Dirrach dropped a pinch of death into the king's flagon. There was enough poison there to dispatch a dozen Bardels. Dirrach would feign illness presently and of course the winebearer would later be tortured for information he did not have.

But there was information which Dirrach lacked, as well. He would never have performed a gestural wardspell, nor given anyone but himself the gift of conversing with other species, had he known just what occult meanings lay in his mummery.

*   *   *   *

The next day was one of sweltering heat, and did nothing to sweeten the odor of the fish Thyssa was filleting outside Panon's smokehouse. "Oroles, turn these entrails under the soil in Panon's garden," she called. "Oroles!"

The boy dropped his new treasure into his waistpouch, hopped from his perch on a handcart and scrambled to comply after muttering something, evidently to thin air.

"Don't complain," she said, tasting perspiration on her lips.

"I wasn't," said Oroles. "Did you know the castle midden heap is rich with last night's leavings and, uh, suc—succulent mice?"

"How would you know," she asked, not really listening.

"Oh—something just tells me."

Despite her crossness, Thyssa smiled. "A little bird, no doubt."

Pausing to consider: "That's an idea," the boy said, and trudged off, head averted from his burden.

Hidden from Thyssa by the smokehouse, Oroles could still be heard as he distributed fish guts in the garden. "Don't take it all," he said. "I'm supposed to plant this stuff." Thyssa thought she heard the creak of an old hinge, clucking, snapping. "No I'm not; you're talking people-talk," Oroles went on. More creaking. No, not a hinge. What, then? "There's a ferret under the cart that can do it too. Funny I never noticed it before." Creak, pop. "All right, if you promise not to steal grain."

There was more, but Thyssa first investigated the cart. A dark sinuous shape streaked away nearly under-foot to find refuge in Panon's woodpile; there *had* been a ferret hiding there! Thyssa crept to the edge of the smokehouse, spied Oroles dividing his offal between the dirt and a raven that was half as large as he. Neither seemed to fear the other. If she hadn't known better, Thyssa would have sworn the two were actually exchanging the polite gossip of new acquaintances. But the boy didn't seem to be in danger, and he had few enough playmates. Thyssa tiptoed back to her work, waved the flies away, and chose another fish from the pile.

Presently Oroles returned, searched around the cart, then began to string fillets onto withes. "I wonder if the shaman is sick in the head," he said.

"Not he," Thyssa laughed. "Why would you think that?"

"He keeps squatting at his window, running back to

leap into bed when servants appear, going back to the
window,—you know," Oroles said vaguely.

Dirrach's chamber upstairs in the castle faced the
dawn, away from Panon's cottage. Oroles would have
had to climb a tree to see such goings-on. "Your little
bird told you," said Thyssa.

"Quite a big one," Oroles insisted, as a raven flapped
away overhead. Thyssa felt the boy's forehead. Such
behavior was not at all usual for Oroles.

                    *   *   *   *

Dirrach did not step outside his chamber until he
spotted Bardel near the vineyards with the outlanders.
The shaman had retired from the feast with complaints
of a gripe in his belly, fully expecting to wake to the
sweet music of lamentations from servants. Told of
Bardel's vineyard tour, Dirrach suspected a ruse; continued to fake his illness; told himself that Boerab must
go next. Dirrach *knew* the poison had gone into the
flagon, had seen Bardel swill it down.

Maybe the fool had thrown it all up soon after Dirrach
took his leave. Yes, that had to be the answer. The only
other possibility was some inexplicable miracle. Well,
there were other paths to regicide. One path would
have to be chosen while the outlanders were still available as suspects.

At the noon meal, the king glowed with health and
camaraderie. "Try some more stew, Dirrach; just the
thing to settle your innards."

"Aye, and to bank your fires for negotiations," Gethae
put in. "Bardel wouldn't hear of serious talk while you
were indisposed."

"Bardel was nearly indisposed himself, this morning," Averae grunted. Noting Dirrach's sudden interest, he continued: "Set your entrails right before your
king runs out of luck."

Boerab grunted at this understatement; but courtesy
forbade outright mention of a king's death. "Made me
dizzy to watch him, Dirrach; climbing like a squirrel to
fetch grapes that were still unripe."

A king, engaged in such foolishness! Dirrach's face mirrored the thought.

"It wasn't the climb that impressed me, so much as the fall," Gethae said, her hand tracing the tumble of a falling leaf. She went on to describe Bardel's acrobatic ascent, the gleam of the hydrophane on his breast as he sweated to the topmost extent of a vine high in a beechtree.

Bardel, deluded that such childish heroics made the right impression: "I don't think I missed a branch on the way down."

"Brought enough of them down with you," Boerab snorted. "What a thump you made!"

Dirrach picked at his food, wondering how much of the tale was decoration. Taking it at half its face value, Bardel should now be lying in state—and in a basket, at that.

From Gethae: "I've never seen better evidence of a wardspell."

At this, Bardel thanked his shaman for his coronation wardspell, now several years old and, in any case, known by Dirrach to be pure counterfeit. Or was it? Dirrach silently enumerated the scars and bruises sustained by Bardel since the coronation; rejected his wardspell out of hand. Still, something was accountable for a flurry of bizarre events—and all since the previous evening. Was the woman teasing him with covert hints? Dirrach allowed himself to wonder if one of the outlanders was a true shaman, and felt his flesh creep. Forewarned, a wise man would take careful note of further anomalies.

Mindful of royal duties, anxious to show himself equal to them in the very near future, Dirrach suggested a brief attendance to local matters before the open-ended negotiations. While emissaries lounged at one end of the chamber, Bardel settled several complaints from citizens of Tihan and vicinity. The runner, Dasio, rounded up petitioners quickly—all but one, for whom Dasio had promised to plead.

When a squabble between farmers had been concluded, Bardel stood up. "Is that the last, runner?"

"Yes, sire, . . ."

"Well, then, . . ."

"And no, sire," Dasio said quickly. "I mean, there is one small matter, but of great import to the girl, Thyssa." Dasio saw the king's impatience, felt the cold stare of Dirrach. Yet he had promised, and: "She begs the special attention of the shaman but dared not leave her work to make petition."

Bardel sat back in obvious pique. Dirrach opened his mouth to deny the petition; remembered the visitors. "Quickly then," he said.

"The girl fears for her brother, Oroles. She thinks he is suddenly possessed; and truly, the cub is not himself. Thyssa craves audience with our wise shaman, and is prepared to pay in menial labor."

"Thyssa? Oh, the daughter of Urkut," Bardel said.

Dirrach's eyes gleamed as he recalled the girl. Prepared to do services for him, was she? But time enough for that when Dirrach occupied the throne. "Next week, perhaps," he muttered to Bardel.

"But her brother was the pup I rewarded last eve," Bardel mused. "He seemed only too normal then. What exactly is his trouble?"

Alarms clamored in Dirrach's mind as Dasio blurted, "He thinks he talks with animals, sire. And in truth, it seems that he does!"

The shaman leaned, muttered into the royal ear. "The shaman will make compassionate treatment before this day is done," Bardel said, parroting what echoed in his ear. So saying, he concluded the session.

*   *   *   *

Following Dasio to the girl's cottage, Dirrach applauded himself for the delay he had caused in negotiations. The outlander runners, in search of boundary clarification, would need three days for round trips to Shandor and Moess. In that time, a crafty shaman might learn more of these evidences of true occult power and perhaps even circumvent the luck of a king.

Dasio had alerted Thyssa to expect the shaman; traded

worried glances with her as Dirrach strode into the cottage. Dirrach waited until the girl and Oroles had touched foreheads to his sandal before bidding Dasio leave them.

"The boy knows why I come?" Dirrach kept the edge off his voice, the better to interrogate them. The more he looked on Thyssa, the more honeyed his tones became.

Thyssa had told the boy, who rather enjoyed his sudden celebrity. "He's never acted this way before," she said, wringing her hands, "and I thought perhaps some fever—."

Dirrach made a few stately passes in the air. A faint chittering reached them from outside. The opal of Oroles nestled in the boy's waistpouch unseen and, somewhere in the distance, a dog howled in terror. Kneeling, Dirrach took the boy's arms, then his hands, in his own. No trembling, no fever, no perspiration; only honest dirt. "His fever is in his bones, and will subside," Dirrach lied, then pointed to a cricket at the hearth. "What does the insect say, boy?"

"Bugs don't say much, 'cause they don't know much," was the prompt reply. "I tried earlier; they just say the same things: warm, cold, hungry, scared—you know. Bugs ain't smart."

"How about mice?"

"A little smarter. What does 'horny' mean?"

Dirrach would have shared a knowing smile with Thyssa, but saw her acute discomfort. To Oroles he said, "It seems that your ability comes and goes."

"It went today while I was working under Panon's raft. You have to strip and swim under. You know those baitfish he keeps alive in a basket? Not a word," Oroles said in wonderment.

Dirrach persisted. The boy showed none of the fear or caution of a small boy perpetrating a large fraud; but to ensure Dirrach of the sister's pliant services, Oroles must seem to be mending. The shaman hinted broadly that cubs who lied about mana could expect occult retribution, adding, "Besides, no one would believe you."

Oroles said stolidly, "You would. A raven told me he watched you running to and fro from your bed to your window this morning."

"The raven lied," Dirrach said quickly, feeling icy centipedes on his spine.

"And the ferret is angry because Dasio is standing between him and a rat nest, right outside."

Dirrach flung open the door. In the dusk he saw Dasio patiently waiting nearby, his feet less than a pace away from a well-gnawed hole in the foundation wattling. No sign of a ferret—but then, there wouldn't be. Dirrach contained a mounting excitement, sent the girl away with Dasio, and began testing the boy further. Though lacking clear concepts of experimental controls, the shaman knew that he must verify the events, then isolate the conditions in which they occurred.

An hour later, Dirrach stood at lakeside with a shivering and very wet Oroles, smiling at the boy. He no longer doubted the gift of Oroles; had traced its mana first to clothing, then to waistpouch, finally to proximity of Oroles with the tiny stone in the pouch. Such knowledge, of course, must not be shared.

Teeth chattering, Oroles tugged his leather breechclout on and fingered his waistpouch. "Can I have my gleamstone back?"

"A pretty bauble," said Dirrach, eyeing its moonlit glitter; "but quite useless."

"Then why can't I have it back?"

Dirrach hesitated. The boy would complain if his treasure were taken, and no breath of its importance could be tolerated. If the boy should drown now? But too many people would wonder at Dirrach's peculiar ministrations. Ah: there were other, larger stones; one of which just might explain much of young Bardel's escapes from death. Imperiously: "Take the gleamstone, cub; I can get all of them I want."

"The raven told you, I bet," Oroles teased.

Dirrach led the boy back to the cottage, subtly lead-

ing the conversation where he willed. Before taking his
leave, he learned that Oroles's winged crony had ad-
mired the gleamstone, had claimed to know where a
great many of them could be found near a warm spring
in the northern mountains. It was not difficult to frighten
the lad into silence, and to enlist him in the effort to
locate a spring whose warm waters might have curative
power. Dirrach returned to the castle in good spirits
that night, resolved to keep his curtains drawn in the
future.

*   *   *   *

After a dull morning spent on details of safe-passage
agreements, the outlanders were amenable to an afternoon's leisure. They groaned inwardly at Bardel's proposal, but the deer hunt was quickly arranged. Dirrach
would have preferred to wait in Tihan, the sooner to
hear what his small conspirator might learn of the thermal spring; but the shaman had been absent from state
affairs too much already; who knew what friendships
Bardel might nurture with outlanders in the interim?
Dirrach's fingers itched for a mana-rich hydrophane;
the sooner he could experiment with them, the better
for him. The worse for others.

A series of small things suggested to Dirrach that the
great stone at Bardel's throat was constantly active.
When Boerab stood in his stirrups by the king's side
and waved their beaters toward a ridge, both men
found themselves unhorsed comically. They cursed the
groom whose saddle knots had slipped, but it was
Dirrach's surmise—a lucky guess—that knot-loosening
spells were easy ones, even by accident. Far better,
Dirrach thought, if he could surreptitiously try spells
while within arm's reach of Bardel—but the king was
much too alert and active during a hunt, and at the
negotiation table such incantatory acts would be even
more obvious. And always the shaman kept one eye on
the winged motes that swept the sky, and thought of
ravens.

The hunt was not a total loss for Dirrach, who cozened a wager from his king early in the afternoon. "One of the Shandorian gems, is it?" Bardel laughed. "Fair enough! If I can't capture my quarry intact, a stone is yours."

"But if he does, Dirrach, you have an iron axhead to hone," Boerab grinned. "Bit of honest labor would do you no harm," and the warrior rode off with his king.

The deer they surprised in the small ravine amounted almost to a herd. His foolhardiness growing by the minute, Bardel was in his glory. His shaggy mountain pony fell on the slope but, with preternatural agility, Bardel leapt free to bound downward as deer fled in all directions. Gethae fumbled for an arrow, but with a savage cry of battle Bardel fell on the neck of the single stag from above, caught it by backsweeping antler tines, wrenched it crashing to earth beneath him in a flurry of brush and bellowing.

Scrambling to avoid the razor hooves, whooping for the joy of it, Bardel strove to choke the stag into submission, and king and quarry tumbled into the dry creekbed. Something arced away, butterfly-bright in the sun, and Bardel's next whoop was of pained surprise. The stag found firm footing. Bardel, now impeded by a limp, was not so lucky. With a snort of terror the stag flew up the ravine and Boerab, bow drawn, feathers brushing his cheek, relaxed and saluted the animal with a smile. It had been too easy a shot.

While Boerab shared his smile with Gethae (for she had witnessed his act of mercy), others were hurrying to Bardel. It was Averae who found the great opal amulet adorning a shrub, its braided thong severed in the melee, and Dirrach who noted silently that possession was nine parts of the mana.

Bereft of his protection, Bardel had immediately sustained a gash below the knee. Bardel accepted the bleeding more easily than Boerab's rough jests about it; jokingly questioned the shaman's old wardspell; retied the gem at his throat; and resumed the hunt. But the king was sobered and his leg a bit stiff, and on their return to Tihan Bardel made good his wager. Boerab saw to the battle wound while Dirrach, pocketing an opal the size of a sparrow egg, retired to "rest" until evening.

*   *   *   *

Trembling with glee, Dirrach set the opal on a table-top to catch the late sun in his chamber. He discovered the knot-loosening spell after sundown, and wasted time gloating while a warm breeze dried the last of the moisture from the hydrophane. Dirrach became glum as the spell seemed less effective with each repetition. The knock at his door startled him.

"Dasio the runner, sire," said a youth's voice. "I bring the girl Thyssa and her brother, Oroles. They said it was your wish," he finished tentatively. Unheard by the shaman, Dasio murmured to the girl: "If you should scream, many would hear. I've heard ill rumors of our shaman with—"

The door swept open to reveal a smoothly cordial Dirrach. With more expertise in sorcery, the shaman could have the girl at his whim; it was the brat who might hold the key to that darker desire for power. Affecting to ignore Thyssa: "I hope your mind is clearer tonight, boy, come in—but come alone."

Thyssa, stammering: "Our bargain, sire, I uh—might sweep and mend as payment while you examine the boy."

"Another time. The cub does not need distraction," Dirrach snapped, closing the heavy door. He bade Oroles sit, let the boy nibble raisins, listened to his prattle with patience he had learned from dealing with Bardel. He approached his topic in good time.

Oroles trusted in the shaman's power, but not in his smile. It became genuine, however, when Oroles admitted that the raven had pinpointed the thermal spring. "He brought proof," said Oroles. "It's at the head of a creek a few minutes west of Vesz. Is there a place called Vesz? Do ravens like raisins? This one wants better than fish guts. Do you have a pet, shaman?"

It was worse than talking with Bardel, thought Dirrach.

"The village of Vesz is near our northeastern boundary, but several creeks feed the place."

"Not this one. It disappears into the ground again. The raven likes it because humans seem afraid to drink there. On cool mornings it smokes; is that why?" Oroles narrowed his eyes. "I think that's dumb. How could water burn?"

Dirrach rejoiced; he had seen warm water emit clouds of vapor. Three ridges west of Vesz, the boy went on, now straying from the subject, now returning to it. Dirrach realized that such a spot should be easy to locate on a chilly dawn.

Gradually, the shaman shaped his face into a scowl until the boy fell silent. "It's well-known that ravens lie," Dirrach said with scorn. "I am angry to find you taken in by such foolishness." He paused, gathered his bogus anger for effect. "There is no such spring or creek. Do not anger me further by ever mentioning it again. To anyone! Pah! You ought to be ashamed," he added.

Oroles shrank from the shaman's wrath as he withdrew a nutshell from his waistpouch. "Maybe there's no smoking water, but there's this," he insisted, employing the shell like a saltshaker.

"And where does the lying raven say he stole this?" Dirrach licked his lips as he spied, in the damp sprinkle of loam, a few tiny nodules of opalescence.

"Scraped from an embankment, fifty wingbeats south of the spring," said Oroles. "Sure is slippery dirt; my pouchstring keeps loosening."

Dirrach feigned disinterest, stressed the awful punishments that would surely await Oroles if he repeated such drivel to others. Dirrach could hear a murmur of male and female voices in the hall. "Your sister fears for your empty head, boy," Dirrach repeated as he opened the door. "Do not worry her again with your gift of speaking with animals." He ushered Oroles through, careful to show ostentatious concern for the boy, caressed the small shoulder as he presented Oroles to his sister.

And then Dirrach realized that the voices had been those of Boerab and the formidable Gethae, who strolled together toward the old warrior's chamber, tippling from a pitcher of wine. Both had paused to look at Dirrach in frank appraisal.

The shaman dismissed the youngsters, nodded to his peers, said nothing lest it sound like an explanation. Gethae only glanced at the spindly form of Oroles as he retreated, then back to Dirrach. One corner of her mouth twitched down. Her nod to Dirrach was sage, scornful, insinuating as she turned away.

Dirrach thought, *That's disgusting; he's only a little cub!* But Gethae would have agreed. Dirrach returned to his chamber and his experiments, Boerab and his guest to theirs.

*   *   *   *

The Shandorian runner was gone for two days, the Moessian for three; ample time for Dirrach to reassure himself that the fresh windfall of mana was genuine and resided, not in outlander sorcery, but in hydrophane opals. By tireless trial, error, and indifferent luck the shaman had enlarged his magical repertoire by one more spell. It would summon a single modest thunderbolt, though it was apt to strike where it chose, rather than where Dirrach chose. In that time he fought small fires, quailed at fog-wreathed specters, and ducked as various objects flew past him in his chamber. But as yet he had not been able to bring any of these phenomena under his control.

It was no trick to arrange a surface-mining expedition "on the king's business"—Bardel rarely bothered to ask of such things—and to stress secrecy in his instructions to the miners. Ostensibly the men sought a special grit which might be useful in pottery glaze. Dirrach was adamant that the stuff must be kept dry, for he had learned two more facts. The first was that the things were potent only when damp. The second was that only so much mana lay dormant in an opal. Once drained by conversion of its potential into magic, the stone might still achieve a dim luster; but it would no longer summon the most flatulent thunderclap or untie the loosest thong. The specimen won from Bardel was still, after many experiments, mildly potent; but the pinpoint motes in the loam sample were already drained of mana.

Dirrach saw his miners off from the trailhead above Tihan, giving them the exhausted grit as a sample. He regretted his need to stay in Tihan, but the outlanders required watching. The ten packass loads, he judged, would easily overmatch the mana of Bardel's great amulet.

"If you succeed, send a messenger ahead on your return," was Dirrach's last instruction before the packtrain lurched away toward a destination a day's hike to the north.

Dirrach turned back toward Tihan, imagining the paltry castle below him as he would have it a month hence, when he'd learned the spells. Stone battlements to beggar the ancient Achaeans; gold-tipped roofs; vast packass trains trundling to and fro; fearsome heraldic beasts of living stone, like those of legend, guarding his vast hoard of opals. And of course, a stockade full of wenches wrested as tribute from Moess, Shandor, Obuda,—it occurred to Dirrach that he was still thinking small. He must, obviously, conjure his great castle directly atop the thermal spring. It would stand on vapor, and soar into the clouds!

All the world would tremble under the omnipotent gaze of the great King Dirrach. Why not the great God Dirrach? Nothing would be impossible, if only he avoided some lethal experiment. A real wardspell was necessary, but so far he had not duplicated his accidental success with Bardel. A hot coal could still blister the shaman's finger; a pinprick could still pain him. Hurrying to the castle, Dirrach pondered ways to steal the great stone from Bardel's breast. He considered seeking out the cub, Oroles, to employ the raven as a spy—yet that would soon be unnecessary, he decided.

For Oroles, the raven was not the only spy. In Panon's smokehouse, the fisherman took a load of wood from the boy, chose a billet. "Don't ask *me* why all Tihan is edgy," he grunted. "Ask your friend, the ferret. Better still, don't. You'll have me believing in your gift, pipsqueak."

"I can't ask Thyssa," Oroles complained, " 'cause the shaman said not to. But everybody's so jumpy . . ."

Panon coughed, waved the lad out with him, brought a brace of cured fillets for good measure. "Huh; and why not? Green clouds form over the castle, fires smoulder on cobblestones near it, thunder rolls from nowhere, —some say the outlanders bring wizardry."

"What do you say, Panon?"

"I say, take these fillets home before the flies steal them from you," smiled the old man. "And steer clear of anything that smacks of sorcery." He did not specify Dirrach, but even Oroles could make that connection.

Panon's smile lingered as he watched the boy depart. If the old tales could be believed, neither Oroles nor Thyssa had much to fear from most magical events. Both had hearts so pure as to comprise a mild wardspell— even though Panon had often seen Thyssa embroidering her tales of the redoubtable Urkut; intoning foreign words of his, copying outlander gestures as her father had done to entertain her once. The girl had a marvelous memory for such things, but little interest in the occult. Besides, Panon mused, if such incantations worked, why was Thyssa not wealthy? Panon shrugged, winced, rubbed his shoulder. If his rheumatism was any guide, all Lyris would soon be enriched by summer rains.

*   *   *   *

Try as he might for the next two days, Dirrach could not entice Bardel into another wager, nor further physical risks. At length Averae exclaimed in the parley room, "I do believe Dirrach craves your amulet, sire, more than he wants a parley. Why not just give it to him and be done with it?" Dirrach maintained his composure while writhing inside.

"Because it's mine," laughed Bardel. "I even sleep with it."

Boerab exchanged a smile with Gethae and murmured, "To each his own."

"To each somebody else's," she rejoined, then cocked an eyebrow at the shaman; "however small."

Because Bardel joined in the general laughter, Dirrach imagined that he was being mocked by all present. The anxiety, frustration, and juggled plans of Dirrach kindled an anger that boiled to the surface; Dirrach leaped to his feet. The moist opal in his waistpouch validated his dignity as Dirrach unleashed his easiest spell with all the gestural strength he could summon, cloaked in verbiage. "Let those who think themselves superior be loosened from conceit," he stormed.

The next instant, all but the invulnerable Bardel were grasping at clothing as every knot within five paces was loosened.

Oil lamps fell from lashings to bounce from floor and table. Boerab and the outlanders fought to hold their clothing—and Dirrach himself was depantsed.

Without a word, eyes flashing with contempt, Gethae gathered her clothing and strode out, living proof that she could combine nudity with pride. Averae sputtered and fumed, his gaunt rib cage heaving with pent rage as he struggled to regain his finery.

As for Boerab, the staunch warrior faced Dirrach over the head of their openmouthed king, leather corselet and gorget at Boerab's feet. "Mana or mummery, Dirrach," he roared, "that was a stupid mistake! You've affronted guests; friends!"

Dirrach retied his trousers, fumbled with waistpouch, a furious blush on his features. "The first offense was theirs," he said huskily. "High time you learned a little respect."

"I'll show respect for lumps on your head," Boerab replied, taking a step forward. "Stop me if you can."

"Hold, Boerab," cried the king, finally on his feet. "What will our guests think?"

"They'll think we need to strangle that piss-witted

child molester," said Boerab. But Dirrach had already fled into the hall.

"Who is king here, you or I?" Dimly, Bardel recognized the need for a regal bearing; for a measured response to this sudden turn. "For all you know, Dirrach could turn you into a toad, Boerab."

Averae, who had watched the confrontation in silence, now spoke. "Well spoken, sire. It strikes me that you may have need for more than one shaman. A balance of powers, as it were."

"But we don't have—" Bardel began, and stopped.

"You have only Dirrach," Averae said for him and added gently, "We know that, Bardel; but mutual loathing and mistrust are brittle bases for a treaty. With Dirrach, I fear—I fear I'm giving counsel where none is asked," he finished quickly.

"No, go ahead and say it," Boerab urged. "Everybody knows our fine shaman is a sodomizer of children."

"Everybody but me," said Bardel, aghast.

"And who was to tell you?" Boerab spread his big hands, then launched into a description of what he and Gethae had witnessed outside Dirrach's chamber. As usual, the tale grew in the telling.

Averae was not surprised. "Dirrach is unwelcome in Moess because he preyed sexually on the young," he said without embellishment.

In the hallway, Dirrach ground his teeth as he listened, enraged at the irony of it. The king was still ignorant of his real transgressions, but seemed ready to punish him for imagined ones!

"Have Dirrach confined in his chamber," said the king sadly, "until I can decide what must be done. If you *can* confine him," he added with sudden awareness.

"Cold iron is rumored to block any spell," Averae said mildly.

"And I have an idea where we can locate another who's adept, or could become so, at Dirrach's specialty. I don't think I really thought it possible until now—the mumbo-jumbo, I mean," Boerab said.

Dirrach heard heavy footfalls, thought of the cast-iron

ax, and ducked into a shadowed alcove as Boerab huffed past. The shaman could not return to his chamber now—but perhaps he would not need to.

At dusk, Dirrach emerged from hiding. By turning his tunic inside out and jamming sandals into his belt, the shaman passed unrecognized in the dusty byways of Tihan. Twice he melded with shadows as men clattered by, clumsy with bronze weapons they seldom used. Dirrach felt certain he could command their fear, or at any rate their trousers, in a confrontation. Yet the uproar would locate him. Thunderbolts might not help. Dirrach made his way unseen to a hayrick near the palisades, climbed atop it, and sniffed a breeze chill with humidity as he burrowed into the hay for the night. He willed the rains to hurry; they kept most folk indoors.

*   *   *   *

Summoned in early morning, Thyssa ran with her friend Dasio before a damp wind as Dirrach, in his perch at palisade height, scanned northern hills for sight of a messenger of his own. While the girl made a fetching obeisance to Bardel, wondering what her sin might be, Dirrach spotted his man astride a packass. Shouldering a stolen mattock, blinking dust from his eyes, Dirrach trudged out from the untended palisade gate into the teeth of the wind to intercept his man.

In the castle, Thyssa was tongue-tied with astonishment. "I, sire? Bubbut, *I*?" Her pretty mouth was dry as she stared up at her king. "But shamans are men, and I know nothing of necromancy or—*I*, sire?"

"Oh, stand up, Thyssa, he's not angry—are you, Bardel?" Boerab dug a gentle elbow into Bardel's ribs. No, not angry, Boerab judged; but perhaps a bit bewitched. How like the dunderhead to notice beauty only when it lay beneath his nose!

"I'm told you might be of great service to Lyris," Bardel began, "if you can but recall your father's ancient spells. Dirrach has crimes to answer for. The question is, could you replace him?"

Slowly, Thyssa was persuaded that this was no trick to convict her of forbidden arts, and no royal jest. She admitted the possibility that Urkut, in his tale-spinning, might have casually divulged knowledge of occult powers which he had learned in distant lands. Urkut's failure to make full use of such knowledge might be ascribed to disinterest, fear of its misuse, or even to a blocking spell. Added Boerab, who did most of the coaxing: "Now it's time to find out, Thyssa. How well do you recall Urkut's tales, and what secrets might they hold?"

Thyssa nodded, then closed her eyes in long reverie. It seemed an age before a smile of reminiscence tugged at her lips. Hesitant at first, Thyssa knelt before cold ashes in the fireplace. A few gestures mimed placement of invisible kindling, whirling a nonexistent firestick, other actions not so transparently pantomimic—and then the barest wisp of smoke sought the flue. With practice, she coaxed a flame upward, but turned in fear toward Bardel who bent near, his huge sweat-stained amulet swinging like a pendulum.

Too dull-witted to consider the dangers, Bardel grinned at her and winked: "Now try it on the flagstones."

Flagstones burned, too. The problem was in quenching them. Thyssa finally thought to reverse her gestures and after some failures, sighed as the flame winked out. Thyssa was, of course, wholly innocent of the oral shorthand equivalents which sorcerers of old had used. Thyssa wondered aloud why Urkut had never put such spells to work around the cottage, then recalled another of her father's anecdotes. She got it right on the third try. Boerab made her erase the spell, laughing nervously as an oak table levitated toward the roof. Again, the reversal worked when she did everything in order; the heavy table wafted down.

Urkut's spell over food was not to be deduced as a preservation spell just yet. Thyssa tried it on their noon meal of bread, beer and fruit, but nothing obvious happened and the experiment was soon consumed. Thyssa had no inkling, yet, that their lunch could have been stored for a century without losing its freshness.

His belly full, Bardel urged the girl to devise some spell of a more warlike nature. "The sort of thing that gave warlocks their name," he said. "We may need it; don't forget, Dirrach is at large."

Boerab shuddered. "And if it goes awry? Thyssa toys with thunder as it is."

"The nearest my father got to a curse, so far as I know, was when he'd speak of shamans and their powers," she reflected. "Then he'd say a prayer for deliverance—and do something like this." She began a two-handed ritual; paused with a frown, reversed it; began anew with a nod of satisfaction.

The trapspell, far older than any of them could know, was very special. Lacking mana to energize it, Urkut had never known—until too late—whether it worked. Fundamentally it was a shrinkspell, positively polarized against evil and those who employed it by magical means. Only those present—the king, the girl, the warrior, and a mouse near the hearth—could be the beneficiaries, and then only in proximity to a source of mana. As with the preservation spell, nothing spectacular happened; but the room grew oppressively warm.

"I guess I forgot something," Thyssa sighed.

Boerab, rising: "You're the best judge of that. But perhaps you'd best stop for now. Think back, and make haste slowly; as for me, I'll just make haste. There's bad weather brewing and we'll never find Dirrach in a storm."

"I hope it cools things off," Bardel nodded; "even my amulet is hot."

Thyssa took her leave, welcoming warm rain on her face as she hurried homeward. It did not seem like the kind of weather that would cool Tihan much.

*   *   *   *

Dirrach's messenger bore the best possible news, and estimated that the grit-laden packass train was no more than a half-hour behind. The man had no way of knowing Dirrach's outlaw status and dutifully returned, on the shaman's orders, to direct the packtrain toward a new destination. Jubilant, Dirrach took shelter from intermittent wind-driven showers under a stand of beeches. From his promontory, he could see groups of Tihaners searching lofts and hayricks. It would be necessary to commandeer an outlying farmhouse and to detain the miners until he had puzzled out ways to make himself invincible.

And how long might that take? Perhaps he should retreat further into the hills with his mana-rich ore. Later he could return with gargoyles, griffons, even armies of homunculi . . .

As the little group of miners struggled from their protected declivity into the open, heading for their new rendezvous, Dirrach allowed himself a wolfish grin. Then his features altered into something less predatory as he watched the packtrain's advance.

The skins over the packs gleamed wetly, and the lead miner fought a cloud of biting flies—or something—so dense that Dirrach could see it from afar. Then pack lashings parted—untied themselves, Dirrach surmised—and both skins began to flap in the wind. The lead packass took fright, bucked, stampeded the animals behind it, and in the space of three heartbeats the procession erupted into utter mind-numbing chaos.

* FLASH * BLAMMmm . . .

A great light turned the world blue-white for an instant, thunder following so close that it seemed simultaneous. Now the miners waved, sought to slow the maddened animals, and fled through clouds of grit as the pack contents whirled downwind, spilled into the air by the leaping beasts.

One miner disappeared in a twinkling. A packass, then another, flew kicking and hawing in the general direction of Tihan—but at treetop level, a sight so unnerving that miners scattered in terror. Paralyzed with impotent rage, Dirrach knew that a trickle of water into one of the packs had triggered a series of events; a series that had scarcely begun.

As the storm waxed, Dirrach hurried toward one pack animal in an attempt to save some of its load without getting downwind of it. Dirrach had seen a man vanish in the stuff, but could not know the man had reappeared safely under his bed in Tihan. The packass saw Dirrach, rolled its eyes, grew fangs the length of shortswords, roared a carnivore's challenge. Dirrach scrabbled into a tree with a bleat of stark horror. From his perch, he could see clouds of fine grit blowing over palisades into Tihan in a monumental manaspill.

*　　*　　*　　*

Old Panon blinked as a grit-laden gust of wind whirled past him at the dock; steadied himself above his nets with outflung arms. He could never recall later what he muttered, but the next moment he stood amid a welter of fish, all flopping determinedly from the lake into his pile of net. Panon sat down hard.

On merchant's row, the bronzeworker followed a reluctant customer outside in heated exchange over prices. A blast of wind peppered them both and suddenly, his heel striking something metallic, the customer sprawled backward onto a pathway no longer muddy. It was literally paved for several paces with a tightly interlocked mass of spearheads, plowpoints, adzes, trays; and all of gleaming iron.

The tanner was wishing aloud for better materials when he ducked out of the foul weather to his shop. He found his way blocked by piles of fragrant hides.

The produce merchant spied a farmer outside, rushed out to complain of watered milk, and braved a gritty breeze. The men traded shouted curses before discovering that they stood ankle-deep in a cow-flop carpet. It spread down the path as they fled, and more of it was raining down.

An aging militiaman paused in his search for Dirrach to surprise his young wife, and found that he had also surprised one of the castle staff. The younger man cleared a windowsill, but could not evade the maledictions that floated after him. He hopped on through the gathering storm, his transformation only partial, for the moment a man-sized phallus with prominent ears. He elicited little envy or pity, since most of Tihan's folk had problems of their own.

Bardel was informed by a wide-eyed Dasio who could still run, though for the time being he could *not* make his feet touch the ground, that the end of the world had arrived. The king howled for Boerab, aghast as more citizens crowded into the castle toward the only authority they knew.

One extortionate shopkeeper, perched on the shoulder of his haggard wife, had become a tiny gnome. The castle cook could still be recognized from his vast girth, but from the neck up he seemed an enormous rat. Bardel saw what the citizens were tracking into the castle, wrinkled his nose, and stood fast. "BOERAAAAB!"

The old soldier stumped in, double-time, sword at ready, but soon realized he was not facing insurrection. "It pains me to say this," he shouted over the hubbub, "but Thyssa may have made some small miscalculation—"

"All this, the doings of one girl?" Bardel's wave took in the assembled throng.

It was Dirrach's erstwhile messenger, breathless from running, who set them right. "No, my lords," he croaked. "The shaman! I saw it begin with my own eyes." Convinced as always of Dirrach's powers, the man attached no value to the windborne grit. Thus he did not describe it, and a great truth passed unnoticed.

"Shaman . . . Dirrach . . . the molester," several voices agreed, as Boerab and his king exchanged grim nods.

Bardel motioned the eyewitness forward, hardly noticing that the knee-high shopkeeper was already beginning to grow to his original size. "Tell us what you know of Dirrach," said the king, "and someone fetch the girl, Thyssa."

*   *   *   *

Sodden and mud-splattered, Dirrach made his way unchallenged in waning light to the unoccupied cottage of Thyssa. He moved with special care, avoiding accidental gestures, forewarned by personal experience that the hydrophane fallout was heavier in some places than in others. He no longer entertained the least doubt that Bardel enjoyed magical protection so long as he wore the amulet.

Face-to-face intrigue was no longer possible, and Dirrach judged that raw power was his best option. It should not be difficult to wrest the small stone from Oroles. Far greater risk would lie in finding the means to steal the king's great opal. Perhaps an invisibility spell; Dirrach had seen the passage of some unseen citizen as footprints appeared in one of Tihan's muddy paths. The shaman had seen Bardel lose his amulet once through accident, knew that it could be lost again through stealth.

Dirrach plotted furiously, filing vengeful ideas as he ravaged the small cottage in search of the waistpouch of little Oroles. He knew it likely that the boy had it with him, but trashing the place was therapeutic for Dirrach.

If the locus of power lay in hydrophanes, then none but Dirrach himself could be allowed to have them during the coming power struggle. Once Bardel was dead—and stiff-necked Boerab as well, by whatever means possible—the shaman could easily fill the power vacuum he had created. Time enough then to organize a better mining foray!

Dirrach paused at the sound of approaching footfalls, strained to pull himself up by naked rafters, and stood near the eaves in black shadow. One of the voices was a youthful male; Dirrach held his one-piece bronze dagger ready.

"I'll be safe here," said Thyssa, just outside.

"So you say," replied Dasio, "but I'd feel better if you let me stay. Why d'you think the outlanders packed up and left so fast, Thyssa? As the Shandorian woman said, 'only fools fight mana.' Who knows what curse Dirrach will call down on Lyris next?"

Stepping into view below Dirrach, the girl shook her head. "I can't believe he intended all this, Dasio." There was something new in Thyssa's tone as she closed the door; something of calm, and of maturity.

Dirrach heard footsteps diminish outside, grinned to himself. He had no way of knowing why this peasant girl's self-confidence had grown so, and did not care. One of the rafters creaked as the shaman swung down.

Thyssa whirled to find Dirrach standing between her and the door. "Where is the cub? No, don't scream," the shaman ordered, the dagger his authority.

"Cleaning a huge pile of fish with a friend," she said. "Perhaps Panon should thank you for them, Dirrach. And don't worry, I won't scream. It may be that you and I have some things in common."

At that moment, Oroles burst into the cottage. Dirrach grasped the lad, enraged both by the surprise and the girl's treatment of him as an equal. Oroles squalled once before Dirrach's hand covered his mouth. Sheathing his dagger quickly, Dirrach wrenched the lad's waistpouch away and cuffed Oroles unconscious. Then Thyssa did cry out.

The shaman was not certain he could silence her quickly and made a snap decision. "The cub is hostage to your silence," he snarled, slinging the boy over one shoulder.

Thyssa's hands came up, churning a silent litany in the air. "I don't think so," she said, and Dirrach found himself rising helplessly into the eaves again. He dropped the boy who fell on bedding, then locked one arm over a rafter as Thyssa reached into a corner. She brought out a wickedly tined fish spear.

Thyssa, advancing, clearly reluctant with the spear: "Even a rabbit will protect her young."

Dirrach saw that the tines of bone were bound to the spearshaft with sinew, invoked his simplest spell with one hand, and barked a laugh as the sharp tines fell from their binding. But something else happened, too; something that startled Thyssa more than the loss of her weapon. She stepped back, hugged the boy to her, gazed up at Dirrach in fresh awe.

Dirrach felt distinctly odd, as if the rafter had swollen in his embrace. "Get me down," he hissed in hollow braggadocio, "or I turn you both to stone!"

Thyssa reversed the levitation spell, naive in her fear of his power—though that fear was fast being replaced by suspicion. The shaman released the rafter as he felt the return of his weight—or some of it, at least. He sprawled on the packed earth, then leaped to his feet and stared up at the girl.

Up? He glanced at himself. His clothing, his dagger, all were to the proper scale for Dirrach; but he and his equipment were all a third their former size. Thyssa's trapspell, dormant until now, had energized in response to his evil intent with magic.

The shaman's fall had been a long one for such a small fellow and, in his fury, Dirrach summoned a thunderbolt. The flash and the sonic roll were dependable.

And so was the trapspell. Thyssa covered her ears for a moment, blinking down at a twice-diminished Dirrach. His dagger was now no larger than a grass blade and fear stayed his steps. Obviously the girl had done this; what if she stepped on him while he was only a hand's length tall?

Little Oroles stirred, and Thyssa kissed the boy's brow. She was shaken but: "I was wrong, shaman," she said evenly. "We have nothing in common."

Her eyes held no more fear, but Dirrach thought he saw pity there. This was too much to bear; and anyway, he already had the boy's manastone. Dirrach snarled his frustration, squeezed through a crack in the heavy wall thatch, hurled himself out into the night.

*   *   *   *

Had the trapspell depended on windblown particles of opalescent grit, Dirrach might have grown tall within the hour. But Thyssa's spell had drawn on the mana of Bardel's amulet, and the shaman had a long skulk to the castle.

His mind, and other things, raced with him before the keening of a fitful wind. He listened for telltale human sounds, found that he could easily hide now, kept his small bronze fang in his fist. Dirrach recalled the vines that climbed past the royal chamber and knew that stealth was a simple matter for one of his size. Now and then he paused to listen. It seemed that even the leaves teased him as they scurried by.

At last he reached the castle wall, planning headlong. Once he had cut his way through the upper-story thatch, he could hide in the king's own bedchamber and wait for the king to sleep. And Bardel slept like the dead. A predator of Dirrach's size and cunning could easily sever the amulet cord, steal the protecting manastone, then slice through a king's royal gullet. After that, he promised himself; after that, old Boerab. It was a shame that Averae had already fled, but a grisly vengeance could be brewed later for that one; for the girl; for all of them.

He sheathed his tiny dagger, tested a rope of ivy, and began to climb. Then he froze, heart thumping as he perceived the eyes that watched him with clinical interest; eyes that, he realized with shock, had been on him for some time . . .

*　　*　　*　　*

Three days after the storm, a healing sun had gently baked away the last vestige of moisture in the dust of Tihan. Citizens tested their old oaths again and found that it was once more possible to enjoy an arm-waving argument without absurd risks.

After a week, Bardel called off the search for his elusive shaman, half-convinced that Thyssa had imagined Dirrach's shrinkage and half-amused at the idea of danger from such an attenuated knave. But he did allow Boerab to post dogs around the castle, just in case.

Boerab's ardor to collar the shaman went beyond duty, for Gethae of Shandor had been spicy tonic for a veteran campaigner, and blame for her leave-taking could be laid squarely upon Dirrach. The garrison joke was that Boerab had exchanged one lust for another.

Thyssa refused to leave her cottage. "I'm comfortable there, sire," she explained, "and Oroles would soon be spoiled by palace life. Besides, my, ah, friends might be too shy to visit me here." She turned toward Boerab. "Intercede for me, old friend!"

Boerab slapped an oak-hard thigh and laughed. "Fend for yourself, girl! Just threaten to levitate your king. Or turn him to stone; you're capable of it by now, aren't you?"

"No," Thyssa admitted sheepishly. "And I don't seem to be inspired unless I'm in my king's presence. But I'll spend some time practicing here daily, if that is your wish."

Bardel kicked at a flagstone. "Why not, uh, spend some time with me just for amusement? I have eyes, Thyssa. Your friends aren't *all* bashful; only Dasio. And all your other friends are new ones. What does that tell you?"

"Just as you are, Bardel," Thyssa replied, "and what does *that* tell me?"

"Damnation! What does my runner have that I don't?"

After a moment: "Long familiarity—and shyness," she said softly. She exchanged a glance with Boerab and did not add, *and wit*.

Bardel pulled at his chin, sighed. "I've offered you everything I can, Thyssa. My larder and my staff are at your orders. What more can we do to seal your allegiance?"

She smiled. "But Lyris has always had that. One day I'll move to the castle, after Oroles has grown and—" she paused. "Oh, yes; there is something you can do. You might have those dogs taken away."

Boerab: "They won't harm you."

"It's not for my sake. Oroles has a friend who lives around the castle. The dogs disturb it greatly."

Bardel's smile was inquisitive: "*Around* the castle?"

"A ferret, sire," she said, blushing. "Oroles no longer claims to talk with animals, except for one. Don't ask me how, but he's convinced me that he really can do it. You have no idea how much he learns that way."

The men exchanged chuckles. "Let's wait for news of Dirrach," Boerab said, "and then I'll remove—"

"Oh, that's another thing," said Thyssa. "Oroles tells me the ferret spied a tiny manlet the other night, and it described Dirrach perfectly. It watched our shaman do the strangest things.

"Oroles told the ferret that it was lucky Dirrach hadn't seen it; that the shaman was a bad man."

"Quite right," said Boerab. "I'll double the dogs."

"I'm not finished," Thyssa went on. "The ferret replied that, on the contrary, it found Dirrach a lot of fun. In its own words: delicious."

A very, very long silence. Boerab, hoarsely: "I'll remove the dogs."

Bardel: "I wonder if you could make ferrets become very large, Thyssa. You know: guard duty, in Lyris's defense."

Thyssa: "I wonder if you would want them thus. They are not tame."

"Um; good point," said the king. "Seems a shame, though. If you can talk with them, looks like you could tame them."

"Only that one," Thyssa shrugged, and bade them farewell in time to meet Dasio for a stroll.

The secret of the hydrophanes was intact. Not even the ferret knew that one of Dirrach's opals remained, permanently damp, in a corner of the animal's belly.

Tihan's folk were to learn caution again during rainy weather, though with each hapless employment the mana was further leached from the glittering motes in Tihan's soil and roof thatches. Meanwhile, Lyrians began to gain repute for a certain politeness, and greater distance from their king. It occurred to no one that politeness, like other inventions, is a child of necessity.

As a consequence of the manaspill, even the doughty Boerab agreed that mana was a hazardous reality which few cared to explore. If a king's presence was fecund with mana, then perhaps royalty bore divine rights. Europe's long experiment had begun.

MALF

Infante nudged his Magnum's front axle against the big tree with that little extra *whump* that said, "grandstander." Old Tom Kelley and I knew that, but Howard Scortia was duly impressed. The lumberman had come to see a hundred and fifty feet of Oregon fir harvested in sixty seconds, between Infante and me, who was more fun to watch.

"Clear?" George Infante's voice rang from his polycarbonate bubble amplified and more resonant than his usual soft delivery.

"Clear," I sang back, louder than necessary for Infante, whose audio pickups could strain a voice out of the screech of machinery. I was grandstanding a little, too, for Kelley's sake.

Everyone jumped when Infante triggered the spike driver. Ten thousand pounds of air pressure will slap your ears when it's shooting a ribbed spike ten inches into a living fir trunk.

All I did was position a quartz fiber strap around the tree just above the paint mark; but it was a crucial operation if the hinge was to sit tight. I dodged out between the tree and one of the eight-foot Magnum tires. Then I ran.

When I replied to Infante's "Clear?" again, I was still sprinting. I knew he wouldn't wait for me to get entirely clear before querying, and he knew I wouldn't make him wait. Machismo, maybe; stupidity for sure. Though Infante had been with us only six months, since November '85, he and I could judge each other pretty well.

Infante's reflexes were honed like microscalpels, or else he started the stripping a nanosec before I cleared him. I scuffed forest humus on Mr. Scortia's boots as I slowed to a stop. He didn't notice; with everybody else, he was watching those gangsaws strip the fir.

Imagine a gang of curve-bar chainsaws arranged in a circle, mounted pincer-fashion on an extendable beam. They're staggered so they won't chew each other up as they pivot toward the center, and God help what's in the center. The saws are run by airmotors, making whoopee noises but with low fire danger.

Infante's eye was good. Correction: it was perfect. He ran his gang of banshees whooping up that fir trunk like a squirrel up a sapling, and branches rained all over the Magnum Seven. Infante had his steel cage flipped over the bubble and stared straight up through the falling junk, hands in his console waldoes, judging how close to strip the larger limbs.

Then he pulled what heavy equipment operators call a Mr. Fumducker, a piece of mechanically amplified horseplay that looks cute if it works, and kills somebody if it doesn't work. He topped the tree.

The Magnum could bring the tree down top and all, gentle as praying. But George Infante, without a line or any other control, topped her so fast she didn't know which way to fall—and that's what makes it horseplay. With six saws chewing at once, any one may bite through first and it's possible the thing will flip. Or it could drop vertically, a great fletched pile-driver on the operator below. And that would ruin Mr. George Infante's whole day, cage or no cage. For an instant, Kelley lost his smile. He muttered, "Barmy little bastard," not loud, but not joking.

Infante hauled the beam back so fast the pneumatics barked, made an elbow of the beam, and sideswiped the top as it fell. My eyes are good, too; I knew Infante could hear admiring feedback from Mr. Scortia's men because he was grinning. I liked the Magnum system; it did a heavy dude's job with precision. Infante—well, I think Infante liked what *he* could do *with* it. The distinction didn't seem large until you had to repair an overtaxed Magnum.

Mr. Scortia rumbled, "Thirty seconds," and I saw him holding a big antique timepiece; railroadman's watch, if I was any judge. I craved it instantly. He stood watching the gangsaws, now stilled, form a ring near the fresh stump a hundred feet up the fir.

But Infante could do that without looking; he was that good. Meanwhile he had his other waldo working the big left front extensor with its single huge chainsaw. Infante flicked the extensor back toward him, the saw snarling as it engaged. He was cutting the tree in one long swipe like a man sawing his own leg off from in front.

He stopped the cut at precisely the right instant. Mr. Scortia obviously expected the tree, all fifty tons of it, to come thundering down on poor little hapless George Infante. Kelley and I knew that poor little hapless George was nearly home free.

As Infante lowered the tree, our simple brawny hinge kept it from kicking off its stump. The entire trunk came down lamb-quiet and Infante placed its upper end in a yoke amid the rearmost of the Magnum's three axles. Time: fifty-seven seconds. I knew we had sold our first Magnum.

I also knew Infante had goddamn-near dented his. In haste to make a record stripping he had left a stub branch long enough that, as he lowered the tree, the stub slammed his cage with shivering impact. *Well*, I thought: *if I can't teach you caution, maybe that will. I'd hate to see you graunched.*

If Kelley noticed he wasn't letting on. Infante magicked the hingepin out with his little extensor. With feet and his other hand, he maneuvered the Magnum several ways at once.

The Magnum's third axle is remoted by a telescoping spiral stainless tube. The idea is to provide mass, leverage, and steerability with the remoting axle and yoke. When Infante had the remote axle tucked closer, he quickly swung the Magnum's legs down. Then, carrying a hundred thousand pounds of cellulose on the hoof, Infante's Magnum stood up and walked the hell out of there. No cheering this time; just unhinged jaws.

The ambulatory feature of the Magnum is mechanically simple, with pneumatics. But feedback circuitry is fiendishly tricky, and nobody made it really work until Kelley learned to calibrate it for a given operator. It's a mite humbling the first time you see it work on heavy equipment. Infante didn't need to walk her out, but a demo is a demo; with one eye on his rear video, he chuffed over a rise and out of sight.

Kelley listened to the turbine doppler down in the distance. "Instant toothpick," he said, chuckling. "Oh: Keith?"

I glanced around. "Sir?"

"Run down with the Six and help George pull a postops check"—he eyed me significantly—"and then grab a beer at the shack."

I grinned to myself at the word. Howard Scortia's geodesic dome was hardly a shack: more a statement of life-style according to the Prophet Fuller. If Mr. Scortia liked making statements of that sort, he was probably an ideal customer for Kelley. With ecology an enshrined word, the big lumber interests were helpless when government annexed "their" private rights to forest, range and watershed. The Department of the Interior might single out a lone prime tree for harvest, and threaten your license if you clipped a twig from the tree next to it. The hallowed jargon was shifting. It was *harvesting*, not *logging*—and very selectively. Snaking was only for pulp cellulose, since it damaged prime logs to drag them with a chain. You didn't snake, you toted. And the Kelley Magnum was just the rig to do it all.

I headed for my rig, the Magnum Six, which I herded around when I could get her to walk straight. The

Seven had more flexible programs and better stability in walk mode. The Six had developed an intermittent malf—malfunction—we couldn't fathom. Kelley wanted it checked out before the Six put a foot wrong and leaned on somebody a little. Eight tons of alloy with the blind staggers isn't much of a selling point. I started the turbine, which was down near the pressure pumps. It was the pumps that did everything; tried-and-true airmotors powered the wheels, gangsaws, and most other subsystems. Like Lear and Curran, Kelley knew when to bluesky and when to opt for standard hardware. That's why he had a working Magnum while AMF was still doping out system interfaces.

I found Infante playing with the damned tree as he tried to balance it upright at the loading ramp. Given time, I think he could've made the big fir stand alone. For a few minutes, anyway—or until somebody nudged it.

He saw me smile and interpreted it correctly: funny, but only as an idea. Impassive, he rolled back and let the huge log fall. Its butt kicked up nearly against the Seven. I silently cursed Infante for gashing the prime wood he had harvested, and risking his vehicle. But his pneumatics coughed, the nearside legs literally bouncing him safely away. That little lunatic could *move*.

"Kelley sending in the second team?" Infante's deceptively mild voice came through my com set.

"Wants us to check out the Six and—I'll tell you while we do it," I said. Ordinarily Infante was happy to drive while I inspected mechanical bits; George at his console, all's right with the world.

But now Infante flatly refused to handle the Six further. "If you ask me, that thing belongs in a straitjacket," he snarled. "You drive; I'll check the leg rams for binding."

As we went through the checkout, I wondered if it were only my imagination that made the Six seem more tractable for me than for Infante. Or maybe his low boiling point interfered with his fine touch. But even granting some difference, the Six had problems. Why *did* the bloody thing stagger? The malf was systemic, I decided: not traceable to any one leg. I hardly blamed Infante.

If Infante was an operator at heart, I was basically a troubleshooter. I'd had most of a five-year B.E. in systems engineering before I learned, during summer work, to make fast money highballing an earthmover. Dumb stunt, but I dropped out and chased the bucks. I wanted to design and build and race against the best Formula cars, and I did—with just enough success to keep me broke and hoping. I was exactly right for Kelley's operation after I sold the race car: just enough experience in vehicle systems, and just sick enough of myself to want somebody to believe in.

It was easy to believe in Tom Kelley. He did his own things, but they were useful things like the Magnums. Having helped him through some bitchin' chassis development problems, I had more time in our two prototypes than Kelley did himself. He was lean and mean for a sixty-year-old, but had the sense to trust younger synapses. They weren't helping me find the malf in the system, though.

Finally I gave up on the checkout and signaled my frustration to Infante. "I could use a ride in something that works," I added, nodding toward the Seven. "Let's see if Scortia really has that beer."

Infante scrambled down from his handholds on the Six. "But why doesn't my Seven act up the same way? They both have the same parts."

"Mechanicals, yes," I hedged. "The differences are mainly in that solid-state stuff Kelley dreamed up."

Pausing before swinging into the Seven's bubble, Infante gave me a wink full of fatherly wisdom. "That's where your malf is," he husked.

I gave a damifino shrug and followed. Those wise nonverbals seemed funny on Infante, but I didn't laugh. When he suspected you were laughing at him, George Infante was not likable. I preferred him likable. He wasn't quite my bulk, two years my senior, with big brooding eyes bordered by the longest lashes I have

seen on a man. Women didn't seem to mind his macho
ways. I liked him too, when he wasn't overcompensat-
ing for looking like a small latin angel.

We rolled back to the Scortia dome and Infante put
the Seven into a run as we neared the place. Kelley and
I had discussed the theoretical top speeds of the Magnum in walk and wheel modes, and it was Kelley's
dictum that we would not try to find out until he'd sold
a few. Infante must've been secretly practicing high-
speed runs, though: we were not merely trotting, we
were running hard and crabwise as we neared the dome.
Infante tooted, in case anyone failed to see us approach.
The toot was redundant. Kelley and Mr. Scortia stood
in the doorway, Kelley's face a study in feigned satisfaction. Infante went in for his beer. I sat in his harness a
few moments, figuring how he had obtained that angled
gait. Infante was given to unpredictable moods and
furies, an abrasive man for teamwork. But as a solo
operator he was brilliant.

As I entered the dome, Mr. Scortia handed me a
beer, holding it like a fragile toy in his great paw. "I
hear good things about your ways with machines," he
said.

Infante started to respond, realized the lumberman
was addressing me, and quickly turned away. I said, "It
may be a case of their having a way with me, Mr.
Scortia."

I perched on a stool near Kelley, who mused, "Keith
and my machines are easy to figure: they think alike."

Scortia chuckled from somewhere deep in the earth.
"That's why I need him, Tom." I glanced up; so did
Infante. Kelley missed neither look. There was a mo-
ment's utter silence.

"As I said, Howard, it's really up to Keith," Kelley
said. He looked alternately at me and Infante. "Howard
Scortia wants to chop costs by having his operator train-
ees learn here on the job. And only from our best man.
That's you, George—or you, Keith. As an operator—
and I'm being up front with you both—George, you're
so good it scares me." I caught the gut-level truth of

that, though Kelley's glance at me was bland. "Another month in a Magnum and you could enter the effin' thing in the Winter Olympics!"

We all laughed to relieve tension. Scortia lifted his beer in silent toast to Infante, who seemed less edgy now. The big man put in, "But I asked who trained *you*, George. And who's the best on-site consultant for maintenance gangs." He turned to me. "And Tom says they're both Keith Ames."

Kelley said wryly, "Keith, I explained we need you on assembly interfaces at Ashland and he could forget about borrowing you. And this Neanderthal says we can forget about the five Magnums while we're at it . . ." Kelley went on banking his rhetorical fires. Five Magnums! Too attractive an offer by far. Scortia was not a bigger name in the Oregon Cascades only because he liked to manage all his operations. If he sprang for a handful of Magnums, everybody from Weyerhaeuser on down would follow suit.

I half-listened to Kelley drip drollery instead of excitement. Like Scortia, Kelley was self-developed and knew his best operational modes. Kelley had started as a cards-lucky kid in the Seabees and never lost his fascination with heavy equipment that functioned with precision. But he also had an eye for what the equipment was all about, the massaging of man's world. When he realized the future of glass fibers around 1950, he sank a month's poker winnings into Corning and didn't regret it. By the time I was born he was building military runway extensions and saw what was about to happen in air travel. He got fatter on Boeing, then on fluorocarbons. Finally he saw he was still gambling with paper when he wanted to do it with hardware and his goofy solid-states. And he took his twenty million right in the middle of the recession and sank it into man-amplifier systems. The Magnum was his heavy bet.

"I know what your contract says, Keith, but I also know what I told you. And if Howard Scortia doesn't take Magnums, his competitors will," Kelley finished, whistling in the dark.

I swirled my beer, thinking. "Well, it's nearly June. By the time we have enough Magnums, there'll barely be time to get 'em in full operation before the rains." Scortia nodded; in Western Oregon you aren't a native until your gill slits begin to function. "Fifty days of familiarization. I can lift down to Ashland in an hour if you need me," I said to Kelley.

"And what if you have to start training with only one Magnum," Kelley asked softly. Infante was perfectly still, listening to something in his head.

"Add thirty days," I hazarded. "I don't see how we can spook up a new Magnum before July, though. Unless somebody slips a cog and we sell a proto."

Now Scortia laughed openly. Kelley made a rueful face: "Guilty as charged, I guess. Keith, I promised him the Seven."

"When?" Infante's question was soft but his corneas were pinpricks in his eyes.

"Is she a hundred percent now?"

Infante hesitated. Kelley glanced at me, and I nodded. Kelley spread his hands. "Then she stays here. Anything wrong with that?"

"I hear rumors you're the boss," I grinned. What bothered me was George Infante. I wished I could read behind those eyes.

"One thing," Scortia said. "Could I hitch a, uh, walk to my Cottage Grove office? I want to enjoy my Magnum before she gets all scruffy. A walk through town is more than I can resist."

"*I* can resist it," I said, counting off on my fingers. "No street license, too wide for state code, and a risk of equipment, for starters."

He winked, "I'll take care of any problems. I want my new rig under my office window for a few days."

Somehow I had never thought of the Magnum as a status symbol. But there it was: the kid in Howard Scortia was loose in our toyshop. "I believe this man has it worse than we do," I said to Infante. "Promise you won't kick any Buicks?"

"It's your show," Infante replied easily. "Why don't you tote Mr. Scortia downtown?"

I was glad to; we had no experience in real-world traffic yet, and this was underwritten. But as we sauntered out to a chill afternoon breeze, I filed a question away. What made Infante so ready to divorce his amplified self, the Magnum Seven? Whatever had been behind his unreadable expression, it had changed when Scortia asked me to park the Seven in town.

I highballed down from Scortia's site to the interstate freeway in an hour, keeping to the verges with all subsystems fully retracted. That way we made a package twelve feet wide, thirty-two long, and scarcely ten high. It was only a bit cramped in the bubble, though I'm average size and Mr. Scortia is a fee-fie-foe-fum type. Naturally we picked up a patrol cruiser as the Seven walked chuffing into town. When he heard the beeper, Mr. Scortia waved joyfully. The cruiser was almost as massive as Caddies of the old days, and dwarfed normal traffic. Yet from the Magnum it seemed a bantam, challenging the cock of the—ah—walk. Whoever said, "Power corrupts . . ." maybe I should give him his due. Sacrifice a goat to him or something. I was uncomfortable with the thought that, momentarily, the police seemed insignificant. Walking a Magnum is walking very, very tall.

The police beeper and beacon went off; the cruiser drew alongside and the big man made sign talk to the effect that this was *his* rig and Gawd, Nell, ain't it grand? They didn't stop us, but they didn't leave us either. My rear video was full of cop cruiser from there to the Scortia offices.

Once in his parking lot: "Waltz us around, this is private property," he said. I did, while he watched me. I knew my first trainee would be Howard Scortia and smiled, wondering how many miles he would perambulate his Magnum around that space in the next few days. Then we set the operator harness for the Scortia bulk and got a half-assed calibration for his particular combination of synapses and rhythms. Once an operator is thoroughly calibrated you can insert a program card for him into the console. But for a new operator, the calibration is rough. Under the lumberman's control, the Seven lurched a few times just as the Six did, until I set the verniers again.

By nightfall my trainee could amble around with reasonable safety. I keyed all extensor subsystems for access only by primary operators, so I wouldn't worry about Scortia accidentally shoving his remoting axle through a brick wall while I was in Ashland. Then he hauled us all into Eugene where we feasted at some place called Excelsior. Then we met a copter at the river and lifted down to the Ashland plant.

Infante, Kelley and I stayed at the plant awhile, burping quiche Lorraine and debriefing. Kelley made notes. Infante shuffled call-ins before deciding to answer a miz and arranging to be picked up. To my surprise, he asked if I would make it a foursome. To my further surprise I said OK. I wanted to say good-bye to a miz, expecting to be gone awhile, and thought it would be less a problem if I did it in company. Besides, it did not seem the right time to make George Infante feel rejected. So much for Keith Ames, boy psychoanalyst . . .

I don't know how long the phone buzzed before I lurched up from a maelstrom dream and slapped the "accept" plate by my bed. I said something nonaccepting.

"Always the last place you look," Kelley grated, not amused. I lay back, glad I had no video on my phone, and tried not to breathe hard. It hurt. The light hurt too. I kept my eyes shut. "How long've you been there?"

I thought for an eternity, and even *that* hurt. "What's the time?"

Kelley delivered a word he keeps for special occasions, then, "Eight-fifteen, and time you answered my question!"

"I—honest to God, I don't know," I moaned. "Mr. Kelley, I need time to think. I feel rotted away."

"You may get fifty years to think while you sure 'nough rot away," he said, and my eyes snapped open. Whatthehell *now?* "Keith, if you're not at the plant in ten minutes you can handle this mother alone! Uh, you're not hurt?"

"I'm mummified. But I don't think I'm—"

"Move your ass, then! And walk. Up the alley. All the way." He slapped off.

Once on my feet I felt better, but nauseated. I struggled into a turtleneck and coverall, nearly passed out while putting my boots on, and shouldered past my back door wishing I had something to barf up. Whatever was wrong, it was screwed up tight and twisted off. I had gone three of the six blocks down my friendly informal alleys when I heard police beepers heading down Siskiyou, and so fuzzy-minded I didn't connect them with Kelley's call.

Tom Kelley opened the alley gate himself and hauled me in with desperate strength, as though the plant meant safety. Maybe it did. Hurrying to his office, he held my sleeve as a truant officer had, once. He kept gnawing his lip and muttering. I began to feel well enough to hit somebody. Infante, maybe; what had I been swilling?

Halfway through a skull-ripping question-and-answer session with Kelley, I was still trying to get his drift when the phone buzzed. The close-cropped curls of a lady cop flicked onto Kelley's video. Kelley made the right decision: yes, I was with him and no, I wasn't their man, and since I was in no condition to visit the station, could they come to the plant?

When police lieutenant Meta Satterlee arrived, I was trying not to spill mocha on the table every time I shuddered. Satterlee reminded me of a loose-jointed math prof I knew. She asked for a blood sample and took it herself, expertly, but I fainted anyway. They both eased up then. The police already knew where I'd been until midnight, from a talk with my miz. Some of it came back to me. I hadn't been drinking heroically, but somehow I got a gutful of something so potent, Infante took me to my apartment. That's all I knew. "Maybe Infante can shed some light on this," I said.

Kelley and the cop exchanged a wry look. "A meeting devoutly to be wished," Satterlee replied, savoring her line. "Mr. Kelley has been less than completely open with us up to now, but I think we can all benefit if I can see some personnel files." She raised a questioning brow toward Kelley, who mooched off through the deserted offices to hunt up our files.

Satterlee sat on the table edge, swinging one trousered leg. It was quiet for a moment, except for the ball bearings someone was grinding in my head. "I'll accept as probable that you didn't know about the APB out on you," she said at last.

"Who told you that?"

"Did you?"

I realized Tom Kelley had known even if I hadn't. "No." The leg began to swing again. "I woke up with—uh—buzzing in my head, and something seemed all wrong, and I got up and walked down to the plant like I usually do."

"Uh-huh. You usually run down alleys every Saturday morning?"

I raised my head, not wanting to shift my eyeballs, and almost managed a smile. "If I had tried to run, lady, my body would've simply disintegrated. You have no idea how I feel."

She caressed the blood sample. "Not at the moment," she admitted. She added something under her breath and left quickly, returning without the sample. I wondered how many cops were milling around in front of the plant. Hell of a public image.

Kelley spread a pair of folders on the table. Satterlee took them, evidently speed-reading, then tapped one with a finger while looking off into the office gloom. Then she said, "I have to take some risks in this busi-

ness, Mr. Kelley. I'm taking one on you now: are you
certain Ames is not involved?"

Tom Kelley stared his best two-pair bluff straight into
her face. "One—hundred—percent."

She registered faint amusement. "I'll settle for ninety-
five," she replied, "if I can place him in your custody."

A nod. I looked from one to the other. "Will you
goddamn kindly tell me *what has happened*," I asked.
"A hit and run?"

"Altogether too good a guess. Using that vehicle of
yours."

I was slow. "My Porsche?"

"Your tree harvester," she said tiredly.

I put my hands over my face. "Oh dear goddy," I
said. Infante!

Satterlee went on. "I'm from Eugene; we have a
copter waiting . . ."

"Hold it," I said and looked up, alert. "Where's the
Seven?" Satterlee was slow this time. "The Seven. The
Magnum. My bloody tree harvester," I cried, exasper-
ated.

"Mr. Infante seems to have it at the moment,"
Satterlee said, "and we have nothing that can catch
him." She saw my alarm and went on quickly, "Oh,
we'll take him eventually; and I understand your concern over your new machine. But right now I wish
there were somebody else with a similar vehicle."

"There is," Kelley said. He jerked a thumb at me.

Satterlee taped my statement as we lifted north to
the Eugene-Cottage Grove strip city. She began to leak
the story as she had pieced it together and Kelley
glumly watched wet green-black forest and fogwisp slip
below the copter. Editing out my questions and some
inevitable back-tracking, Satterlee put it roughly this
way: "Sometime around three a.m., a poker crowd in
Cottage Grove heard chainsaws ripping through a third-
floor wall nearby. All they knew was, it was one awful
racket for a few seconds. This was near the city limit
where the cities are snarling over jurisdiction.

"Turned out someone was after a payroll in the Daniel mill. Don't ask *me* what it was doing there on a Friday night, some of these old outfits keep a bushel of raw cash around with only a steel-faced door between themselves and bankruptcy. About eighty-five thousand in cash was taken, minus the change.

"Then a Eugene prowl car spotted something proceeding east at high speed. The officer gave chase. Very excited. Said the thing ran *on legs* across a suburban mall but that he was catching it.

"And then it caught *him*. It evidently grabbed his cruiser near the front window and picked it up, judging from the debris, and threw two tons of prowl car into the Safeway front window, setting off the alarm. And incidentally," her jaw twitched once, "killing the officer.

"We were fit to be untied after that hot-pursuit crash. A bright cadet found oval depressions big as coffee tables in the mall and surmised it truly was a hellacious big machine on legs. Road blocks all negative. Then Pacific Tel reported vandalism on some old phone lines over a street in the east outskirts of Cottage Grove. Something tall as a telephone pole took the lines down like a grizzly through a spiderweb. But no oval tracks. Then a drunk convinced us there was a gaping hole up on the Daniel Building.

"From then until now, it's been our biggest Chinese fire drill since the Bowles escape in the Seventies. A Mr. Howard Scortia reported the theft of his Magnum from his very own personal parking lot in the night, and you can imagine the confusion then." Kelley and I swapped miserable chuckles. She continued, "When we realized he was talking about a big vehicle instead of a handgun, we first hypothesized Scortia was involved. But he had some things going for him: an alibi, a local rep any politician might envy, and the nearest thing to a genuine speechless rage I ever expect to hear. He put us in touch with Mr. Kelley. I was already airborne so I lifted for Ashland.

"We got some fingerprint ID's then, but prints can be planted. Mr. Kelley couldn't believe either of his top operators had done anything offbase, but he gave us a pair of names. The Ashland force is very sharp. I suppose it helps when they know everyone in town."

She gave a little snort. "Oh, yes: there's a traffic control officer in Cottage Grove who verified that Scortia could've driven your monster machine. Said officer is in deep yogurt for failure to report your attractive nuisance meandering through congested traffic yesterday. If he'd logged a description in, we'd've been hours ahead."

I explained the traffic incident, adding, "There are lots of odd agriculture rigs. Since we *didn't* by-God disturb traffic, maybe he dismissed us as just another new plow or something."

"He may shortly face another kind of dismissal. I can't even guess all the ways your new plowshare can be used as a sword."

I was in a better position to guess. Even in darkness, Infante could use infrared video to guide an extensor through a hole in a wall, using his gangsaws. I didn't see how an extensor could scoop up cash, but since Infante's prints were in the cash room, that one was simple enough. He had shinnied up the duralloy beam and personally ransacked the place. "If he filled his plenums first," I offered, "he could do it all on air pressure for several minutes without using his turbine. Quieter, except for going into the wall. You could park nearly a half-block away and run the gangsaws out to a wall, so long as there was room to extend the remote axle as a balancing moment."

Meta Satterlee broke out a sheaf of faxed maps, confirming that Infante could have done it that way. "Your inferences are awfully good," she said, "for someone who hasn't seen an aerial map of the scene."

"Maps," I yelped. "You have charts of the terrain east of here?"

She did. Kelley came alive then, and we began tracing the likely paths Infante might take. Satterlee was optimistic about the Six and called to get its fuel tanks topped off by Scortia's crew. As we swung up a valley I

could see Cottage Grove to the northwest. Copter lights
blinked in and out of a low voluptuous cloudbank advancing on us from the Cascade range. Patrol copters
were running search patterns with IR, radar, and gas
analyzers, but had turned up nothing promising. That
wasn't surprising, our pilot announced. The Cascades
are so steep, with so many sources of heat and emis-
sions to check, it might take days to find a Kelley
Magnum. Especially if Infante was smart enough to
minimize the use of his turbine. The heavy weather
front made it worse. It doesn't rain all the time there in
May; only half the time.

It was an hour to lunch when the copter whirred
down in the clearing next to the Magnum Six. Satterlee
shook her head in dismay, perhaps beginning to realize
the full destructive potential of the beast we hunted.
With lifting heart, I saw Scortia in the Six's bubble,
manfully trying to hotwire her ignition. Standing alert
in the drizzle were a dozen of his gang. Not one lacked
a shotgun.

While I checked out the Six and filled her plenums,
the others lifted to Scortia's dome to confer with remote
units by com set. My head was clear by then and, best
sign of all, I was hungry. I highballed back to the dome
and was met outside by an oddly different Meta Satterlee.

"Whether your friend Infante is working alone or
not," she said, "I'm happy to report he is not your
friend."

"Where were you yesterday," I grumped.

"It's where the Ashland lab people have been that'll
interest you," she said, matching strides with me toward
the dome that shed rivulets of Oregon rain down its
faceted flanks. "You, sire, were drugged like a horse.
Ah—it's safe to say you didn't brush your teeth or
gargle this morning."

"Jeez, is it that bad?" I tried to smell my own breath.

"Could be worse, dear. Somebody hypoed more alka-
loids into your toothpaste, and made an interesting
addition to your mouthwash."

"For Christ's sake! What for?"

"To zonk you out the minute you became functional again. A cute little notion favored by the Families back east, I'm told. Which ties in nicely with George Infante—if you call that nice."

"Mafia?"

"Splinter groups of it. The man with George Infante's fingertips was believed to be wheelman on a major crime last year in Gary, Indiana. Not arraigned; lack of evidence. They gave him a long, long rope and it led here. Nice of 'em to warn us. Oh, hell, too much of that and I suppose we'd have a police state."

Infante a getaway driver: it figured. The sonofabitch was a natural. I began to shake with anger as well as low blood-sugar. In the dome I calmed down with sweet coffee and eggs served up by Scortia himself. My only cheering thought was that Satterlee seemed to be accepting my innocence as very likely.

A burly captain of the Oregon Highway Patrol mumbled with Satterlee over the high-relief area charts. He had some trouble with her gender; not because she was all that attractive a miz, but because she insisted on doing her job like any other cop.

Reluctantly he offered her a heavy parcel, which she pocketed. "Pretend you're using a carbine," he said. "Forget about long leads or aiming high. And watch that recoil," he sighed, with a glance at her narrow shoulders.

"I've qualified with boosted ammo," she said a bit crossly. "I only wish we had some of the new API stuff."

"It's coming from Salem," he said helplessly. "Can you wait?"

I interrupted her negative headshake as I approached their work table. "I still don't see why Infante tried to poison me when he could've just as easily cut my throat," I said.

"He wanted you alive but on ice," Satterlee explained. "My guess is, he didn't expect to be seen, and thought he'd have until Monday before we connected the pay-roll job with a missing Magnum. Since you could've done it as easily as he did, he wanted you as a live decoy. By the time you were on your feet, he could be back in Ashland, maybe having switched your mouthwash. Then he could wallop himself with his own drugs and have a story at least as good as yours. He just didn't plan on his murder spree."

The OHP man rasped, "Sure as hell didn't shrink from it."

"Lieutenant, you really think George Infante planned to stick around after the job, with his known background, and put his word against mine? Does that make sense?" I asked.

Satterlee tapped a finger against the projection of the Three Sisters wilderness area in impatient thought. "Not really. From the profile we're developing on him it's hard to say. I could give you a long academy phrase for Infante, but let me give it to you without the bullshit: I think we're dealing with a crazy man."

"Foxy crazy," the captain reminded her. "We may never find out how he got from Ashland to Cottage Grove so fast; and you don't know how he got a fix on that payroll. But he damn well *did it*. And unless the forestry people are crazy too, he tried to get up here to your other unit—the Six?—early this morning."

This brought Howard Scortia onto his feet, his stool over backward. It suddenly occurred to me that this old gent had started in his business when it was a brawler's job. "You didn't tell me that," he roared.

"Betcherass I didn't." The OHP man grinned. "You'd be chasin' around up there with a willow switch—"

"And my eight-gauge!"

Kelley spoke up from his well of gloom. For the first time since I'd known him, he was sounding his age. "Barring luck, Howard, you might as well have one as the other. They're right, it's plain stupid to go after the Seven without special weapons. But what's this about it being around here?"

Infante was no longer roaming the heights above us, but there were fresh prints skirting a nearby ridge, and they hadn't been there the day before: prints only a

Magnum's feet could make. I calculated this would've
been about dawn if Infante went cross-country. And he
would not have kept to the roads. Infante wasn't *that*
crazy. "One thing sure," I said. "Infante didn't intend to
switch to the Six. Hell, he won't even operate it, he
thinks it's hexed. Maybe he wanted to destroy it."

"Probably something scared him off," the captain
said.

"Beats me what it would've been," Scortia mused. "I
called and put a crew on guard only after I realized my
Magnum was gone, around eight a.m. or so."

"Damn, that's right." Satterlee was tapping like mad.
"This is rough country; knowing it halfway is infinitely
better than not knowing it at all." Scortia nodded.
"What if he wasn't interested in the other vehicle?"

"Then why come up this way?" This from Kelley.

"I don't know. He could buy time by evasion in these
wilds. He probably has the money with him. All he
needed to do was ditch the vehicle and catch the valley
monorail to Portland. *Unless he had further plans for
the Magnum!*"

Kelley and I burst out talking, convinced she had
doped it right. The OHP man was vehicle-oriented,
sending us back to the relief charts with: "If that thing
can do only seventy on wheels, how does he expect to
escape in it?"

One answer was, he could select a mountain lake and
ditch the Magnum in it. But he might not get it back. A
second was, he had a rendezvous with an equipment
carrier within fuel range of the Magnum. The third
answer was that Infante was nuts.

If it were number one, the Magnum was already underwater. I didn't think Infante would drown his alter ego.
If number two, we might try searching every road that
could accommodate a semi-rig or transporter. And if
number three, logic could gather dust on the shelf.
Infante might be reasonable all the way, or some of the
time, or not at all. Or he might change modes every
time a bell rang in his noggin. The OHP and Eugene
forces were patched into the captain's neat com set and,

given time, would have all the people needed to comb the area. But Satterlee decided against waiting and prepared to lift up to some nearby lakes in her copter, to check on the "drowned Magnum" hypothesis.

She had already lifted off when the OHP announced paydirt. A hint from copter radar was followed in dense fog by a highway cruiser. An old diesel transporter was stashed away not far off Highway 58 near Willamette Pass. It was on firm ground, fitted with wheel ramps, and had jacks under one set of duals but nothing evidently wrong to justify the jacks. It could have been there a week or more.

We heard Satterlee's cool contralto ask for a stakeout at the transporter, and she was trotting back to the dome a few minutes later. "This looks likely," she said, "but could Infante have parked it himself during the past ten days? It's crucial: he may have help in this, and there are"—her gaze flickered past me—"complications if a second equipment operator is in on this."

I knew, but let Kelley think it through for himself. Satterlee would value it at zip, coming from me. "Yes," Kelley said slowly, "last weekend. We all knew we'd have both Magnums up here for the Scortia demo."

"So did fifty people in my organization," Scortia rumbled. "It wasn't exactly a state secret."

Satterlee smiled, a brief sunburst of good teeth. "Which gives us fifty more suspects—but no matter. The patrol officer took microscan prints from the transporter, and we can get positive print ID by video." She was standing as if relaxed, but if I had said boo she would have ventilated me by reflex action. I realized Satterlee had returned with the idea that somehow I was, after all, tied in with Infante. I liked her, and I didn't like her. Perhaps it was just that I couldn't blame her, but I wanted to.

I walked to the coffee pot, a huge old veteran that had seen campfires long before it saw the inside of a geodesic dome. I was nervous as a rabbi in Mecca, knowing that Meta Satterlee was gauging my every move.

Then the com set displayed a pair of apparently identical thumbprints. Eugene confirmed: George Infante had recently driven the transporter—and placed the jacks, too. The OHP man whistled. Satterlee shook her head wonderingly. "This little man has had some busy days, and some luck. How much is the Magnum Seven worth, Mr. Kelley?"

"Six hundred thou," Scortia replied instantly, accusingly.

"Or to some other firms, ten times that," Kelley answered the accusation.

"No telling how much it might be worth to factions of the underworld," Meta Satterlee said. "Keith Ames, I apologize for some reservations about you. I didn't say so, but . . ."

"The hell you didn't, it was all over your face. 'Act natural, Ames, or I'll letcha have it,' " I said, aping the old Bogart style.

She tried not to grin, failed, then sobered. "Sorry. But you have been in rough company. Bear in mind that your Mr. Infante has intimate connections among the Families."

"Meaning?"

"Meaning his reference groups are pretty restrictive," she said. "More simply: he is as likely to care about most human life as he is about a bug on his windshield. I don't want you to be in any doubt about that."

"Why me, especially?"

"Because this weather front is going to impede air search for days. Because Infante might run across dozens of hikers or workers during that time. And because you're the only person trained and able to cut that time short, if you're willing to be deputized to run him down with me."

It was Satterlee's idea to use the transporter as a jumpoff point, and mine to run the Magnum Six in wheel mode up Highway 58. We estimated that Infante could already be nearing his transporter after several

hours' head start in heavy rains across the Diamond
Peak wilderness area. There were no navigable trails
short of the highway, so we'd be unlikely to cut him off.
If we simply trailed him, we could only learn what he'd
done after he'd done it. Better, thought Satterlee, to
intercept him. I had a half-formed notion I could reason
with him if we managed to confront him from a position
of more or less equal footing. I believed as Satterlee
did; real or spurious, the equivalence of the two Magnums might alter Infante's plans to muscle his way
through, leaving still more grief in his wake.

Kelley was right; with no load but Satterlee and her
riot gun behind me in the bubble, the Magnum Six
exceeded seventy miles an hour on level stretches. An
OHP cruiser ran interference for us most of the way
and at two p.m. we were at Infante's transporter. The
lone stakeout man was considerably more nervous when
we left him, having seen from ground level what kind of
vehicle he was to stop. Satterlee's ammunition did not
fit his weapon. His orders were to blow tires if possible,
then aim for the air plenums. Without a prime mover
Infante was only a hundred and sixty pounds of maniac,
instead of eight tons of it. Or he could make it sixty tons
if he chose to use a tree for a battering ram. Satterlee
put in an urgent call for more help at the stakeout.
They were promised within the hour.

Satterlee made an obvious target perched up behind
me. *If* he had a weapon capable of penetrating the
bubble, and *if* his own bubble were raised, Infante
might bushwhack us from cover. She saw the logic of
hunkering down in the equipment hopper. She didn't
have to like it. I could receive police frequency, but
dared not reply and we had not thought to patch in an
extension for Satterlee outside the bubble. Infante could
monitor us, and I didn't want him hearing my voice or
the strength of my signal.

A damnable dialog kept looping through my head.
What would I do if I were Infante? The refrain was
always . . . *anything at all*. Still, Satterlee made sense. If
Infante did something really wild it would probably

impede him. If her quarry were smartest he'd be most dangerous—and he'd rendezvous with the transporter.

I went to walk mode en route to a knoll a half-mile from the transporter. Poised on the forty-five-degree talus slope, sliding only a little, I heard a patrol copter pass in the low overcast. A few moments later a strong negative report signal reached my com set. And if they couldn't detect us with our turbine running, they might pass over Infante the same way. The ugly handgun Meta Satterlee gave me seemed like useless weight in my coverall. I had more confidence in the boosted slugs her riot gun carried. Though far from muscular, she handled herself with grace and confidence. The twelve-gauge would be a double armful but she was one smart, tough miz and I never doubted she could use it. If she got the chance. Trouble was, Infante was sheer entropy on wheels; one of those people who lives on uncertainty.

We shifted vantage points twice, getting further from the transporter as we eased toward where we thought Infante might approach. As I walked the Six carefully to keep the pneumatics quiet, my hopes went in both directions. It was like preparing for a race in chancy weather, you don't know whether to count on rain or shine, so you choose your equipment and hope. And get the butterfly-gut syndrome. And you live with it.

I was on the point of suggesting another move when Satterlee made a startled motion. I followed her out-stretched hand and saw George Infante scrambling into his harness, not half a mile off in a creekbed. The Seven had been there—how long? I wondered if he knew we were there. It seemed he didn't; he came up from the gully on legs, but cautiously. As the Seven approached the transporter, Infante showed less caution. Satterlee guessed why.

I accelerated for the transporter and saw exhaust pluming from its old diesel. "He has it running," Satterlee shouted, pounding on my bubble. "He took our man out! Go, goddammit, *go!*"

I reached the road and went to wheel mode just as Infante vaulted from his Magnum. It was already on the transporter, but he hadn't chocked or strapped down. When he saw us he stiffened in recognition as if from electric shock. We were already too near for him to reach the cab-over. I wished we'd waited until he got started; a Magnum can outrun a transporter and eat holes through it.

Infante opted for his Magnum, pouring back into his harness as we neared shooting range. Ever see a quarterhorse rear back? When Infante rolled backward off that ramp, he went to walk mode so fast the Seven actually went up on her hind legs before setting off down a ravine.

Satterlee risked a shot and missed, nearly falling with the recoil. We exchanged glances as I whirled the Six on wheels down a gentler incline, hoping to snag Infante with something. Both of us saw the terrible, bleeding lump of meat wearing tatters of a police rain slicker. Infante had run over the stakeout man. I hoped it was after he was already dead.

I broke radio silence and called for everything in Oregon. Then I brodied as hard as I could. Infante had neatly suckered me into building up velocity downhill and had his magnificent, deadly goddamn Seven running *backward* toward the road.

I stayed in wheel mode but without pausing to think about it, momentarily engaged the legs to stilt us over a narrow gully. It saved us a few seconds. I dared not give Infante time to select a tree or he would have a bat and we, the baseball. We reached the road two hundred yards behind Infante and both Magnums went howling toward the main highway, turbines like sirens. Satterlee somehow put a shot directly into Infante's rear video sensor. To me it looked as though the sensor had simply exploded. Infante raked his duralloy gangsaw beam back, elbowed it, and made it a shield for his bubble. I saw a long clean scar appear along the beam as Satterlee fired again. She might as well have hit a bridge pillar.

Infante saw the patrol cruiser's flasher before we did; he crashed off into the brush parallel with the road. I shouted a warning on my com set. Too late. As the cruiser rushed toward us, Infante swept his extensor beam out across the road and the driver barely had time to duck before a set of wailing gangsaws took away his windshield and roof. They tell me the officer lived.

I had gained over a hundred yards. On a hunch, I motioned Satterlee out of the way and manipulated my beam out ahead about fifteen yards. *What would I do if I were Infante?* Run that third axle back as a feint to make us swerve, maybe. I hoped he would, so I could hook onto it and set my brakes.

Craning his head back as he reached the road, his rear video only a memory, Infante saw my strategy. Then he saw the campers. Ahead, parked in disarray along the shore of a small lake, a group of Oregonians were going about the lovely business of fishing, rain or no rain.

Satterlee shouted something. All I caught was ". . . hostages!" If Infante got among those poor devils he could grind all but one to powder and still have himself a ticket out. He turned sharply but had to avoid an arroyo. I stilted it, by God, something I could still teach him. Then I held my breath and drove straight through a grove of aspen. Both Infante and I saw that I had the momentum. I might, could, I surely *would* ram him scant yards from the nearest camper. I shouted for Satterlee to jump.

Angling his course off behind the parked vehicles, Infante unlimbered a silenced handgun and fired through his bubble. A mistake; the polymer turned the slug and gashed his own bubble. Then he swung his duralloy beam out as if to sweep three kids and a woman toward him. It probably would kill them outright, at the rate he was moving. Racing parallel with him, a covey of horrified campers screaming between us, I lashed my extensor out and parried his with a jolt that nearly tore me from my harness. With a cry of anger, Satterlee flipped clear of my rear wheels. Her riot gun got thoroughly graunched but it proved one thing: the slug it fired in the process, blew out the right rear tire on my remoting axle.

Infante's gangsaw extensor waved in an arc, bent at its elbow. In one wild swing his gangsaws cut a swath through the back of his bubble. My parry had side-swiped the length of his duralloy beam, taking limit switches with it. For the first time, now, Infante had a real mechanical malf. Those switches prevent the beam from swinging back to hit the vehicle—but only when they work. Infante ducked away from the shards of plastic that spewed around him in his bubble, then turned away from me as he stopped the extensor beam.

I thought he intended to run, but instead, he fired at me through the hole his own gangsaws had made. A hole appeared in my bubble with the toll of a muted bell. The slug stopped on its way out. I thrust my gangsaw beam ahead as a shield and tried to accelerate, intending to ram him from behind. Part of me was scared puckerless, remembering what Infante would do to a man. And part of me, looking past that bullet-hole, just didn't give a good goddamn. Now I saw I could engage his rear axle if he slowed, or pursue him toward the lake if he went ahead. In either case he was beyond taking hostages. I rolled smashing through a litter of unattended camp equipment, boats and all. Infante ran for it in wheel mode, not realizing the trouble I had just to move straight with that deflated rear tire. I saw I would have to give it up, and went to walk mode faster than I thought possible. The Magnum Six leaped up on her legs with hard pneumatic coughs and I ran her straight at him. Still on wheels, looking back without his rear video, Infante laughed as he easily outdistanced me.

And found himself boxed.

He faced the lake on the right side, and an almost straightup bluff on the left. Fifty yards ahead, the bluff came to the water's edge. It was thirty feet up, much too vertical even for a Magnum. And directly behind, I loped the Six with a spine-jarring stride. She staggered, but she was highballin'.

Infante risked going into the water to get around the bluff. Another mistake. It was a steep dropoff and even with her right-hand legs on full extension, the Seven tilted over at a dizzy, crazy angle. Her turbine swallowed water and seized explosively with a flashing exhaust spray. But he still had his air plenums. Popping his bubble back, Infante set his gangsaws howling as I raced down on him.

I ran my duralloy beam out and above him like a great arm to wave him back as he leaped and clawed up the brush-covered precipice, money spilling from his jacket. His gangsaws moaned just over my bubble and continued the arc Infante had programmed. He saw my beam and made a lightning decision to dive for the lake. With no limit switches, his beam elbowed at precisely the wrong angle, George Infante met his own gangsaws in mid-air.

Kneeling at the lake's edge, I lost the meal Scortia had fed me. Satterlee had the decency to let my brief spasm of heaves and tears pass before she approached. I washed up in the icy clear water and stood shaking, judging the path of Infante's murderous—and suicidal—weapon. It was still swinging in the same arc. There was no danger to me, so I climbed the chassis to the ruined bubble and flicked off the pneumatic valve switches. I did not look at the gangsaws again.

Satterlee refused to let me rig a sling on the Seven until a crew arrived to make the necessary police videotapes. I couldn't argue with a bruised miz who had, in a way, poked out Infante's eye when she obliterated his rear video. I owed her. I would've kissed her if she hadn't been a cop. After the first camera passes, the police asked me to move the Six back a bit, and I made myself think about something else. It had been gnawing at me since my first inkling that Infante himself was erratic.

And in a half-hour I isolated the malf in the Magnum Six. I erased all calibration programs, including mine and Infante's, and carefully recalibrated myself. The campers watched me with suspicion, unaware that I was only making a checkout. Well, maybe I played a little, running backwards and essaying that slanting gait Infante had used.

When Tom Kelley arrived in the police copter, I had good news. "Hey, your new solid-states in the Seven did more than you thought," I hailed him. "They damped out a malf that we put in, ourselves."

As I explained, Kelley furrowed his brow. "But it doesn't work that way," he complained. "Dammit, it won't program a random error, Keith."

I nodded. "I didn't say it was random. In some complex way it was predictable and not a random aberration. It was picked up and integrated by the multigraph functions monitoring his behavior. I checked out in the Six first; but remember, Infante was the first one you calibrated closely because his reflexes were so sharp."

Kelley was silent for a long moment. "So I built in a malf that the damping circuits cured in the Seven. Huh! I'm smarter *and* dumber than I thought I was. Well, we don't know enough about psychophysics, but systems theory should'a told me," Kelley grumbled. "When you have a sane man who overrides a master control, the *real* master control is the man. That's why you were better in the Six than Infante was."

"Come on," I said, remembering Infante's panache in a Magnum.

"Infante was flashy; you were predictable, Keith. Your manual override was really a mental override. That makes a malf fundamentally a feedback-correctable item. No wonder Infante thought the Six was nuts, it was feeding his own aberrations back to him amplified—worse than it was for you. That kind of feedback might push a man over the brink; I dunno. I do know that the original malf was Infante."

I gazed out on the lake, where calm gutty Meta Satterlee watched police gather most of eighty-five thousand dollars in bills, like leaves on the quiet water. "I wonder if his malf could've been traced," I said.

But the real world is not a neat circuit. As the OHP

captain predicted, we never learned how, or even if, George Infante managed so much by himself. Nor what plans he had for the Magnum Seven.

Kelley's crystal ball wasn't bad, either. By the time I trained Scortia's operators, there were Magnums enough to go around and orders enough to please him. Kelley got his bonus in media coverage. And I got mine. It cost Howard Scortia a bundle to get his pocketwatch duplicated.

THE FUTURE OF FLIGHT:
COMES THE REVOLUTION

All futures are *not* created equally.

Of course, all of those futures are educated guesses. Guessers who assume that all long-established trends must continue will, with Thomas Malthus, often show us gloomy futures; evolution with a vengeance. Yet we know that trends are not always continuous.

The extinction of most dinosaurs, about 64,000,000 years ago, was a natural revolution on Earth; a sudden discontinuity in a *very* long-established trend. Evidence is mounting that a sizeable asteroid struck this planet with such violence that the ecological carpet was suddenly jerked from under the feet of the great reptiles. Early mammals benefited from this sudden change and a different future evolved. The human race is a beneficiary.

Occasionally a new idea rekindles the human spirit, reverses trends, and creates real changes in the quality of life. When the change is discontinuous, a sharp break from predictable step-by-step evolution, we have *revolution*. It may be political and violent, or it may be technological and peaceful.

The future we "create" in these pages has an unfair

Excerpted from The Future of Flight *by Dr. Leik Myrabo and Dr. Dean Ing* advantage over some others because ours plugs in the revolutionary stuff. We think that is proper because, when people's backs are against the wall, they turn to any revolutionary help that's handy. As it happens, much of our world is nearing disaster in its energy needs—and we are not finding permanent peaceful solutions in conventional ways. Some leaders are beginning to look hard for revolutionary solutions (in several senses!). We're in luck because, among others we will describe, there is one that left the realm of "pure" science fiction around 1960 and it does not require violence or a new government. But it may cause a few governments to evolve in useful ways.

Revolutionary change is relatively rare. It's also less predictable than the weather, which explains why leaders often greet it with gritted teeth. The best they can do is rush to see how the new revolutionary change might affect them because, after the revolution, evolution takes over again, and that's more predictable.

Thanks in part to outrageous claims by advertising flacks, we have just about wrung all the juice from the word *revolutionary*. Every new kitchen gadget, diet fad and teaching aid is a candidate for the tag, despite the fact that almost all of them evolve, step by painstaking step, from previous ideas without much discontinuity. The marvelous airships of Alberto Santos-Dumont are often mislabeled this way.

Santos-Dumont, an eccentric little Brazilian, became the toast of Europe in the 1890's with his dirigible (which means directable, or steerable) balloons. As a boy, he had read the science fiction of Jules Verne to his saturation point, tinkered with engines on his father's coffee plantation, and built toy hot-air balloons of the type pioneered by the Montgolfiers a century earlier. Arriving in Paris in 1891, he found that cigar-shaped balloons had already been tried; hydrogen and other gases were used to inflate some craft, and one Henri Giffard had tried driving balloons with a steam engine. The young Brazilian suspected that existing gasoline engines might be better.

Santos-Dumont saw the high-tech hardware evolving, and put it together with care and courage. By 1899, after gradual improvements, he was putt-putting over Paris rooftops, steering his little dirigibles where he liked. The Zeppelins and blimps of a later day owed much to the daring and gadgeteering of this tiny aeronaut. His autobiography reveals how he proceeded with detail improvements until, years before the Wright Brothers succeeded at Kitty Hawk, Alberto Santos-Dumont could circle the Eiffel Tower. He won worldwide renown, and deserved it; but his work was not revolutionary.

We cite the case of Santos-Dumont to show the steady march of evolutionary design, and to applaud it. But the future of flight involves something more: truly revolutionary discoveries, technologies that are discontinuous from earlier work where Santos-Dumont's was not.

Now we take a case that *is* revolutionary, even though its discovery was predicted in Santos-Dumont's day. The Russian futurist, Konstantin Tsiolkovsky, wrote during the early years of this century that ". . . energy may even be supplied to a missile, from the Earth, in the form of radiation of one or another wavelength. . . . This source of energy is very attractive to contemplate, but we know little of its possibilities." Of course, there's a huge gulf between predicting something, and demonstrating that it works. Tsiolkovsky risked his reputation by predicting revolutionary changes, with only the sketchiest notion how those changes might be achieved. Many scientists of his time dismissed him as a candidate for a strait-jacket.

Then Albert Einstein, in 1917, wrote a paper on stimulating radiation. On the cover of one issue of Gernsback's *Wonder Stories* in 1932, science fiction fans saw a propulsion beam; but no one had any firm ideas how power might be beamed without tremendous losses in the beamspread. (Every time the area of the beam doubles, its intensity must drop by half.) During the 1930's at least one man, the inventor Nikola Tesla, pursued his dream of wireless transmission of power.

Tesla proved himself a genius in his early years with Edison but later became secretive and scornful of criticism. We know that Tesla sought to beam power, but we must suspect that he never succeeded.

But by 1954, experimenters managed to amplify microwaves through a scheme they called "Microwave Amplification by Stimulated Emission of Radiation." They soon reduced this jawbreaking phrase to its initial letters: "maser." Then one of the discoverers, Charles Townes, co-wrote a paper suggesting that the scheme should also work for radiation of visible frequencies: an "optical maser." This created a lot of excitement in laboratories, as scientists worked to demonstrate *light* amplification by stimulating emission of radiation. Of course they soon adopted the short term: "laser."

The first laser was fired by Theodore Maiman of Hughes Aircraft, using a ruby crystal and a flash tube to jolt the crystal with a great wallop of energy. Within a few months, Ali Javan of Bell Labs succeeded using gases instead of rubies.

Both approaches drew instant attention. The amplified beam of light did not spread out like a flashlight beam or even a searchlight. A beam of light as thin as a pencil could be sent for long distances without fanning out much, and had obvious uses such as optical alignment and communication devices. The beam transmitted very low power, but it did transmit a tight beam of wireless power that could be collected by a distant lens. The race was on to develop lasers for special uses— especially lasers of higher power. The revolution had begun.

The Soviets claim that in 1962, Askaryan and Moroz were first to draw attention to the fact that a laser, when vaporizing part of a target, can produce thrust. But researchers credit the U.S.'s Arthur Kantrowitz with the first serious suggestion, in 1971, that lasers might furnish enough power to boost vehicles into orbit. Both in print and in an annual AIAA (American Institute of Aeronautics and Astronautics) meeting, Kantrowitz pointed to the fast-rising power levels of lasers. He suggested that launches to space could be made enormously cheaper by this revolutionary use of beamed power. The AERL scientist added that we were letting naive pessimism put false limits on our future. Always the cautious optimist, Kantrowitz said it might be possible to increase the power of lasers by perhaps *six orders of magnitude*.

A multiple of ten is only one order of magnitude; six orders of magnitude increase meant that a laser transmitting, say, ten watts in 1971 might be the forerunner of *million-watt* lasers one day. History is proving him right, perhaps sooner than he thought. Thanks to stepped-up activity in several related fields—some of it provoked by the redoubtable Kantrowitz—we are now developing lasers measured in megawatts of power output. We see no reason why we cannot keep boosting their power to the gigawatt range. Ten billion watts, furnished for a few minutes' duration, could boost a payload half that of NASA's shuttle from launch pad to orbit at the cost of thirty thousand dollars' worth of electricity. In other words, we could put a payload into orbit for a dollar per pound, instead of nearly a thousand dollars per pound!

Maybe this kind of optimism has a domino effect. In any case, a few scientists began to look around for other ways, in addition to lasers, that we might power vehicles of the future. By now they've come up with several schemes that may rival lasers in the future of flight.

Well then: why aren't we rushing to do it? There are several answers, some of them political. The point to remember is that while the remaining hurdles are real, none of them appear to be basic. This future of flight is a future we can all share. On the other hand, by a general failure of vision or determination, Americans may share a flightless future while others soar above us.

Alan Lovelace, Deputy Administrator of NASA, described part of the problem, and the promise, in 1979. Writing in *Astronautics and Aeronautics* he said, in part, "Let me sketch for you two possible world 'options.' One I will call a fully flight-integrated society. In it everything and everyone flies—not just 65% of the U. S. population, but 100% of the world population. . . . Wherever a person finds himself, there will be a landing site, and he can call for this transportation easier than you can call a cab. . . .

"The other possible world I will call a flight-regressive society, a society that has found no affordable solution to the problems of energy, noise, and pollution, a society in which aviation reverts to the status of a technology too expensive to use. . . .

"The major issue is one of national will. . . . The Wright Brothers did not stick with the bicycle, and I do not think we will either."

Lovelace, in so many words, was calling for a renewal of what historian Joseph Corn calls the "winged gospel." From the early Wright flyers to shortly after World War II, the U. S. raised the dream of flight to something beyond a cult; we viewed flight almost as a religion. We lionized Doolittle, Lindbergh, Earhart, and Halliburton. We doted on our aircraft such as the JN-4 "Jenny," the workhorse DC-3, the advanced little Ercoupe, and strange hybrids like Kellett's autogyro. And if we loved aircraft like those in which we might actually hope to fly, we virtually worshipped the B-29 "Superfortress," the twin-tailed P-38 "Lightning," and the Bell X-1, with the shape of a winged artillery shell, that hangs today in the Smithsonian like a giant's toy. Very few people born after 1945 share the gut-level excitement of their elders whenever a restored P-51 streaks overhead, its in-line Allison snarling a challenge that raises hackles on the old-timer's neck, and perhaps a catch in his throat. Oh yes; we knew a winged gospel in the first half of this century. . . .

Then, somewhere between the German V-2 and the Soviet Sputnik, most of us discarded that fervor. Some have never replaced it with anything. Others replaced it with dreams of wealth, or prowess in sports. True, a few parishioners kept the faith with tiny single-seat air racers or model aircraft. Of those, a very few went on to design hang-gliders and then, like Santos-Dumont, evolved new craft which we call ultralights.

Just as Martin Luther once stirred the world with his new wrinkles on an old religion, the ultralights have produced a storm of controversy among followers of the winged gospel. By now it is becoming clear that ultralights will fill an important niche in the future of flight. Perhaps more important, they have inspired another, more advanced type of new aircraft; the aircraft recreational vehicle, or ARV. That is not to say that everybody likes them yet.

But a latter-day gospel of flight is growing now, and Princeton's Gerard O'Neill is one of its prophets. When Tsiolkovsky predicted manmade worldlets in space, growing their own food, his contemporaries considered him a mad Russian. When Robert Heinlein wrote of a huge spacecraft with a complete ecological system in his 1941 story "Universe"—well, everybody knew science fiction people were a little strange.

O'Neill, however, is a professor of physics at a prestigious university. Since 1969, with the vital help of young scientists who share the dream, he has been working out the problems of living in space. Not just taking brief visits from our planet, but living and working there, in habitats that provide all of Earth's benefits without some of its drawbacks. O'Neill and his colleagues have shown that most hurdles on the way to space habitats have already been cleared; our primary lack now is the will to do it, because it will be very expensive at first. And faced with huge deficits here on Earth, many people ask: why do anything that expensive?

Answer: for the same reason Queen Isabella hocked her jewels for Columbus. Spain was repaid ten thousandfold in riches from the new world, and the countries that create new worldlets in our solar system will reap wealth so tremendous as to make all that Spanish gold look like pocket change.

Soviets know those details as well as we do. Does the word "cosmograd" ring a bell? It's a Russian word meaning "space city," and cosmograds are a Soviet goal. Stefan Possony, an often-quoted scholar of the Hoover Institute, tells us that the Soviets are expanding their space capabilities well beyond anything needed to support their current military *or* civilian work. A moon settlement and a huge space station, says Possony, are among the few things that would explain all this furious activity by the USSR; and they have already told us they intend to build such things. James Oberg of NASA, author of *Red Star In Orbit*, tells us that all this Soviet activity may include a manned Mars mission.

Everyone knows that the Soviets have serious economic problems. They would not be outspending us in the effort to build space cities unless they expected huge returns. They proceed as if they had memorized the books of American engineers like Stine and Pournelle, who are telling everyone who will listen that the wealth is out there, and that it's up for grabs.

A growing fraction of Americans is already impatient to get on with it, to spread the latter-day gospel of flight. The L5 Society is an organization of people working toward permanent settlements beyond the Earth, and toward commerce plying between Earth and those settlements. Anyone can join; its monthly *L5 News* repays the dues handsomely, and its articles are written for ease of understanding. Its board chairman is Arthur Kantrowitz and its officials include world-famous scientists, publishers, legislators, and futurist writers. A careful reading of the *L5 News* shows that members are at odds over the support of military space funding. One side of the issue claims that the U. S. should fund only nonmilitary space efforts. The other side replies that space has already been weaponized by the Soviets, and that the U. S. will reap huge peaceful benefits from military space programs—particularly those that are genuinely defensive, not offensive. [For more on this topic, see *Mutual Assured Survival* by Drs. J. E. Pournelle and Dean Ing, Baen Books, Nov. 1984.—Ed.]

What does "L5" mean? The mathematician Lagrange noted that, in the case of two celestial bodies positioned as the Earth and its moon are, there are five points nearby where much smaller bodies can be stationed where they will stay in position, perhaps oscillating slightly around that "libration" point. Some of those points (such as the gravitational midpoint between Earth and the moon) are not very stable; we might have to keep nudging a satellite to keep it there. But libration points L4 and L5, in the same path as the moon but 60° ahead and behind it in Earth orbit, are very stable. Even if we snagged an asteroid a hundred miles thick and placed it at the L5 position, it would stay there, influenced by the gravitational pulls of Earth and the moon.

The L5 Society expects commonplace flight to worldlets in such positions; they say that once you escape Earth, in terms of energy you are halfway to anywhere. Mining the asteroids and colonizing Mars will be fairly straightforward tasks then. Cheap nonpolluting power beamed to Earth from orbit will be a cinch because we already know that structural metals and solar cell chemicals can be extracted from moon dirt—which is known formally as "lunar regolith," and informally as "green cheese," by the way.

O'Neill and his colleagues have developed working models of a device called a "mass driver," a sort of electric catapult which could fling materials up from the moon into lunar orbit. The mass driver is much more efficient in vacuum; though it probably will not be used to hurl payloads up from the Earth, it may be just the thing to boost materials up against the moon's gravity.

Prophets of future flight back their claims with convincing figures, though some claims seem a bit farfetched at first blush. How can we solve earthly pollution from space? By making fossil fuels obsolete, collecting solar power beyond our atmosphere where it is *eight times* more available and beaming it down to us. How can it help solve overpopulation? By creating so many off-Earth colonies and with flight so cheap that within a century, emigration might well stabilize Earth's population. How will we get there? Several ways, beginning with the present chemical fuels while we develop HEL

(High Energy Laser) propulsion systems and some others even more advanced.

Carl Sagan, testifying before a U. S. Congressional subcommittee, has said that the engineering aspects of space cities seem perfectly worked out by study groups. He added, "It is practical."

Still, it will be tremendously expensive until we develop those cheap, clean propulsion systems. Some systems will boost huge payloads to orbit, while others will power the family flivver to Athens for dinner and back to Topeka afterward. Much of the revolutionary work has already been done; now we need to evolve them in practice. That will take more funding of advanced designs.

Astronaut Gordon Cooper, never one to mince words, summed up the situation in conversation last year with one of the present authors. "In the field of propulsion systems," he said, "most of the scientific establishment is about fifty years behind a few little groups of geniuses. I think we should reassess the whole funding process."

LIQUID ASSETS

Because she'd had an exhausting week training a young bottlenose, Vicki Lorenz dallied in her bungalow over the standard Queensland breakfast of steak and eggs. And because it was Saturday, the Aussie marine biologists had trooped off to Cooktown, leaving Cape Melville Station to her for the weekend. Or maybe they just wanted to avoid her fellow Americans scheduled to fly in; she couldn't blame them for that. She did not know or care why a research site near the nor-east tip of Australia had attracted visiting honchos.

Though it was midmorning in September, the sun had not yet forced its way through the pile of cumulus that loomed eastward over the Barrier Reef like the portent of a wet summer. She chose her best short-sleeved yellow blouse as concession to her visitors, and faded denim shorts as refusal to concede too much. She flinched when the sun searchlighted through her bed-room window to splash her reflection in the full-length mirror. Short curls, intimidated toward platinum by tropical summers, complemented the blouse, bright against her burnt-bronze skin. In two years, she thought, she'd be as old as Jack Benny, and her deceptive youthful epidermis would begin its slow sea change into something like shark leather. She tucked the blouse in, assessing the compact torso and long thighs that gave her a passable, if angular, figure with less than average height. It would do, she thought. If Korff had liked it so much, it had to be in good taste.

Against her will, her eyes searched out the curling poster she had tacked against the bedroom wall two years ago, after Korff's boat had been found. Sunlight glinted off the slick paper so that she saw only part of the vast greenish tube of a surfer's dreamwave which some photographer had imprisoned on film. At the lower left was a reprinted fragment from Alec Korff's *Mariner Adrift:*

> *The wave is measured cadence*
> *In the ocean's ancient songs*
> *Of pélagic indifference*
> *To mankind's rights and wrongs . . .*

And knowing that indifference as well as anyone, he'd made some trifling mistake along the treacherous reef, and it had cost him. Correction: it had cost *her*. Well, no doubt it benefited the reef prowlers. Korff would have been pleased, she thought, to know that his slender body had finally become an offering to the flashing polychrome life among the coral. She turned then, self-conscious in the sliver of light, and made a mocking bow toward the sun. Scuffing into sandals, she padded out to her verandah. It was then that she saw Pope Pius waiting before the sea gate far below, a three-meter torpedo in gray flesh.

She called his name twice, trotting down the path. She knew it was her old friend Pius even though his identifying scars were below the water's surface. The slender mass of the microcorder, on its harness just ahead of the high dorsal fin, was unmistakable. He heard and greeted her, rearing vertically, the sleek hairless body wavering as tail flukes throbbed below. He was an adult *griseus*, a Risso's dolphin, with exquisite scimitar flippers and a beakless prominent nose that made the name *Pius* inevitable. Inevitable, that is, if you had Korff's sense of the absurd.

Soon she had activated the pneumatics, the stainless grate sliding up to permit free passage from Princess

Charlotte Bay into the concrete-rimmed lagoon. She whistled Pius in, whistled again. Then she clicked her tongue and spanked the water to urge him forward. The cetacean merely sidled near the planking outside the sea gate, rolled to view her with one patient eye, and waited.

Vicki sighed and fetched the lightly pickled squid, tossed one of the flaccid morsels just inside the gate. No response—perhaps the slightest show of impatience or wariness as if to say, *I'm jack of it, mate; it's dicey in there*. Except that Pius was cosmopolitan, no more Aussie than he was Japanese or Indonesian. As usual, she tended to append false values to the people of the sea, and then to chide herself for it.

Eventually Vicki went outside the sea gate and knelt on the wood. Pius rolled to assist her, breathing softly to avoid blowhole spray that could soak her with its faint alien rankness. She fed him one small squid, earning a rapid burst of friendly Delphinese complaint at her stinginess, and she knew he would wait for her to return.

The videotape was fully spent. The batteries should be good for another cartridge but Vicki took fresh nicad cells from the lab with a new blank tape cartridge just to be on the safe side. She was hurrying back to Pius when she saw the aircraft dip near. Sure enough, it was one of the Helio Couriers which, everybody knew, meant that the passengers had clout with American cloak-and-dagger people. On the other hand, there'd been a lot of that kind of air traffic in the area for the past fortnight. She was increasingly glad that McEachern and Digby had gone to Cooktown to get shickered. *Plastered,* she told herself; *must revert to American slang for the day*.

Something seemed to be bothering the big *griseus*, she thought, fumbling to replace the equipment on Pius's backpack. He had never refused to enter the sea gate before. *Don't get shirty,* she thought; *if I'm late it's my bum, not yours*. And because of Pius, she was clearly going to be late. The fact of his early return made the tape important, though. The microcorder operated only when triggered by calls made by Pius himself, and it pinged to remind him of squid when the cartridge was expended. That meant he might return once a month—though he was very early this time. Two years ago it had been once a week, and no one was sure why Pius communicated with his fellows less as time passed. Perhaps he was growing laconic with age, she thought, giving him a pat before she upended the squid bucket.

Pius whirled and took a mouthful of delicacies in one ravening swoop, pausing an instant to study Vicki, then seemed to evaporate into the bay, leaving only a roil of salt water in his wake. Water and uneaten squid. *Boy, you must have a heavy date,* she mused. It did not occur to Vicki Lorenz that the big cetacean might be hurrying, not toward, but away from something.

She wheeled the decrepit Holden sedan onto the taxi strip, chagrined to see that the pilot had already set his chocks and tiedowns. The portly fellow standing with the attache case would be Harriman Rooker, from the cut of his dark suit and the creases in his trousers which might have been aligned by laser. The little weather-beaten man sitting on the B-four bag, then, had to be Jochen Shuler.

Vicki made breathless apologies. "I had a visitor who wouldn't wait," she smiled. "Dolphins can be a surly lot."

So could State Department men. "At least you make no secret about your priorities, Dr. Lorenz," Rooker said. "It *is* Dr. Victoire Lorenz?" The hand was impeccably manicured, its grip cool and brief, the smile a micron thick.

"I truly am sorry," she said, fighting irritation, and turned toward the smaller man. Shuler wore rumpled khakis and no tie, his voice a calm basso rasp leavened with humor. "Forget it," he said, with a shoulder pat that was somehow not patronizing. "It's not as if we were perishable."

The imp of extravagance made her say it: "Everybody's perishable in tropical salt. You come here all bright and shiny, but you leave all sheit and briny." Shuler's control was excellent; his wiry frame shook silently but he only put his head down and grinned. Rooker was plainly not amused. Well, at least she could relate to one of them.

The pilot, Rooker explained, was prepared to stay and take care of the Courier. He looked as though he could do it, all right. The bulge in his jacket was no cigarette case. Rooker selected three of his four pieces of luggage for the Holden's boot (*trunk, dammit; trunk,* Vicki scolded herself). One, a locked leather and canvas mail sack, required both men to lift. Shuler lugged his one huge bag into the rear seat. The bag clinked. Perrier water? Booze?

Vicki appointed herself tour guide without thinking and drove along access roads until she was pointing out the salt water pens where young dolphins and other cetaceans were monitored. "We know Delphinese has dialectal differences, just as people and honeybees have local variants of language. We're using recorders to identify various subspecies by sonic signatures. I've made friends with a big Risso's dolphin that roams around loose with a video recorder, sort of a linguistic shill. Maybe we can get some idea whether a *grampus orca,* a killer whale, sweet-talks a little *tursiops* before he swallows it. Generally, larger species communicate in lower frequencies—." She broke off, glancing at Harriman Rooker who sat erect beside her, his right arm lying precisely along the windowframe. *Straightens pictures,* she guessed. His left hand was in his lap and— inexcusable for a trained observer—Vicki realized only then that a wrist manacle bound the man to his equipment. She pulled to a stop, killed the engine. "You didn't come here for a tour," she accused. With sudden intuition, she did not want to know why they had come.

Rooker's pale eyes swept her face, hawk-bright, unblinking. "No," he agreed. "We are here for an exchange of information—and other valuables. A matter of the most extreme urgency, Dr. Lorenz."

"Vicki, please," she urged with her most engaging smile.

"If I must. I suggest that *you* tell *us* what our next move should be."

She searched the implacable features, puzzled, then faintly irked. She felt as if she had been thrust into the middle of a conversation she hadn't been listening to. "Well, you could try telling me what information you need, and why the urgency."

He stared until she grew positively uneasy. And that made her, unaccountably, angry. Then, "Tell us about Agung Bondjol," he said. Softly, but cold, cold.

"Uh. A kid from Djakarta, wasn't he? Right; he was with that Wisconsin senator on the *R. L. Carson* when she sank a few hundred miles south of here last month. One of the four people lost."

From the back seat: "Some kid."

"Thank you, Jo," Rooker said quickly, in that'll-be-enough tones. "Nothing more, Dr.—Vicki?"

"If there was, I didn't read it. I don't pay much attention to the news on any medium, you know."

"Apparently. Now tell us about Alec Korff." The transition was verbally smooth, but for Vicki it was viciously abrupt.

She took a deep breath. "Poet first, I suppose; that's how he liked it. And because he could be acclaimed at that and starve at the same time, he made his living as a tooling engineer.

"Korff got interested in interspecies communication between cetaceans and humans; his mystic side, I guess. He didn't give two whoops about explicit messages. Just the emotional parts."

Low, but sharp: "You're sure of that?"

Long pause, as Vicki studied the sea for solace. Then she said, "Certain as one person can be of another. He once said that the truth is built from gestures, but words are the lumber of lies. He hated phonies and loved cetaceans.

"You know, of course, that I lived with Korff. Met him while I was getting my doctorate at Woods Hole and he was designing equipment for whales and dolphins. Prosthetic hands they could work with flipper phalanges, underwater vocoders, that sort of thing. When I landed the job here, he came with me."

She waited for Rooker to respond. When he did not, she sighed, "Korff was happy here. I knew when he was really contented because he'd compose doggerel on serious topics and laugh his arse off about it. Hiding his pearls like a swine, he said. Everybody's heard *Mariner Adrift*, but did you ever hear *Fourteen Thousand Pounds Of God*? Pompous *and* self-deprecating, and hides a great truth right out in the open.

> *The orca's fangéd dignity*
> *Fills me with humility.*
> *One is wise to genuflect*
> *To seven tons of self-respect.*

The killer whale doesn't really have fangs, of course. Just teeth a tyrannosaur would envy. Korff knew that. He knew a hell of a lot about cetaceans."

Still no response. Rooker was not going to let her off the hook. "And two years come November," she recited quickly, fingernails biting her palms, "Korff took his goddamn sloop along the goddamn Barrier Reef and caught a goddamn tradewind squall or something and goddammit, *drowned!* Is that what you wanted to hear?"

"Quite the contrary," Rooker said, still watching her.

Instantly she was out of the car. "I don't know why I let the consulate talk me into this pig-in-a-poke hostess job on my own time, and now it's become cat-and-mouse insinuation, and I won't have it! If you know anything, you know how I felt about Korff and—and you can go piss up a rope, mate," she stormed. She slammed the door so hard the Holden groaned on its shocks.

Halfway to her bungalow afoot, she looked back to see Shuler patiently following. He had a bottle in each hand, so she waited. It seemed a good idea at the time.

Given that they knew her fondness for mezcal, how did they know she couldn't get it locally? Vicki considered many such nuances in the next hour, sitting cross-legged with Jo Shuler while they plastered themselves into a thin film on her verandah. At first he answered nearly as many questions as he asked. She learned that he was detached from the U.S. Mine Defense Labs in Panama City, Florida; an expert in experimental sonar video and no ignoramus on dolphin research either. He had read her papers on cetacean language, but his own papers were classified. He did not elaborate.

Shuler even managed to explain his companion's cryptic manner, after a fashion. It wasn't nice, Vicki decided, but it made sense. "Okay," she said, stifling a belch, "so some nit at Rand Corporation figured Korff was alive and that I knew it. I'm sure he isn't, and if he is, I don't." She shrugged: "You know what I mean. So much for heavy thinkers at Rand."

Shuler regarded her gravely, listing to port a bit. "Why are you so sure?"

"You want it straight?" Why was she so willing to bare these intimacies? Something beyond her normal candor was squeezing her brains. "Okay: Alec Korff had a few leftover sex hangups, and very tough standards, but he was highly sexed. Me, too. My mother hated him for his honesty about it. She was a tiny little thing, always trying to prove something by vamping him. Then one day she phoned—I was on the extension and I don't think either of them knew it. She implied she might fly up to see him alone. Korff suggested she could ride a whiskbroom and save the price of a ticket." She spread her hands wide. "How could I not love a man like that? Anyway, the point is that we clicked. It was like finding the other half of yourself. He played poet for me and I played floozy for him." With a sly grin: "It'd take him years to develop a replacement, I think. Oh yes, he'd have got in touch with me, all righty." She took a mighty swig, remembering. "You can go back to the car and tell Mr. stiff-corset Rooker all about it."

"I bet he's blushing about the corset," Shuler laughed, then looked abashed.

Vicki squinted hard. "You're bugged, aren't you? He's

been listening!" She saw guilt, and a touch of truculence, and went on. "You two have been rough-smoothing me, haven't you? He's really the rough and you're really the smooth. How many of my old friends did you bastards interview before I fitted into your computers?" She stared grimly at her bottle; she had consumed over a pint of the stuff and now she had a good idea why Shuler was drinking from another bottle.

"I dunno about that, Vicki, I was briefed just like Rooker was. He's used to representing the government, negotiating with some pretty weird groups. I'm just a technician like you. Lissen, lady, we're hip-deep in hockey—all of us."

She flung the bottle far out over the turf, watched it bounce. "Not me, I feel bonzer."

"You're just high."

"High? I could hunt kookaburra with a croquet mallet," she boasted, then went down on hands and knees near the immobile Shuler, shouting, "That's a bird, Rooker, you twit!" Then she saw past Shuler's foolish grin, realized that he carried a shoulder holster too, and sat back. "You people scare me. Go away."

"We're scared too," he said, no longer playing the drunk. As though Rooker were standing before them he went on, "She's about to pass out on us, Harriman. Why can't we drop this interrogation farce and accept her at face value? Or d'you have any nasty little questions to add to mine before the drug wears off?"

Australian slang is compost-rich with unspeakable utterance. Vicki Lorenz had heard most of it, and found it useful now. She had not exhausted her repertoire when she began to snore.

Jo Shuler waited for a moment, moved near enough to tap his forefinger against her knee. Snores. "Drive that heap on over here," he said to his signet ring. "She's out. We can put a call through while she sleeps it off. For the record, I say we take a chance on her." Then he managed to carry Vicki inside to the couch, and waited for Harriman Rooker.

*   *   *

Late afternoon shadows dappled the verandah before
Vicki had swept the cobwebs from her mind. To Rooker's
apology she replied, "Maybe I could accept those vague
insinuations if I knew what's behind them. What's so
earth-shaking about that kid, Bondjol?"

"He's small loss in himself," Rooker agreed. "He's a
renegade Sufi Moslem—pantheist, denied the concept
of evil, embraced drugs to find religious ecstasy, learned
he could purchase other ecstasy from the proceeds of
his drug-running—tricks that'd get him arrested in Djakarta if he weren't the pampered son of an Indonesian
deputy premier."

"I take it a deputy premier's a real honcho."

"Oh, yes; roughly equal to half a vice president for
openers. But the elder Bondjol is quite the pivotal
figure. He's made it very clear: if the United States
wants to keep some leased bases, Bondjol gets his son
back."

Vicki considered this. "If you think I can round up a
million dolphins and send them out to find the body—
forget it. I'm not sure I could even get such complicated messages across in Delphinese—"

"Somebody sure as hell can," Jo Shuler put in.

Rooker: "You still don't understand. Western media
haven't broken the story yet, but it's all over Indonesia:
Agung Bondjol is alive, sending notes on driftwood—or
was, ten days ago. I think you'd better view this tape,"
he added, patting the attache case.

It took an interminable twenty minutes to locate a
compatible playback machine in the lab. The men stood
behind Vicki as she sat through the experience. The
R. L. Carson had been a four-hundred tonner, a small
coastal survey vessel inside the great Barrier Reef with
Australian permission, under contract to the United
States Navy. The vessel carried unusual passengers: the
swarthy young Bondjol with two camp followers and
Bondjol's host, Wisconsin Senator Distel Mayer. This
part of the tape, chuckled Jo Shuler, had been surrep-
titious film footage saved by a crew member. The good
senator had paid more attention to one of Bondjol's

young ladies than he had to the wonders of the reef. Thus far it was an old story, a junketeering politician with a foreign guest on a U.S. vessel far from home.

Shuler cut through Vicki's cynical thoughts: "Now you know why Mayer's so helpful in persuading our media to hold the story. The next stuff, I put together at M.D.L. from the ship's recordings. It's computer-enhanced video from experimental sonar equipment."

The scene was panoramic now, a vertical view of sandy bottom and projecting coral heads with preternatural color separation. Visually it seemed as if animation had been projected over a live scene. It was a hell of a research tool, she thought longingly. The audio was a series of clicks and coos, with a descending twitter. Vicki punched the tape to "hold" and glanced toward the Navy civilian. "Don't ask," Shuler said quickly. "I promise you'll be the first nonmilitary group to get this enhancement rig. It may take a year or two, we're working on better . . ."

"That's not it," she said. "The audio, though: isn't it ours?" She re-ran the last few seconds as Rooker shrugged his ignorance.

"The Great White Father signal," Shuler nodded. "Sure. It's becoming standard procedure for the Navy in such treacherous channels, when they don't mind making the noise. But it won't be any more," he added darkly.

Cape Melville Station had developed two messages in Delphinese that, in themselves, justified every penny spent on research. The first message was a call for help, repeatedly sent by a battery-powered tape loop whenever a modern life jacket was immersed in salt water. During the past year, over a hundred lives had been saved when cetaceans—chiefly the smaller dolphins but in one documented case, a lesser rorqual whale—towed shipwrecked humans to safety. The device had come too late for Korff, though.

The Great White Father signal had a very different effect. It seemed to make nearby cetaceans happy, to provoke playful broachings and aerobatics as though performing for a visiting dignitary. "I hope you don't let whalers get a copy of this," Vicki said ominously. "It was intended as a friendly greeting. The people of the sea are too trusting for their own good."

"Is that a fact," murmured Harriman Rooker, his eyebrows arched. "Roll the tape."

The tape repeated its record, then proceeded as the *Carson* swept over sandy shallows, reef fish darting into coral masses that projected nearly to the hull. Then Vicki saw a thin undulating line of bright brown cross the video screen, rising slightly as the ship approached. Something darted away at the edge of the screen; something else—two somethings, then others, regular brown cylindrical shapes—swerved into view, attached to the brown line like sodden floats on a hawser. One of the cylinders disappeared, suddenly filled the screen, moved away again. Then the varicolored display turned brilliant yellow for an instant.

"Concussion wave," Shuler explained.

Nearby coral masses seemed to roll as the picture returned, hunks of the stuff crumbling away with the reef flora and fauna.

Vicki stopped the tape again. "Did the boilers explode?"

"The *Carson* was diesel," said Shuler. "It took us hours to identify those drums and the cable, but there's not much doubt it was some of our old munitions. A mine cable barrier, the kind we used in the Philippines forty years ago. Five hundred pound TNT charges intended against assault boats. We're not sure exactly how it got to Australia, but we're not ruling out your cetaceans, Vicki."

A silent *ahh*, then quick re-runs of the underwater explosion. Vicki's fingers trembled as she flicked the tape to "hold" again. "Much as I hate to say it," she poked a finger against an ovoid gray blur on the screen, "that could be a cetacean. Big one, maybe a *pseudorca*— false killer whale."

"The sonar says it was live flesh," Shuler responded, "possibly big enough to haul a cable barrier into position."

Vicki drummed her fingers against the screen, then flicked off the display. "Could this be the work of terrorists?"

"I was picked because of modest experience in that arena," Rooker said. "Yes, it obviously *is*. But up 'til now we've counted on human leadership."

"Didn't someone take Bondjol away? You said he was alive."

"We thought you might have some ideas," Rooker said apologetically. "There are thousands of islands to check, and not enough aircraft. We've tried. The witnesses—all citizens of the United States except for Bondjol and his two child concubines—agree on some uncanny points the Indonesians don't know. One: there was a second blast while they were filling the inflatable lifeboats. Perhaps the *Carson* wasn't sinking fast enough?

"In any case, two: almost the moment she went down, every one of the lifeboats was capsized. Not by sharks, in spite of what some of the crew claimed. No one drowned or sustained a shark attack. Two nonswimmers have toothmarks proving they were carried *back* to the lifeboats by dolphins. Distel Mayer himself says he was buffeted, ah, rudely, by something godawfully big and warm. He shipped a bit of water while it was happening, I'm happy to say."

"Same thing happened to most of the crew," Shuler added.

Vicki, to the stoic Shuler: "You think they were being visually identified?"

Rooker: "Don't *you?*"

"Maybe." Vicki stared blindly at the video screen, testing hypotheses, thinking ahead. "But this presupposes that a big group of cetaceans knew exactly whom they were after, and culled him out of a mob. That's— it's not very credible," she said politely.

"We are faced by incredible facts," Rooker agreed. "Of course Bondjol's junket of the *Carson* was previously announced on Radio Indonesia. And in the non-Moslem press, his picture is better known than his father would like."

Vicki was tempted to offer acid comment on pelagic mammals with radios and bifocals, then recalled that Pius had a video recorder of the latest kind. She tried another last-ditch devil's advocacy: "What proof do you have that Bondjol didn't drown?"

Jo Shuler moved to retrieve the classified tape from her. "Show her the glossies, Harriman." Then, as Rooker exchanged items in his tricky attache case, Shuler went on, "Out of fifty-six people, four were missing when they got to the mangroves near shore. Three were crewmen. They were found in the *Carson* when divers retrieved the ship recordings. Bondjol wasn't found. Nobody saw him go under, or knows how he was taken away. But if you can believe our Indonesian friends, here's what was tossed from the sea into a little patrol boat off Surabaya a week later when everybody figured young Bondjol was only a bad memory." He flicked a thumb toward the photographs that Rooker held.

The first three photographs showed a scrap of metal, roughly torn from a larger sheet. It looked as though it had been subjected to salt corrosion, then roughly scrubbed, before someone covered it with cryptic marks. Vicki took a guess: "Malayan?"

"Bahasa, the official Indonesian language," said Rooker. "Roughly translated, 'Saved from American plot by whales. I am on island in sight of land, but sharks cruise shoreline. Living on coconut milk and fish that come ashore, I am, et cetera, Agung Bondjol, son of et cetera, et cetera.' I hardly need add that there was no American plot that we know of."

She ignored his faint stress on his last four words. "I'll bet there aren't any sharks around, either. Some dolphin dorsal fins look awfully suspicious to most people." In spite of herself, she was beginning to accept this awesome scenario. "Dolphins often scare whole schools of fish ashore, right here in Queensland. The aboriginals divide the catch with them, believe it or not."

Silent nods. She turned her attention to the other glossies, fore and obverse views of a second metal fragment. It looked much like the first one, except for a pattern of dots and lines incised on the obverse side, and Vicki admitted as much.

"The jagged edges appear to fit together," Rooker said, using a finger to trace torn and evidently matching sides of the metal sheets. "This piece showed up a week ago. Poor little rich boy: 'Third day, sick of fish and coconuts; small whales will not let me swim. Death to evil Senator Mayer and American imperialists responsible. Finder please remit to Deputy Premier Bondjol, et cetera, signed Agung Bondjol, ad nauseam.' At least he seems to be rethinking his ideas about evil," Rooker finished. His eyes held something that could have been cold amusement.

Vicki tapped the last photograph. "How was this one delivered?"

"Thought you'd never ask," Shuler said. "It was literally placed in the hands of a research assistant near the study pens at Coconut Island, last Saturday. By a bottlenose dolphin."

Vicki could not avoid her yelp. "Oahu? The marine labs?"

"You got it. Halfway across the Pacific at flank speed—maybe just to prove they could do it. The pattern on the back is the simplest code you could imagine: one for "a," two for "b," but in binary. Easier to peck it out that way. It reads in clear American English."

As gooseflesh climbed her spine: "Bondjol didn't encode it?"

"No-o *way!* Analysis shows Bondjol scratched his message with sharp coral fragments, but our metal sheet was torn and the obverse incised with some tool. The tool was an alloy of iron, lots of chromium, some manganese, a little selenium—in other words, austenitic stainless steel."

"Now," Rooker put in, "do you see why we wonder about Korff?"

She nodded, letting her cold chills chase one another. More than once, cetaceans wearing Korff's experimental manipulators had escaped the pens—a fact she had mentioned in scholarly papers. "But you're implying a lot of—of subtlety. For one thing, that they've somehow learned much more about human languages than we have about theirs."

"Unless Alec Korff, or someone like him, is behind it," Rooker insisted softly. "He could have two motives: money; politics."

Vicki moved away to the lab's crockery tea service because it gave her hands something to do while she considered these bizarre ideas. The men accepted the strong brew and waited until she met Rooker's gaze. With fresh assurance: "Not big money, because he ran from it. Believe me, I know," she smiled ruefully. "Politics? He didn't want anyone governing anyone, which is why he used to say ours was the least of a hundred evils. No," she said with conviction, "I wish— God, you don't know how I wish—I could believe you. But Korff is—dead. I know it here," she added, placing a small fist near the hard knot just under her heart.

A searching look passed between the men. "She's probably right, you know," Shuler muttered at last.

"So much the worse," said the diplomat. "We are forced to concede the possibility that cetaceans must be classed as hostile, tool-using entities who can interdict us across three-quarters of the globe."

"Oh, surely not hostile," Vicki began, then paused. "All the same, if I were whaling I might seriously consider some less risky line of work. Starting today. Oh: what was the binary message?"

Rooker's mirth was faint, but it came through. "Assurance that young Bondjol was safe, and a demand for ransom in exchange for his whereabouts."

"What do they demand, a ton of pickled squid?" Vicki was smiling back until she thought of the gradual attenuation of data on the Pius tapes. If cetaceans were getting subtler, they would reveal only what they wanted to reveal. And Pius had behaved strangely—. She strode to the forgotten tape she had taken from Pius this morning, but paused in disbelief as Rooker answered her question.

"They demand ten million Swiss francs, in hundreds. They promised to contact us again, and gave Melville Station's co-ordinates."

In a near-whisper, Vicki Lorenz held up the Pius cartridge between thumb and forefinger. "I have a terrible suspicion," she said, and threaded the tape for playback.

She was right, as she had known she would be. Not only did they see an unshaven Bondjol from the viewpoint of Pius just offshore; they could hear the man's excited cries as he struggled with his dinner. The rest was sunlight filtered through deep water, eerie counterpoint to a long series of flat tones and clicks. Vicki shared unspoken surmise with Shuler as they listened: binary code.

Vicki and Jo Shuler easily programmed the lab computer to print out the simple message as Harriman Rooker stood by. There were a few mistakes in syntax, but none in tactics. They would find a red-flagged float, attach the ransom to it, and tow the float into the bay. They would find Bondjol's co-ordinates on the same float, after the ransom was examined.

"I've been going on the assumption that it's counterfeit," Shuler grinned to his companion.

"Unacceptable risk," Harriman Rooker said blandly. "We don't know how much they know. It's marked, all right—but it's real." Shuler's headshake was quietly negative, but Vicki saw something affirmative cross his face.

It was not yet dark. Vicki hurried from the lab and was not surprised to spy a small channel marker buoy bobbing just outside the sea gate, a crimson cloth hanging from its mast.

Vicki drove the Holden to the sea gate with Harriman Rooker while Shuler, in a dinghy, retrieved the buoy. Rooker unlocked the mail bag, shucked it down from the sealed polycarbonate canister, and smiled as Vicki glimpsed the contents. Vicki mentally estimated its weight at a hundred kilos, obviously crammed with more liquid assets than she had ever seen. The clear plastic, evidently, was to show honest intentions. She turned as Jo Shuler, breathing hard from his exertions, approached them from behind. Something in her frozen attitude made Harriman Rooker turn before, silently, they faced the little man holding the big automatic pistol.

Shuler was not pointing it at anyone in particular. A sardonic smile tugged at his mouth as Jo Shuler, staring at the equivalent of nine million dollars in cash, took one long shaky breath. Then he flung the weapon into the dusk, toward the tall grass, as hard as he could. "Let's get this crap onto the buoy," he grunted as the others began to breathe again.

They towed the world's most expensive channel marker into the bay, hurrying back without conversation, half expecting some dark leviathan to swallow them before they reached shore. They had all seen the buoy plunge beneath the surface like a tiny cork float above a muskellunge.

The trio stood very close on the wharf, sharing a sense of common humanity and, a little, of deliverance as they peered across the darkling water. "Don't worry," Vicki said finally. "They'll keep their end of the bargain."

"That's what I was thinking," Jo Shuler replied, "back at the car. I couldn't very well do less."

As though to himself, Rooker murmured, "The most adept seafarers on the globe, and they could have been such an asset. I don't share your optimism, Vicki. Isn't it time you finally gave up on them?"

"I'm more worried about how they intend to use *their* assets," Vicki said softly. "And how they'll raise more money when they want it. Anyway," she said, turning back toward the Holden, "you ask the wrong question. The real question is, have *they* finally given up on *us*?" She wondered now if Korff had outlived his usefulness to the sea people. One thing sure: his surviving work included more than poetry.

Given language, she had said, cetaceans would develop other tools. But given other tools, Korff had argued, they'd develop further linguistically. Since she and Korff had worked to develop cetacean assets at both ends, she knew the argument would never be resolved. But which species would be caught in the middle?

She could almost hear the laughter of Alec Korff.

LOST IN TRANSLATION

"Howie's dumped a deadline again," Hawke sighed. "Sorry, Jus', but if he won't write progress reports for Delphium, we'll just have to do it for him."

"We, meaning Justine Channing," I said, and slapped a sheaf of notes between my breasts. "I'll never get my work done if I have to nurse that little creep through every waking hour."

Cabot Hawke fondled his mustache, a period piece that went with his graying sideburns and tweeds over big shoulders. All of it lent him the panache of a twentieth century colonel. While clawing my way above the ranks, I'd learned to read every one of Hawke's nuances. Whenever he stroked that brush, he was reminding himself who he was: Projects Director of Delphium Corporation. "More like once a week," Hawke grunted, leaving his half-acre desk to drape an arm over my shoulder.

I knew that move, too: he was showing me the door. But nicely; when Hawke wasn't nice during business hours, I could be bitchy at night. Who was it said, "Reciprocity works both ways?"

"Try and forget how the man looks," Hawke rumbled softly. "To board members, he's beautiful. The day Howard Prior leaves Delphium, our best CanAm Federation contract goes with him. So you wipe his flat nose for him, find him more old tapes of Vivaldi and Amirov if he wants you to. Whatever." He patted my rump as if identifying "whatever."

I stopped in the entryway, using a haute couture stance from modeling days, regarding Hawke through my fall of auburn hair. Narrowing my eyes, I said, "Maybe I will."

Hawke showed me his strong teeth—half of them implants—and refused the bait. "You're the most overpaid administrator in CanAmerica," he slandered, "because you prod my prima donnas to create their polymers and scenarios and translations. I don't always tell you how to do it, and I refuse to worry about it. So don't *be* a prima donna, baby; be an administrator. Go minister."

"By God, maybe I really will," I muttered, trying to believe it.

"Just don't forget to spray," Hawke's basso chuckle followed me, loud enough to be heard down the corridor. "God knows what musty corner Howie's hands have been in. Some of his germs must be centuries old."

I headed for the lower-level complex and out of executive country, reflecting that Hawke was only half joking. Once, a year before, I'd driven Howie from Baltimore to the remains of a Library of Congress annex—Howie couldn't find Delphium by himself, much less a specific ruin around Washington—and I'd waited while Howie snooped for records of the Sentinel project. That was after the news that the Tau Ceti expedition had found leavings of a dead civilization.

Delphium had signed Howard Prior up before other thinktanks realized what that news meant in terms of study contracts. But working with Howie was a nightmare: the man could *not* keep things in proper order. And I key my life to the observance of order. Hawke could joke that I made neatness into a vice, but one day he'd find himself outmaneuvered by my sense of order. Taking *my* orders.

Nothing will ever divert me from that goal, by that path.

On the annex trip, Howie hadn't emerged for hours. All his cassettes were used and he looked like he'd been crawling through conduits—grimy, smelly, tear-streaked. Evidently they were tears of joy because the little twit had found a cache of music recordings. Howie's degrees from Leeds and Yerkes had made him a world-class expert in interspecies communication problems, but his mania was old music.

He was delirious over his finds, music by Purcell and Porta and one, Haydn, I'd heard of. Never mind that he upset my schedule, never mind that the Sentinel Project of the 1980's was a wipeout—small wonder, since the Tau Ceti civilization had quit transmitting five thousand years before. Still, little Howie began regular forays into those archives. But not with me. Hawke teased me later when I complained. But I say, once burnt by a four-hour fiasco with a filthy little nigger, *forever* shy!

Actually, Howie was mostly Caucasian, with a British scholar's accent and a sallow complexion, lighter than Hawke who quicktanned religiously. But Howie's maternal grandmother had been an aboriginal in Queensland. Those mixed-up—disorderly!—genes made him the image of a loser. Knobby little body, squashed nose, and hair almost kinky enough to be sculptured. The one time I suggested cosmetic surgery to him was the last time Howie tried to get cozy with me for months. I can't ever forgive the look I saw on his crumpled features.

All he said was, "It's fatuous to brag about what you can't help, Justine. It's worse to apologize." But what I saw in his expression was not self-pity.

It was clemency. The hell with him. . . .

Let's face it: Howie wasn't interested in bettering himself. That's another reason why I wasn't interested in keeping my options open with Howie. I stopped outside the door to his tiny office, took a few sniffs from my compact, and feeling suitably mellow, stepped inside. Into chaos.

*   *   *

Fax notes everywhere, cassettes underfoot, Howie in shirtsleeves capering at his data terminal with a light pencil like some scrawny shaman crooning a non-tune. That would've been enough by itself, but humming and twanging through it, the speakers played something just far enough from sensible music to set my pearly-whites on edge. "Howie, have you gone . . ." I began.

His wave cut me short and suggested I shut the door in one motion. Before he turned back to the terminal, I caught his glance. It was whimsical, guilty, appraising. And like a fool I thought his office bedlam was the reason.

Howie was talking. Or rather, his terminal was, synthesized from his voiceprint and contrapuntal to the music. But it didn't have Howie's educated Yorkshire diction; it spoke in standard CanAm, which didn't seem to bother Howie but nearly drove me wild. How could I tell which voice should take precedence?

". . . not sure whether the Greeks did it first. But Porta proved you can write music to be played right side up or upside down," said the Howie terminal.

"Invertible polyphony," the real Howie said to me, eyes agleam, his light pencil marking time. "Bach tried it in this fugue." He punched an instruction. His grin invited me to enjoy it.

Instantly the terminal voice stopped and instead we were hearing what Howie claimed was Bach. I could take it but preferred to leave it and said so.

"Ah, but listen to it inverted," he begged. Another punched instruction. More Bach—I guess.

Howie closed his eyes in bliss. I closed mine too, and raised my fists and shouted, "HOWIE, WHEN WILL YOU LEARN SOMETHING AS EASY AS A PROGRESS REPORT?"

Finger jab, and a silence of anechoic chambers. Then as I waited for his apology: "Justine, when will *you* learn something as easy as calling me 'Howard'?"

"If the diminutive fits, wear it," I snapped. "I'm here to do your paperwork, since you prefer to play with your stolen ditties."

"Ah, no," he breathed, smiling at a private whimsy, no longer appraising. "Not stolen; lost, and now found." He let the smile fade while I whiffed at my compact again. It's easy to overdo a hit from a compact, which is why Howie disapproved of my doing it, which is why I pretended to overdo it. Instead of an apology, I detected patronage. Nobody patronizes Justine Channing. *No*body.

"So you must work, because I play," he murmured finally. "If you hate that so much, Justine, why do you do it?"

I shrugged. Why did *everybody* do it? To get somewhere. Too elementary to repeat.

"Answer one question," he prodded gently, "and then I promise to help you draft a report synopsis."

"I'm listening," I said.

"Why do you do it? Help me draft the report, I mean."

Well, he'd promised a *quid pro quo*. "The federation gets your report, Delphium gets its quarterly check, and Cabot Hawke gets off the hook." Howie just looked at me. "All right, and then Hawke lets *me* off the hook! More or less," I hedged.

"Hawke and you. More and less." He nodded like a wronged parent. "And I, less still."

"Life is a billion-way parlay, Howie. To be a winner, you pick winners. I don't care what you think about me and Hawke."

"I didn't mean that. I meant, we fool ourselves about our motives. A good turn has a selfish component; we try to be more, while the system is biased to make us less."

"Hell, if you don't push for number one, you'll never amount to anything."

Howie looked at, then through me, and then began to laugh a soft hollow-chested wheeze that lasted a long time. "We obviously wouldn't be as we are," he said at last, terminating his private joke. "Very well; into the breach of the report, as it were. What tale did we spin for the analysts last time? Must have a clear sequence," he added, as if he'd said something clever.

I passed him "his" last progress report—I had written it—and waited while Howie scanned it. Half of his work was unraveling Cetian arts. Every child knew that the quasimammals on Tau Ceti's major planet had been nuts about communication. Their color sense had been so acute that the Cetians could leave a complex message with a single dot of color. Hue, shape, size, sequence of spots; all affected Cetian message content. The trouble was that nothing that remained of Cetian media told us why they weren't still there.

Picture a planetful of garrulous ground sloths, carefully documenting each war and yardage sale, every farce and footrace of a dominant culture. Now picture them disappearing suddenly without trace or announcement, centuries before our Egyptians built Abu Simbel. Cetian science yielded no clue. Cetian art, someone guessed, might yield some hints.

Howie worked, or rather played, overtime for months before he discovered that Cetian communication went to hell just before their disappearance. The Cetians produced one final piece of abstract visual art, a huge blob of varicolored tiles by some philosopher-priest, and they reproduced it as proudly and as often as we copy the Mona Lisa. And then their commentaries began to decay fast.

Howie's last report had concluded: "Cetian language became more chaotic with each sleep period. The hue variable was abandoned, and we infer that the Cetians fell prey to some epidemic that first confused, then consumed them. During the next quarter we will run content-analytical surveys of late Cetian story mosaics," and made other vague promises I'd added.

"Hawke must be glad that I'm not making much progress," Howie mused as he read the last paragraph.

I donated a cool smile. "Just enough, not too much. The riddle's been there a long time, Howie. Why work yourself out of a job overnight?" Wink. Even if he rarely made heavy passes at me anymore, Howie liked my little winks and nudges—and they didn't cost me much.

He studied me without expression except that the broad nostrils flared and contracted, reminding me of a skinny little hippo lost in thought. Then he grunted and began to read my write-up of his Proxima Two translations.

The Proximans had disappeared several million years ago; so long ago that it took two expeditions to discover remains of a race that had vanished, like the Cetians, suddenly. They'd been sea-dwelling invertebrates with enough savvy to build pearlescent craft that explored their land-masses, then build others that took them into orbit. We hadn't a clue to Proximan language until a xenologist suspected there was meaning in all the bubbles.

I mean, of course, the bubble generators that were still blurping away in the coral cities Proximans had built. Give our pickaninny his due: it was Howie who thought to run analyses of covariance of the size, frequency, gas composition, and absorption rates of the bubbles. Those little isotope-powered bubble generators, he figured, hadn't been put there just for decor. And Howie was right. They'd been for entertainment and news; Proximan media broadcasts.

Thanks to Howie, we knew the Proximans had a strict caste system, high art, and a suspicious nature, even in those bubble messages. Howie's current work was often a case of guessing what the Proximan sea-cities *didn't* want to talk about.

Howie sighed while reading my last paragraph: ". . . further study of a long, curiously-wrought sequence that was found programmed into bubble generators in widely-separated cities. The sequence may have been a rare cooperative effort by Proximans to unify several mathematical theories. The effort was barely underway when, after a brief period of linguistic decay, the Proximans vanished."

"Most of that is eyewash, you know." Howie tapped the fax page without rancor. "Oh, it's glossy enough, and harmless—but who told you all that sodding rubbish about unifying theories? My work suggests the Proximans were studying a single message."

"Pity you didn't write this yourself, then," I flared, and waited for my apology.

And got it. "True. If I leave it for someone else I must expect something to get lost in translation. I really do apologize, Justine. We might do better this time, eh?"

I remarked that it was up to him. He edited what I'd written, then spent the next hour extracting bits on the Ceti problem from his computer terminal, putting them in order for me. Sure enough, Howie had fresh surmises which I arranged, then rechecked.

At first I thought I'd misplaced a fax page. "Damn, this passage isn't Ceti. It's Prox stuff."

"No, you've got it spot-on," he said with a final inflection that teased me to continue.

"But—it was the Cetians, not the Proximans, who went gaga over a piece of art."

"The Cetians," he replied, nodding and leaving his chin up as he added, "*and* the Proximans." And he watched me with that damnable catch-me-if-you-can smile of his.

I made a dozen intuitive leaps, all into black holes of confusion, in ten seconds. I could feel the hair begin to rise on the nape of my neck until I decided Howie was kidding me.

He decoded my glance and began quickly: "That massive Cetian colorburst? Its title translates roughly into 'Rebirth' or equally well as 'Climax.' The work of one individual who couldn't explain it. Pure inspiration. Also," he added slowly, "pure message. Our Cetian artist just didn't understand his own message at first."

I tapped an extravagant fingernail against my faxes, denying the gooseflesh creeping down my spine. "But *you* understand it?"

"Lord no," he laughed. "It has a level of abstrauction that escapes me." More seriously then: "Exactly the same as the Proximan problem, Justine. It involves a different idiom."

I swallowed and sat down. Mostly, I wondered how to tell Cabot Hawke that his prize egghead had cracked his little shell. "No. You can't seriously imply that—that the Ceti mosaic has any connection with a string of bubbles. In another star system. *Five million years* apart. It's beyond reason, Howie!"

The little monkey was grinning. " 'Tis, isn't it? I keep trying to decode that mosaic and what the Proximans called their 'Coronation Lyric,' but so far I haven't the foggiest."

"The hell you don't." My mouth was dry. I compared his conclusions again. "The short bubble message commentary that preceded the Coronation Lyric: any room for error in your translation? I mean, saying their lyric thing was an inspired piece of art?"

"Not much. I gather it unfolded like Coleridge's vision of Xanadu—only our Proximan wasn't interrupted. He got to finish undisturbed."

"Just before the Proximans all disappeared."

"Not quite. Proximans considered it only great art at first. They didn't tumble immediately, as the Cetians did; they had a puzzle to solve."

In the back of my head, a small voice reminded me that none of this was on my faxes. Howie didn't want it in the reports. What else had he held back? I half-closed my eyes and smiled. "You think the Cetians and Proximans were communicating," I said.

"Unlikely. There are other possibilities."

I persisted. "But a direct connection between the art and the disappearances?"

"Between the *messages buried in the art* and the disappearances," he corrected. He was glancing at me: hair, cleavage, mouth.

I moistened my lips with my tongue and said softly, "If you're right—Howard—how big is this news?"

He was still focusing on my mouth, pole-axed with desire. "Pick a number," he said like a sleepwalker. "Quite a large one."

"But only if you can translate those messages."

"Can you keep a secret, Justine?"

"Try me." If he missed that *entendre* he was no translator.

"I suspect neither message can ever be decoded by humans. There's something missing, as if each message were tailored exclusively for a given species. A Cetian, I suspect, could never have translated the Proximan message. And so on."

"But who could have sent such messages?"

"Ah," he said, a forefinger raised, and then turned the gesture into a wave of helplessness.

I let it all sink in, and let Howie take my hand while I raced over the possibilities. If Howie chose to report that the translations couldn't be made, his study contract might be terminated. That meant major problems which Hawke would pass down to me. If Howie did break those codes, assuming he wasn't march-hare mad with his whole scenario, it might mean a Nobel.

There had to be some way I could profit from this thing, without risking anything. As Howie interlaced his fingers against mine with his sad, tentative smile, I squeezed. "You realize I'm obligated to report all this," I said.

He jerked away. Carefully, voice shaking: "You don't have to report pure oral conjecture, Justine. That's all it is right now. I shared it with you in strictest confidence."

Time to set the hook. "If it's ever discovered that I held back crucial information, it will ruin my career," I said. As though Cabot Hawke hadn't shown me that the reverse is true! "You're asking me to be a full partner in this, Howard."

"I suppose so," he said. "All right. Yes, I am."

I'd landed him. Ruffling his kinky thatch with one hand, I stood up. "You won't be sorry, Howie. Just keep trying to decode those messages." I stacked my faxes neatly and headed toward the door.

"You're assuming," he said dreamily, "they haven't already been decoded for us." I must've stared, because he started ticking items off on his stubby fingers:

"Brancusi's 'Bird in Space' can be expressed mathematically. Maya glyphs. Altamira cave paintings. It may have been what Hesse had in mind with his bead game in *Magister Ludi*. Or"—he gave a happy giggle—"I could just be bonkers. But I'm in training for the search, Justine. That's what I was doing when you walked in."

"Training for the Interstellar Olympics," I teased.

"Or for the twilight of the gods," he replied thoughtfully. "You understand that secrecy is vital if there's danger?"

Well, I thought I did: to keep some other weirdo from jumping his claim. "Trust me," I said, and left him.

Two minutes and a broken anklestrap later I was with Hawke, babbling so fast he had to help me open my compact for a settle-me-down.

As usual, Hawke traded me fresh perspectives for what I gave him. As we lay on his apartment watercouch he blew one of my curls from his lips and reached for a cheroot. He lit it, and fell back beside me puffing happily.

Wrinkling my nose: "I've come to think of that stink as the unsweet odor of your success," I gibed. At Hawke's age, he wasn't always successful.

"Be glad it doesn't smell like Howie Prior," he replied, and I could feel his furry barrel chest shaking with amusement.

I bit him. "That's for your innuendo. And for refusing to explain this afternoon."

"About Howie's fear of *gotterdammerung?* Seems clear enough, Jus'. He thinks there could be some magic formula that wiped out two entire civilizations." Hawke dragged on the cheroot, studied its glow. Then, reflectively, "Well, well; what a weapon in the wrong hands."

Trust Hawke to think in those terms. He was still chuckling to himself as I prompted, "And in the right hands?"

Long silence. Then, "There probably wouldn't be any right hands. Classic paranoid fantasy—and I'm not

at all surprised to find our little Howie entertaining it."
After a moment he added, "Watch him, Jus'."

The idea of Howie Prior being violent was absurd,
and I laughed. "I probably outweigh him."

"You miss the point. He doesn't need muscle to be
dangerous. Humor him. Keep an eye open for his private computer code. I don't want to wake up one morning and find him bootlegging full translations to the
highest bidder because he thinks it's all that important."

What good would it have done me to insist that
Howie was not capable of such sharp practice? To Cabot
Hawke, the world was populated only by Cabot Hawkes—
and certainly not many Howies. I promised I'd give all
the support Howie asked for, and then changed the
subject. My mistake.

Howie Prior wanted to lie on his bony arse high up in
the Sistine Chapel. Not on a muffled skimmer, which
wouldn't have required so many permissions, but on a
rickety scaffold which took me weeks to arrange. But
Delphium has clout, and Howie got to play Michelan-
gelo. It got him nowhere.

Howie had more fun as Constantin Brancusi and I
had hell finding sculpture replicas. But we found photos of the man's studio and the airy, white sunsplashed
rooms had charm—until Howie put dust covers over
the pieces I'd collected, to recreate the ambience the
sculptor had kept. When Howie donned outmoded
funky clothes and a little pointy woolen cap, I walked
out. He said he needed to be Brancusi for his work, but
hadn't told me how far he was willing to take it. Well,
Brancusi didn't take *him* very far.

When Howie asked me to find him a place in Clarens,
Switzerland, I almost called Hawke. Then Howie showed
me photos of the view he wanted, and I agreed. A tiny
pension in a Swiss hotel was easy enough to locate.
Why shouldn't I make the arrangements over there and
enjoy Howie's madness before Hawke realized how much
it cost?

"Which Swiss are you going to be?"

"Try and find me some Mahorka tobacco. It's Spanish," he unanswered,

"Picasso?"

"And get me an appointment with an internist," he added. "I must know the proper dosage."

"For what?"

"For just a touch of nicotine poisoning, if you must know. We don't want to overdo it, do we?"

"*We* don't know what the hell you're up to. *We*," I stressed it again, "get queasy thinking about postmortems. So no, goddammit, *we* aren't going to find you any poisonous tobacco."

I hated that look of his, the gaze of a saint caught with his hand in the till. "I don't want to pull rank, Justine. I know what's needed. I promise not to get very sick on nicotine. I intend to get well with it."

"You're ill? That doesn't surprise me—"

"We all are. Please don't act the nanny; the role ill-suits you." He didn't have Hawke's subtlety; he just pointed at the door.

I went. I could already smell Alpine meadows.

The Swiss were an enterprising lot who understood money better than most. In a week I was back with a real tan and an itch to return. Meanwhile, Howie had collected a trunkful of manuscripts and custom-tailored old formal clothes. And yes, he was already dosing himself with nicotine and smoking strong tobacco as well.

Handing him the packetful of travel vouchers, I tried to get him to endorse another trip for me. Lowering my voice for vibrancy: "There's a nice room below yours at Clarens. Surely you'll need me for, um, *some*thing."

"I'll need all my concentration, thanks. I couldn't do justice to the problem if I were constantly thinking of a lovely woman just downstairs."

I tried once more: "It could be so romantic, Howard."

"Too right," he muttered, tasting me with his eyes, but sadly—like a man craving cheesecake who fears he'll miss the last rowboat out of hell if he stops for a nibble.

"You really must think you've got it this time," I said.

The little chin came up. "Yes, I do. Seems obvious now. Ah— where're my tickets?"

"In your hand, fool. What will you do without me? Well, give me a call when you're through with your Swiss mystery," I said quickly, and made a *toujours gai* exit.

So Howie went alone to Clarens carrying his damned Mahorka tobacco and his double-damned, old-fashioned manuscripts and high-collared shirts, and I didn't see him again for almost a month. But I know he went there because I spoke with him by vidphone several times. I even had to wire money to a doctor who visited Howie in his *pension*. The man confirmed that Howie's neuralgia was probably from nicotine poisoning. I sent money to Howie's concierge, too, as a bribe to keep her from taking the muted upright piano from Howie. It wasn't loud, she admitted; merely calamitous. She might have been describing the nightmares I was having by then. In each of them, I was kept marking time while tacky little people passed me.

While Howie was gone I backtracked him. His Delphium account showed he'd taken a taxi to the old library annex before deciding on his Swiss trip. I unearthed no hint of what he went there for. I got Howie's passplates—Delphium's personnel files are *thorough*—and wasted hours searching his grungy little apartment for a gap in his files, notations of his computer access codes, anything to build a scenario on. I found nothing of interest, beyond the poster-sized blowup of a candid holo that faced Howie's desk. I wondered when Howie had taken it; nice, but it hadn't captured the real me.

I figured there was an even chance that Howie would wind up in a loony bin, in which case Cabot Hawke would seek some heavy explanations from me. And I hadn't any, until it occurred to me that Howie might be ignoring his personal bills while in Switzerland. Paying his bills gave me slender reason to search his apartment. The rent bill would include the number of times his door passplate was used, so Howie would eventually know someone had been there.

Utility companies can be so-o-o understanding when you offer to pay overdue bills. They weren't angry at Howie. CompuCenter wasn't, either; his bill for the past few weeks had been hardly more than the base rate. *Hardly* more? Well, his apartment terminal had been used for only thirty-nine minutes since his last payment. A trifling sum, which would be carried over since it had, after all, been spent within the past few days.

Within the past few days?

I kept the tremolo from my voice, thanked them, rang off. Somebody had been using Howie's apartment, and very recently.

I called his apartment manager and offered to pay his rent. Yes, Howard Prior was slightly delinquent. Gentle, sweet man, honest to a fault; not to worry.

I simpered into the vidphone, "Howie wanted me to take care of things, but he's an absent-minded dear. Did he sublet the place or let any of—our friends use it?"

The manager consulted her terminal, then said, "No. His door passplate's been used only once in the past few weeks."

"Would you know when that was?"

"Uh—just today, about noon." She cocked her head. "Something wrong?"

Something goosefleshcrawlingly wrong. "No," I smiled past my chill, then thanked her and rang off again. That single entry at noon had been *mine*. No one else had passed through that door in weeks.

Yet his apartment terminal had been used very recently. And CompuCenter long ago stopped permitting remote processing through private terminals.

I stood gazing down at Howie's desk terminal, then at my picture on Howie's wall, until my neck began to prickle. I sensed a presence. Maybe not exactly human.

What if someone had been in his apartment all this time? In fact, what if someone were *still there with me*, watching me, silently waiting in the shadow-haunted bedroom? The sensation of an unseen presence became a hobgoblin that forced me out of Howie's apartment at a dead run.

By the time I reached Delphium, my panic had transmuted to rage and I knew just the pickaninny to take it out on. I passplated myself into Howie's office, intending to call him from his own office for a little therapeutic Swiss *sturm und drang*.

I didn't need to make that call. Howie Prior, in the flesh, sat on his desk, swinging his legs and grinning like an imp with a forefinger across his lips. He didn't need the gesture. I tried to speak but couldn't find the breath for it.

"Don't you ever tell anyone I started hyperventilating," I said, still leaning against his door, willing my hands to stop shaking as I found my compact. "I don't know what industrial espionage you're up to, but I could blow your whole show. You're going to tell me about it right now, Howard Prior. Right *now*," I repeated.

"You again called me 'Howard'," he said smiling. His face, ugly as it was, bore a frightful beauty, his dark eyes shining deep under his brow ridge, teeth bright between pale lips. I mean, he looked—haunted, but unafraid. Exalted. All right then: beatified.

I keyed Cabot Hawke's emergency priority code on the vidphone, leaving it on *hold* so that I needed only to press the *execute* bar. "You look like hell frozen solid, Howie. And you've got me suspicious, and you don't want to do that unless you're after big trouble. Set me at ease."

"That's why here am I."

"You can start by telling me who's been using your apartment terminal this week."

"I did. A few things there to verify were, and easiest it seemed—"

"A lie. You haven't been through that door in weeks.

Anyhow, you can't afford to shuttle back and forth from Europe and Delphium sure as hell hasn't bought you more tickets, and your concierge has orders to call me if you disappear or start acting crazy. And stop talking funny, you're beginning to scare me."

"Sorry. I hadn't thought how to you it might look. But I assure you, I several times my terminal used. Maybe a half-hour."

Again that unspeakable sunburst smile of a madman or a bright angel: "However, yes I *can* afford anywhere to go I bloody please. And so can you, Justine."

My suspicions made a quick test-connection. "You broke the Cetian code and sold it!"

Softly, lovingly, so quietly I almost missed it: "Broke I the *human* code." He caught himself garbling the phrase and slapped his knee. "Human communication breakdown: it's wonderful. Don't you want to know where was hiding our message?"

"I want to know what it said," I hedged.

"Life lastingever," he said, obviously amused now by his own speech patterns that suggested an unhinged mind. He opened his arms, palms up, and continued: "Freedom to discover, to anywhere go. To pain an end. That is part of what it said. Forgive my troubled syntax," he chuckled. "I must sound a bit queer but—but you see, once you, um, internalize the translation, you needn't obey any of the nasty little hierarchies that hag-ride us until we can't see Godhood staring us in the face.

"We even make languages into stumbling blocks; help it we cannot! This word must go here, there another, yonder that phrase. Change the sequence, the pecking order, and you may impair the meaning. Precedence. Status. The stuff of our shell protective."

"What's wrong with protection?"

"Nothing—if you're an embryo. The translation is our egg tooth." Seeing my headshake, he added, "We can use it to peck our way out of the egg of the hereandnow."

He had all the earmarks of a loser who had hit on some nutcake rationale for giving up the good fight. By

now he'd probably drained his savings, telling himself it
didn't matter. If and when he came to his senses again,
Howie was going to be damned sorry. "Howie, do you
suppose neuralgia from a self-poisoning could just possibly have a teeny weeny something to do with your
outlook?"

"Indirectly—but the translation the crucial thing is.
To share it with you first I chose. Than yours, no one's
need could be greater."

"Enough of your ding-y bullshit! You should've said
nobody's single-minded determination could be greater,"
I said proudly.

"Wrong-headed determination amounts to the same
thing," he sighed.

"I know my priorities," I said in anger, "and I'll tell
you yours. First let me see the damned translation."

"Lor' love you, Justine, you don't see it, you—empath
it. The code was based on cardiac rhythms our. I think
was Stravinsky too much the cold intellectual to realize
what with the *Sacre* he had done. Didn't have crypt-
analysis to guide, poor man; and suffering he was from
his tobacco habit in Clarens." A sense of sorrow and
wonder suffused Howie's face. "Imagine how he might
have exulted once the *Sacre*—the *Rite*—translated was
into his own human rhythms."

"Talk sense! Once the right *what* was translated?"

"*The Rite of Spring; Le Sacre du Printemps!* Stravinsky said it was really a coronation of spring. Proximans
had their Coronation lyric to free them; Cetians had
their Rebirth mosaic. And since primitive times, socie-
ties human have to something like this tuned into.
Frazer, in *The New Golden Bough*, said the celebration
of spring is to the expulsion of death a sequel. Frazer
just let notions of sequence bugger him up. Stravinsky
didn't—until later rewrote the music he." Animated,
pleased as a kid, Howie rushed on. "If the *Rite of
Spring* you've ever heard, you know it's from metric
patterns liberated."

"I wish you knew how *you* sound to me," I warned
him.

"Only at first," he said chortling. "Monteux the conductor thought raving mad Stravinsky when the piano score first he heard. Himself Stravinsky complained that badly overbalanced were some parts. So rewrote it he. Harmonies were more than dense; impenetrable they were. Until now," he said, as if in prayer, and looked at me shyly. "Gibberish to you this is, suppose I."

I had to rearrange Howie's chatter in my head, and the thought that he might be teasing me tempered my confusion with fury. "So you've been playing Stravinsky; that much I understand. And it sent you around the bend."

"Listened—truly listened—to the translation, I once only." He turned to his keyboard. "Fed it I into memory with a recording old of the composer's recollections. Listen." He punched an instruction.

The voice from the speaker was aged, unemotional, precise. Old Stravinsky's accent sounded more German than Russian. And with it, beneath it, was a soft thudding asymmetry that I took to be an abnormal heartbeat.

Except that it was *informing* me, its message as clear as speech.

Howie had run two audio tracks together. On one track, Igor Stravinsky was saying, "Very little immediate tradition lies behind the *Sacre du Printemps,* however —and no theory. I had only my ear to help me. I heard; and I wrote what I heard. I am the vessel through which the *Sacre* passed . . ."

Then only the second audio track, the drumbeat whisper of some thunderous concept I hadn't been listening to, emerged into the silence beyond the old man's words. I thought, *And Howie listened had to it once only,* and then I screamed.

It couldn't have been more than a few moments later when I felt Howie's skinny hands stroking my shoulder. I lay in a fetal crouch on his floor hands over my ears, and there was a dampness between my legs that had nothing to do with sex. I could hear my torturer murmuring, "Let it free you, Justine." At least he had stopped that subversive mindbending throb of—knowledge? Heresy? I didn't have a label for it, but I loathed it.

I swiped at his arm as I struggled up, waiting for my strength to return. "Free me from what, you stupid abo? My sanity?"

"Your shell of needs," he said, still kneeling uncaring that I towered above him. "Needs that into a cage we made. Restrictions terrible of imprisonment in hierarchies, and time, and space."

I reached for my compact; checked to see that its gas cell had nearly a full charge, and took a nice long hit to quell my tremors. "All my life I've trained and fought to be somebody, Howie. Now I'm halfway up the ladder and you want to do me the favor, the FAVOR, of mindwashing me into—what? Some kind of born-again Buddhist?"

"Anything timeplace you choose," he said. "Forever," he said. "It offers such freedom that honest to be, I'm growing restless with you. You heard some of it. You know, too."

He was right. It had taken only a minute of that telepathic thudding seduction to push me to the brink of an internal precipice. Another few moments and I knew, positively, I wouldn't have given a damn for my job, or getting Hawke's job, for as long as the madness lasted.

Well, I'd been strong enough to resist. But what if I could get Hawke to listen! Ah, yes; just as Howie wanted *me* to listen. "Howard, is your translation stored in your private access code?"

"No," he said with a smile, and showed me. "It is for access free. It no longer to me belongs, Justine. Returned I to arrange its broadcast, and to first with you share it."

He turned away to his terminal. I triggered my compact, holding it under his nose while gripping his head with all my strength. For only an instant he struggled, then relaxed against my breast, head back, smiling up into my face. "More proof, my love?" He inhaled deeply, deliberately.

He kept on breathing the stuff until I felt the thumping in his little body diminish, falter, quit. Even before that, though, something abandoned his gaze.

As long as his lungs were pumping, I held on. He'd gone berserk, I rehearsed, but I'd been too strong for him. Kept my compact hissing too long out of pure terror. It would be self-defense, and I was sure Hawke would back me. I was sure because I would soon have Hawke working for me.

Howie's heart was still. That had a message for me, too; it told me I'd go on winning, no matter what.

I checked Howie's terminal again, momentarily horrified that I might not be able to retrieve that demonic message. It was there, all right. I changed its address so that only I could locate it again—or so I thought. I stretched the body out on the floor, then remembered to rip my blouse and to use the dead fingernails to drag welts along my throat. When I left Howie's little office I staggered convincingly.

Hawke left a conference in midsentence when he saw me on his vidphone. In his study, he fussed over me in real concern. Gradually I let him understand what I'd rehearsed. I've always been able to evoke tears on demand.

At the crucial point, Hawke showed no suspicion. "Dead? And you didn't get a copy of his translation? Damn, damn, *damn*," he muttered, then patted me distractedly. "I'm not angry with you, Jus'. You can't be blamed."

I made it tentative: "I—might be able to find it. In his office. Uh—hadn't we better get rid of . . . ?" I waved my hand instead of saying it. Hawke knew very well there are some things I'd prefer not to say aloud.

"You sure you're up to it?"

I took a deep breath, smiled my bravest smile, nodded. I said, "We wouldn't want the police stumbling onto Howie's translation before we do."

A few minutes later I had something more to worry about. Howie Prior's body was gone. "Look," I said to Hawke, balling my fists, "I did not imagine it. I—may have been wrong about his heart stopping." I hadn't been.

"Or else someone removed his body. I'm trying to figure out how and why," Hawke said.

I moved to Howie's terminal, readied my fingers at the keys. "I'm feeling barfish," I said as preamble in a vulnerable little-girl voice that seldom failed. "I may have to . . ." I had intended to "find" Howie's translation and then leave quickly while Cabot Hawke absorbed it. But I swear, I never touched a key.

"We pause for a special bulletin," said a familiar voice; Howie's, of course. If he wanted people to listen, he had to ease them into it in a familiar way. "If carefully you listen, this is the very last bulletin special you will ever need."

The next voice was Stravinsky's. I heard the ravishing velvet hammer of propaganda beneath it, thrust my thumbs into my ears, and hummed while I tried not to feel the message vibrating through me.

Hawke didn't notice me. After a moment he sat down, his face transformed in something beyond sexual rapture. I could almost understand, dimly, the message throbbing through my shoe soles. When I eased out of the room, Cabot Hawke was lost in Howie's translation.

En route to Hawke's office, I kept hearing stray bits of that voiceless communiqué from every open doorway, and hummed louder. By some power I couldn't yet guess, Howard Prior had plugged his translation into every channel of every terminal and holovision set in existence. I had to put my heel through Hawke's speakers but finally, insulated by his plush pile carpet and my loudest soprano, I could feel free of that hellish persuasion.

Two hours later I left Delphium. There wasn't anybody there anyway. Then I left Baltimore. There wasn't anybody there, either.

I slid into the driver's couch of a roadster, abandoned like many others with its motor still whirring, and sang "Ain't We Got Fun" at the top of my voice until I could rip the wires from the dashboard speaker. I saw no traffic as I sped north.

I'm not sure why I stopped for the hitcher; maybe because he was the only person I'd seen in an hour. Maybe because he was a good-looking hunky specimen. But when I say he acted altogether too goddamn familiar, I'm understating. He talked as if he were my alter ego. "Free choice have you. No one's going to force you to listen, Justine." Those were his first words as he settled in.

I was already accelerating. "How did you know my name?"

"I listened," he said with the ghost of a wry grin. "To give it a try you ought before the machines run down," he went on. "You wouldn't want stranded to be."

"It's you who gets stranded," I said with finality and braked hard. "Out, buster."

He shrugged. "Losing interest I'm, anyway. Like Prior Howard," he said, stepping out.

It seemed perfectly natural that this total stranger knew all about Howie. "That one's lost interest in *every*thing," I said.

"Did you think that you Howard killed?" His hand described a capricious fillip in the air. "Howard translated."

"Why are you doing this to me?"

"Expiation. I'm—*was*—the Omaha Ripper. Mind never, you don't want the details."

I already knew them. Who didn't know about the manhunt in Omaha? "Got it," I said; "you're a hallucination. Why aren't you in Nebraska?"

"Good question," he said, and winked from existence without even a pop of displaced air. I drove on, a bit more slowly. My odds-on favorite explanation was that my mind had begun playing tricks. To punish itself, maybe? "Nice try," I told it.

Near Harrisburg I was running low on fuel when Cabot Hawke flagged me down. I was quite cool; I'd half-expected something of the sort. I switched off the motor and lounged back, very much in the driver's seat.

"I'm expiating too," Hawke said with no previous greeting. "I'll even try to speak this ridiculous language in a way that won't spook you."

"Spook is the operative word," I said. "I'll settle down, Hawke. And then I'll be flying high in the number one slot, and with all your motivations peeled away, where will all you poor bastards be?"

"Everywhenandwhere. The Eocene. The Crab Nebula. What's the point of being number one, Jus', when there's no number two?"

"Plenty of folks who don't speak CanAm," I said.

"They don't have to," Hawke said gently. "The message is perfectly clear if you only *listen*, whether you speak Tagalog or Croatian. Or Hohokam. Or if you're newborn or deaf," he said in afterthought. "The vibrations, you see."

I'd never heard of a Hohokam, and that bothered me. How could something be dredged from my subconscious if I'd never heard of it? Oh: I'd simply invented it, like the whole conversation. Simple. "You'll come around," I said pleasantly. "And I'll be waiting."

"I wish you were all that interesting," Hawke said mildly. "Anything I can do to convince you? You're starting to bore me."

My tummy rumbled. "Sure. I could use a ham and cheese on rye, and a cola. Oh, and some fuel."

"Don't wait too long," he said, and turned away. And vanished. In the seat beside me was a thick juicy sandwich and a cola; my fuel gauge read full.

I stayed at an inn on the Susquehanna where the machines had already stopped, and spent a few days unwinding in the Executive Suite. That got to be tiresome; no maid service.

Finally I drove back to Baltimore. My fuel tank is always full, and there's always a sandwich and a cola when I want one.

No one else roams the Delphium complex to keep me from clearing out Hawke's desk for myself, reading his private journals, learning how trivial the sonofabitch thought I was before I showed them all. I keep in shape with a fire ax whenever I find a locked door in Delphium. Or anywhere else in Baltimore. Now and then I see a shimmer of something down a silent hallway, or against a moonlit sky, and it makes me think of great shadowbirds at play.

I keep reminding myself that they'll get tired of it pretty soon. Then they'll have to start all over again at square one. Bottom rung of the ladder. That's my most comforting thought, so I think it a lot. At other times, I reflect on the truth of one of Hawke's old phrases.

It's lonely at the top.

EVILEYE

Dr. Victoire Lorenz stood in the shadowed twilight silence of the visitor display room, cradling her kitten, and studied her enemy in the big floor tank. The light from high windows above the aquarium displays was scarcely enough illumination for human eyes. It was more than enough for the nocturnal vision of Evileye. Prowling rocky sea-bottom haunts, his kind had fed in darkness for ten times a million years. Crowded up against the heavy clear plastic of his circular tank, clearly aware of her scrutiny, her enemy stared back. Though the tank was over twenty feet across, its acrylic wall waist-high to a woman of Vicki's small size, it was barely enough for Evileye to move about freely.

It had been Gary Matthews, mate of the *Yaquina*, who'd suggested adding the inward-curving tank lip with sharp edges. The angular, rawboned Matthews had shown interest in Vicki from the first, despite the fact that her responses were barely civil. Gary had taken her turndowns with an easy grace that irritated her, yet he could still take an interest in her work. That acrylic lip idea had, at least, stopped Evileye from prowling.

Now and then, when some idiot visitor tossed popcorn or a candy wrapper into his open pool of sea water, Evileye might move off in a sidelong crawl, sand and tons of water roiling in his wake. At such times he used a lidlike structure to squint. But at other times he could open his eyes round as a barracuda's. When at rest, for example; or occasionally when studying prey.

He was doing that now. *Think I don't know what goes on behind that pitiless gaze?* she thought. *But this concrete floor is my turf. And I know you, mister . . .*

In fact, most marine biologists knew him—or his kind. Proper name: *O. dofleini*. At her last research station across the Pacific in Queensland, they'd pronounced it "doe-flain-eye." Here in Newport at the Oregon State marine science center they said "doe-fleen-eye." But he'd earned his private nickname from Vicki by destroying a month's painstaking work with his insatiable lust for crab flesh.

A lab assistant had walked in one morning, horrified to find Vicki Lorenz's experimental tanks overturned, one smashed, with bits of *Cancer magister,* Dungeness crab, strewn on the concrete and too many carapace fragments in the octopus tank. Though the *dofleini* was again in his tank, the seawater trail was plain and the vast brute sported a cut on his mantle. Much of Vicki's salary came from a sea grant to study the diminished commercial crab catch. The ravenous *dofleini,* in one midnight foray, had wasted a third of her grant money and forced her to start anew. It *would* be a male! And afterward, to Vicki, he was Evileye.

His common name: Pacific Giant, the colossus of octopi. Larger specimens existed, but his body was the size of a medicine ball and at full span, those leathery tentacles could reach nine feet in any direction for the food, bits of crab or squid, introduced into the big display tank. Depending on his mood, Evileye might adopt a rusty hue or a grayish brown to match the sand. Few visitors appreciated his most subtle camouflage trick, the change of his surface texture from smooth to rough or even to nodular, as it suited this subtle hunter of the deep. He was a great favorite of the visitors.

"Oh yes," Vicki murmured, "they love a good safe scare. But what if they were your size, Scrapper?" At the sound of her name, the dozing tiger-stripe kitten waked for a languid glance at her mistress and, lying on her back in the crook of Vicki's arm, flexed tiny orange-furred paws.

"Think you're a predator, huh?" Vicki freed her left hand; moved it above Scrapper's face to tempt playful claws. "Well, that smart sonofabitch in the tank has two hundred pounds, and a lot of brain-power, and a few million years of evolution on you. You'd last about as long as a hermit crab." Her mind flashed in an unwelcome hallucination of the great beast plucking little Scrapper from her arms, encircling the tiny spitting ball of fur with a sucker-lined tentacle, plunging the kitten below to his own watery turf, pulling the pathetic sodden prey toward the beaklike jaws, lethal toxin from his salivary glands flooding the small body—She felt an unprofessional shudder; turned away toward her office and the experimental equipment it held. Acrylic lip or no, she would never again leave her tanks of gravid female *C. magister* specimens in the display room with Evileye.

Scrapper yawned and closed her eyes. "Yeah, me too," Vicki said. "And if I don't get those egg counts done tonight I'll be in a cock-up." While setting her desk in order she smiled to herself at the Aussie slang, an old habit of hers that grad students sometimes gently mocked.

Though Vicki was American, she'd found the peak of her life during her thirties after she and Korff landed jobs in Australia. Birding on unspoiled Heron Island near the small exclusive marine labs there, listening as Korff recited his latest poem—his "most recent literary offense," as he put it—and making love on the Tropic of Capricorn. When his tiny knockabout day-sailer was found capsized on the barrier reef, she could not believe at first that her best years were over.

The memory brought a familiar grief and, with it, a reaction that experience had caught her unaware. Anger, at least, she could handle. "Goddammit, get away from that," she muttered as Scrapper showed interest in the multicolored bottles of recording pen ink. The bottles were secure and the kitten had committed no offense but: "Make my desk a sack of arseholes, would you," Vicki said, lifting Scrapper by her scruff. She dropped the kitten a few inches to the waterproof carpet and resumed setting her notes in order for the morrow.

She knew that her anger was really at Korff, who'd betrayed her by dying. She'd learned from her mother that males weren't to be trusted, but she'd made herself deeply vulnerable to one, bedazzled by his mind, enraptured with his body. *He should've been more careful for my sake!* But he wasn't. Korff had been a gambler. And when he'd lost, *she* had lost. She sent the savage thought back across the years and the pelagic deeps to her long-dead lover: *Thanks for a valuable lesson, mate*.

Vicki slammed the upper left desk drawer too hard; heard a hard thump, probably the little nickel-plated Smith & Wesson she used to dispatch a thrashing shark when working at sea from one of the research vessels. An empty Nansen bottle, its heavy brass hidden with white epoxy paint, nearly toppled to the floor but Vicki caught it just above Scrapper's head. The massive specimen collection bottle would have obliterated her only friend. Certainly the only one she slept with. "Eight lives to go," she said with a shaky laugh, and swept the kitten up again.

A quick look at her wrist: past seven p.m. She hurried to lock up, thrust Scrapper beneath her frayed peajacket, and headed for her rusted-out Datsun. The rules against dogs or cats at the marine center were supposedly strict. But because they had a problem with ants, the joke went, aardvarks were okay. One of these days an undergrad would show up with a real anteater, and then the joke would be ruined.

She took Bay Boulevard, ignoring the lingering Pacific glow that outlined Yaquina Bay Bridge, now a series of sinister spans arching against the bloody palette of the evening sky. Vicki hadn't time to drive to her cottage halfway to Waldport. But neither could she afford dinner at the nearby seaside places, so she turned toward The Anchor in Newport's heart. The food was good and, because they knew her, they'd ignore Scrapper so long as she stayed inside that pea-jacket. They offered other advantages too; when times were as hard as these, pride was your enemy.

She took a rear corner booth; made an effort to produce a smile because she knew the waitress slightly. "No menu, Fran; we're not all that hungry so, uh, a hamburger steak and iced tea. Make it a child's portion," she added, more defiant than pleading.

"You could eat a horse and chase the driver, honey," Fran accused, adding, "and child's portion it is."

Vicki nodded her thanks, knowing the finely drawn lines in her own face were more from overwork than from undereating. Besides, Fran obviously took pride in curves as exaggerated as an overstuffed sofa. Fran made no secret of her view: if you weren't blowsy, you were sickly. For a moment, Vicki's smile became genuine as she watched Fran's ample behind. By most standards, Fran was twenty pounds too healthy.

Then Vicki leaned back and closed her eyes, her hand stroking the fidgety kitten inside the jacket. She couldn't blame Scrapper; the restaurant smells had her juices flowing, too. It was probably the shadow across her eyelids that made her jerk them open.

"I bet you eat in bed, too." Gary Matthews's voice was husky but light for a man of his size. He saw the spark kindle in her face and raised his hands, drawing back. "Cancel that. I mean, if you sleep in restaurants, why then, ah—"

"Ho," she said gravely, "ho. And I wasn't sleeping."

"Minor surgery on your navel, then?"

She realized she was still stroking Scrapper and jerked her hand from the jacket. One tiny paw shot out, answering the challenge of quick movement, and by mischance caught Vicki's forefinger. "Damn," said Vicki, and put the finger in her mouth.

Matthews had seen the kitten. Still, "Ah; minor surgery *from* your navel. It's little differences like this that make you so intriguing, Lorenz."

He was still standing, because she was gauche, because she needed to think about her grant work, because it was all she had, because—"You're in Fran's way," she said, "Sit." He did.

After an interminable pause of perhaps two minutes he leaned his chin on his knuckles. "You don't talk me to death either. That's good."

"Maybe I just don't have much to say to you."

"Sure you do. How's the larvae count coming?"

The man had an unerring knack for divining what was uppermost in her mind. Like Korff. One strike against him. "Beg pardon?"

"Those Nansen bottles we brought you from the escarpment. You know, planktonic larvae? From *Cancer magister?* Basis of the local econ—"

"So I've heard," she replied drily. "It's too early to tell, and thanks for doing your job, Matthews. There's lots more lab work to do, mostly at night. I wish I knew why you cared."

"I've got friends in Newport, Lorenz. If the crabbing doesn't improve, a lot of furniture gets repossessed." His own job, of course, would be secure in any event; yet he spoke as if he really cared about people. Again, like Korff; strike two.

"Not about the crabbing. About me. I don't want to be bitchy, but why me?"

Fran was beside them, sliding a small plate with a suspiciously large aromatic meat pattie onto the table. She cast an appreciative eye toward the newcomer with his wide-set gray eyes and sun-bleached hair. "Something for you?"

"Doesn't look like it," he grinned up at her. He waited, watching Fran move off, amused at the cats-in-a-sack movement of her rump, and caught Vicki's glance before answering. "Why you? Well, you're dedicated; students claim you're tough, but fair. And you're a loner like me. You stay in shape. You don't party a lot." He paused to watch her separate a bite-sized piece of meat, saw Scrapper devour it from her hand. "And you read damned fine poetry, and you take in strays." He spread his hands again for her.

"Scrapper happens to be a female. No, I'm not lezzo," she added quickly.

"I never dreamed you were. I know about Korff," he said softly.

Now he was riding sidelong on a dangerous Pacific swell. "Then leave me alone with him!" She hadn't intended to say it that way, or that sharply. More subdued: "I really just need to be left alone, Matthews. I really, really—" Momentarily, without knowing why, she was near tears with frustration.

"Forgive me," he said, rising. "You don't need this. I just thought you might enjoy hunting agates on the beach sometime, or a steak at The Moorage now and then."

"I can't afford it."

"I can."

"I can't afford you, either."

"Ah." His answering smile was bleak now. "I suppose there's something to be said for traveling light. We *could* keep it light, you know." He got up slowly, favoring his back like an older man.

"Looks like you've put in a long day, too," she said to change the subject.

"They seem to get longer as we get older," he said.

" 'We are all her children, and age too soon; Yet our witch-mother sea is still bride of the moon.' "

A fragment of Korff; strike three. "Mister Matthews, you are now invading my privacy," she said, staring at her plate.

"I suppose it never occurs to you that others might miss him," Matthews said. "Or that his work belongs to us all—even if he did dedicate it to you."

He had already turned away when she spoke. "He gave himself too easily to the sea."

Pause. Then, over his shoulder: "Maybe you'll explain that sometime."

"Maybe I will. But I'm rotten company tonight, Matthews. I'm sorry."

He nodded and left her. Presently she withdrew a square of filmy plastic from her jacket; folded the remainder of the meat inside. "You'll want a midnight snack before I'm done," she muttered to the kitten, and counted out the coins for Fran's tip.

It was almost ten p.m. before Vicki had enough data on the *magister* egg counts. It was messy work with its own special odors. She washed up, setting out a few fragments of crab for Scrapper, and carried a tray of remains into the display room.

"Never say I'm not fair," she muttered as she emptied the tray into Evileye's tank. He reached one tentacle out, suckers flattening against the clear acrylic to anchor him, and sent two more of his powerful limbs after large morsels. He was in no hurry, but watched her warily as he began to feed.

Why had she told Gary Matthews she might explain her bitter memories of Korff? It would only make a bad situation worse. It was her firm conclusion that, among the more intelligent species, the female became the giver; a genetic bias, perhaps, in caring for the young. The male, biased toward the hunt, became a selfish taker.

She watched Evileye reach far across his tank for a remnant of *C. magister* with the tentacle that proved his maleness. Its underside had a faint groove from which, at mating time, a special appendage grew. This detachable pseudopod was his gift to the female. "And you wouldn't do it unless it felt damned good," she said, wondering for the first time about that particular tentacle.

Big specimens of Evileye's kind were in special demand for dissection, precisely because everything was so large. Fine structures, the optic nerve, even the circulatory and neural systems. Perhaps someone had already made a study of the nerve pathways of *O. dofleini* with respect to that special tentacle. If not, perhaps she would sacrifice Evileye to that end. It would be a great pleasure.

She noted the series of faint lines, perhaps abrasions from the stones in his tank, that marked the tips of three tentacles that were most directly in line with those evil eyes. "One day soon, you may give your all for science," she warned, and took the tray back to her office.

The far end of her narrow office held lab hardware and the sink. Presently she began to chuckle as she completed her cleanup. It might be possible for a man as honest as Gary Matthews to admit that he had a selfish purpose in paying court to a woman—herself, for example. But even under torture he wouldn't allow the comparison of his own flesh, his sex tentacle as it were, to that of Evileye. Still, that was clearly how it was. Basically, all he wanted was his own selfish pleasure, regardless who got destroyed in the process. Take a step or two across the evolutionary ladder and you had a cunning, highly intelligent male predator who made not the slightest effort to please anyone in his lust-driven pursuit.

You had Evileye.

Her wry amusement lasted until she had fed new figures into her desk computer, saved the updated data on a spare disk, and filed the disk away. Then she remembered Scrapper's late snack, and sitting, reached for her pea-jacket. She'd forgotten to shut the door to the display room, a common occurrence. But then her gaze followed a long trapezoid of light into the big room. In the edge of the blade of light, a saffron bundle of fur gamboled, fell over its feet, reared, pounced.

A runnel of water, a very small thing really, edged into the light. Vicki wondered if the big tank had sprung a leak, and then something else flicked into the light for a bare, ghastly, enervating instant, and in that tick of time her heart went as cold as primeval ooze.

She knew how suddenly, and with what lethal precision, Evileye could lash out with that tentacle which now lay stretched over the lip of his tank, its tip flicking in the edge of the light, tantalizing the innocent Scrapper into mock attacks. If she screamed or bolted into the big room, she would be too late. Evileye might have been luring the kitten forward for long minutes. Noiselessly, not daring to look away, Vicki pulled open the top left drawer of her desk and groped for the revolver.

But the cold metal object she grasped was not the revolver; it was merely a paperweight, long forgotten until this moment of mortal need. Now, straining to see into the gloom, she could see Evileye, crowded hard against the near wall of his tank, one huge eye wide, staring down at the kitten which was busily stalking the lure and did not see the second hawser-thick rope of muscle sliding along the floor behind it.

Biting her lip, mewling with desperation, Vicki wrenched open a second drawer, then a third, and then remembered with thunderclap clarity that she'd left the goddamn revolver in her apartment a month before. In her middle drawer was a dissection knife that she used as a letter-opener. If that was all she had for an attack on a monster twice her size, then that, by God, would have to do. She leaped to her feet, grasped the heavy Nansen bottle with her free hand and prepared to toss it against the tank in the wild hope that it might prove an instant's diversion. She took two steps, raised the metal canister, and paused.

Scrapper had already found her goal. The kitten had wrapped both forepaws around one leathery tip, and kicked with both hind feet against the tentacle in pretend ferocity. The second flanking tentacle had reached the kitten. Slowly, repeatedly, the tip of the second tentacle rubbed the back of Scrapper's neck, moving up between her ears and back again.

Vicki Lorenz, her knees failing, slid against the near wall of her office, so near collapse that she dropped the Nansen bottle. At the muffled clang, Scrapper came to her feet in a liquid gymnastic, then turned again to resume her little game. Evileye, staring expressionlessly from his world, seemed equally willing. Moments later he had the kitten on its back as he tickled its almost hairless belly.

As Vicki walked on unsteady legs into the room, slipping the dissection knife into a back pocket, Evileye moved one eye to keep her in view. Simultaneously, he slid his tentacles back with such guilty speed that one of them actually made an audible "plop" into the water. The kitten sat up and began to lick its breast.

"You didn't know I was watching, Evileye. So I believe you." Her voice shook so much, Vicki scarcely recognized it as her own. "Now I see how you got all those scratches. How many nights, I wonder."

Now he wrapped three of his rearmost tentacles around heavy stones in the tank; solid purchase for a quick retreat. Yet he stayed near the wall of the tank, watching as Vicki stooped to pull Scrapper into the crook of one arm.

"Scrapper doesn't know how sharp her little claws are; why do you let her scratch you up like that? Hell, why do I? Maybe friends all have claws, now that you mention it. You just have to be willing to bleed a little." Her voice, echoing in the big room, sounded doubly foolish. She didn't give a damn; at least it wasn't so shaky anymore.

Then she laughed aloud. "Let me tell you something, Evileye; I've pigged out on crab, too. Maybe we should pick friends for what they're selfish *about*, hm?" She didn't really expect the big brute to take her hand when she placed it in the water; and he didn't.

But when she squatted and eased Scrapper up against the clear plastic of the tank—the kitten did not care for its chill surface—one careful tentacle snaked out along the acrylic inside the tank, its tip moving as if in symbolic caress. Vicki placed her hand flat, fingers apart tentacle-like, opposite the appendage.

Later she would wonder if she had imagined it; but as the tentacle became still, Evileye did two things: he opened both eyes wide, and he changed from gray to a hue that was ruddy as her own sunburnt skin.

"That does it, buster; but it'll have to look like an accident."

Among the list of emergency numbers she found Matthews, Gary. He answered at the fifth ring. "If you're only watching Johnny Carson," she said, "how would you like to help me out here at the lab? Yes, tonight. The sooner the better."

During his reply she rubbed Scrapper's neck. Then: "It's not illegal, but you'll think it's crazy as hell. . . . Okay, twenty minutes, but one more thing: you must never, ever, tell anyone."

She listened a moment more. Then, with a sigh: "All right then: we're going to fishnap a two-hundred-pound octopus. Still with me? Right; fifteen minutes," she said, laughing.

She put down the receiver and strolled back into the display room with its horrific central exhibit. She leaned forward on the tank lip, certain that no member of *O. dofleini* could understand her words, saying them anyway. "I could set up subtle lighting and get videotapes; I know, don't tempt me. Maybe I will, with one of your brothers. But not with you, Evileye. It'll be a bitch to fake your trail, but we've got all night."

And maybe, she thought, one day she would tell the details to Gary Matthews, While sharing a London broil, or combing Agate Beach some summer evening. She nuzzled her kitten and winked at Evileye, her buoyancy an almost physical sensation. After long years of self-imposed exile in green twilight depths, she was rising now, soaring upward to the light and to her own element; to life. The least she could do was return Evileye to his.

VEHICLES FOR FUTURE WARS

Long before the first ram-tipped bireme scuttled across the Aegean, special military vehicles were deciding the outcomes of warfare. If we can judge from the mosaics at Ur, the Mesopotamians drove four-horsepower chariots thundering into battle in 2500 B.C.; and bas-reliefs tell us that some Assyrian genius later refined the design so his rigs could be quickly disassembled for river crossings. In more recent times, some passing strange vehicles have been pressed into military service— Hannibal's alp-roving elephants and six hundred troop-toting Paris taxicabs being two prime examples. Still, people had seen elephants and taxis before; application, not design, was the surprise element. Today, military vehicle design itself is undergoing rapid change in almost all venues: land, sea, air, space. Tomorrow's war chariots are going to be mind-bogglers!

Well, how will military vehicles of the next century differ from today's? Many of the details are imponderable at the moment, but we can make some generalizations that should hold true for the future. And we can hazard specific guesses at the rest.

It's possible to list a few primary considerations for the design of a military vehicle without naming its specific functions. It should have higher performance than previous vehicles; it should be more dependable;

and it should be more cost-effective. Those three criteria cover a hundred others including vulnerability, speed, firepower, maintenance, manufacturing, and even the use of critical materials. Any new design that doesn't trade off one of those criteria to meet others is likely to be very, very popular.

It may be fortunate irony for peace lovers that the most militarily advanced countries are those with the biggest problems in cost-effectiveness. Any nation that pours billions into a fleet of undersea missile ships must think twice before junking the whole system—tenders, training programs and all—for something radically different. That's one reason why the U.S. Navy, for example, hasn't already stuffed its latter-generation Polaris missiles (after Poseidon and Trident, what's next?) into the smaller, faster, more widely dispersed craft. A certain continuity is essential as these costly systems evolve; otherwise, costs escalate like mad.

Still, new systems do get developed, starting from tiny study contracts through feasibility demonstrations to parallel development programs. There is probably a hundred-knot Navy ACV (Air Cushion Vehicle) skating around somewhere with an old Polaris hidden in her guts, working out the details of a post-Trident weapon delivery system. Even if *we* don't already have one, chances are the Soviets do—and if we can prove that, we'll have one, all righty.

The mere concept of Polaris-packing ACV's says little about the system design, though. We can do better but, before taking rough cuts at specific new designs, it might be better to look at the power plants and materials that should be popular in the near future.

POWER PLANTS

Internal combustion engines may be with us for another generation, thanks to compact designs and new fuel mixtures. Still, the only reason why absurdly powerful Indianapolis cars don't use turbines now is that the turbine is outlawed by Indy officials: too good, too quiet, too dependable. In other words, the turbine doesn't promise as much drama, sound and fury—perfect reasons for a military vehicle designer to choose the turbine, since he doesn't want drama; he wants a clean mission.

Turbines can be smaller for a given output if they can operate at higher temperatures and higher RPM. Superalloy turbine buckets may be replaced by hyperalloys or cermets. Oiled bearings may be replaced by magnetic types. Automated manufacturing could bring the cost of a turbine power unit down so low that the unit could be replaced at every refueling. In short, it should be possible to design the power plant and fuel tanks as a unit to be mated to the vehicle in moments.

The weapons designer won't be slow to see that high-temperature turbines can lend themselves to MHD (magnetohydrodynamics) application. If a weapon laser needs vast quantities of electrical energy, and if that energy can be taken from a hot stream of ionized gas, then the turbine may become the power source for both the vehicle and its electrical weapons. Early MHD power plants were outrageously heavy, and required rocket propellants to obtain the necessary working temperatures. Yet there are ways to bootstrap a gas stream into conductive plasma, including previously stored electrical energy and seeding the gas stream with chemicals. If the vehicle needs a lot of electrical energy and operates in a chemically active medium—air will do handily—then a turbine or motor-driven impeller of some kind may be with us for a long time to come.

Chemically fueled rockets are made to order for MHD. If the vehicle is to operate in space, an MHD unit could be coupled to a rocket exhaust to power all necessary electrical systems. The problem with chemical rockets, as everybody knows, is their ferocious thirst. If a vehicle is to be very energetic for very long using chemical rockets, it will consist chiefly of propellant tanks. And it will require careful refueling, unless the idea is to junk the craft when its tanks are empty. Refueling with cryogenic propellant—liquid hydrogen and liquid fluorine are good bets from the stored-energy standpoint—tends to be complicated and slow. By the end of this century, rocket-turbine hybrids could be used for vehicles that flit from atmosphere to vacuum and back again. The turbine could use atmospheric oxidizer while the vehicle stores its own in liquid form for use in space. The hybrid makes sense because, when oxidizer is available in the atmosphere, the turbine can use it with reduced propellant expenditure. Besides, the turbine is very dependable and its support equipment relatively cheap.

Some cheap one-shot vehicles, designed to use minimum support facilities, can operate with power plants of simple manufacture. When their backs neared the wall in World War II, the Japanese turned to very simple techniques in producing their piloted "Baka" bomb. It was really a stubby twin-tailed glider, carried aloft by a bomber and released for a solid rocket-powered final dash onto our shipping. The Nazis didn't deliberately opt for suicide aircraft, but they managed something damned close to it with the Bachem "Natter." Bachem hazarded a design that could be produced in under 1,000 man-hours per copy, a manned, disposable flying shotgun featuring rocket ascent and parachute recovery. "Hazard" was the operative word—or maybe they started with factory seconds. On its first manned ascent, the Natter began to shed parts and eventually blended its pilot with the rest of the wreckage. Yet there was nothing wrong with the basic idea and a nation with low industrial capacity can be expected to gobble up similar cheapies in the future using simple, shortlife power plants.

There's reason to suspect that simple air-breathing jet engines such as the Schmidt pulsejet can also operate as ramjets by clever modifications to pulse vanes and duct inlet geometry. In this way, sophisticated design may permit a small have-not nation to produce air-breathing power plants to challenge those of her richer neighbors, in overall utility if not in fuel consumption. A pulsejet develops thrust at rest, and could boost a vehicle to high subsonic velocity where ramjets become efficient. Supersonic ramjets need careful attention to the region just ahead of the duct inlet, where a spike-like cowl produces exactly the right disturbance in the incoming air to make the ramjet efficient at a given speed. A variable-geometry spike greatly improves the efficiency of a ramjet over a wide range of airspeeds, from sonic to Mach five or so. We might even see pulse-ram-rocket tribrids using relatively few moving parts, propelling vehicles from rest at sea level into space and back.

For a nation where cost-effectiveness or material shortages overshadow all else, then, the simplicity of the pulse-ram-rocket could make it popular. A turbine-rocket hybrid would yield better fuel economy, though. The choice might well depend on manufacturing capability; and before you can complain that rockets absolutely demand exacting tolerances in manufacturing, think about strap-on solid rockets.

MHD is another possible power source as we develop more lightweight MHD hardware and learn to use megawatt quantities of electrical energy directly in power plants. An initial jolt from fuel cells or even a short-duration chemical rocket may be needed to start the MHD generator. Once in operation, the MHD unit could use a combination of electron beams and jet fuel to heat incoming air in a duct, and at that point the system could reduce its expenditure of tanked oxidizer. We might suspect that the MHD system would need a trickle of chemical, such as a potassium salt, to boost plasma conductivity especially when the MHD is idling. By the year 2050, MHD design may be so well developed that no chemical seeding of the hot gas would be necessary at all. This development could arise from magnetic pinch effects, or from new materials capable of withstanding very high temperatures for long periods while retaining dielectric properties.

It almost seems that an MHD power plant would be a perpetual motion machine, emplaced in an atmosphere-breathing vehicle that could cruise endlessly. But MHD is an energy-conversion system, converting heat to electricity as the conductive plasma (*i.e.*, the hot gas stream) passes stationary magnets. The vehicle would need its own compact heat generator, perhaps even a closed-loop gaseous uranium fission reactor for large craft. A long-range cruise vehicle could be managed this way, but eventually the reactor would need refueling. Still, it'd be risky to insist that we'll *never* find new sources of energy which would provide MHD power plants capable of almost perpetual operation.

Whether or not MHD justifies the hopes of power plant people, other power sources may prove more compact, lighter, and—at least in operation—simpler. Take, for example, a kilogram of Californium 254, assuming an orbital manufacturing plant to produce it. This isotope decays fast enough that its heat output is halved after roughly two months; but initially the steady ravening heat output from one kilo of the stuff would be translatable to something like 10,000 horsepower! No matter that a kilo of Californium 254 is, at present, a stupefyingly immense quantity; ways can probably be found to produce it in quantity. Such a compact heat source would power ramjets without fuel tanks, or it could vaporize a working fluid such as water. In essence, the isotope would function as a simple reactor, but without damping rods or other methods of controlling its decay. Like it or not, the stuff would be cooking all the time. Perhaps its best use would be for small, extended-range, upper-atmosphere patrol craft. There's certainly no percentage in letting it sit in storage.

For propulsion in space, several other power plants seem attractive. Early nuclear weapon tests revealed that graphite-covered steel spheres survived a twenty kiloton blast at a distance of ten meters. The Orion project grew from this datum, and involved nothing less in concept than a series of nukes detonated behind the baseplate of a large vehicle. As originally designed by Ted Taylor and Freeman Dyson, such a craft could be launched from the ground, but environmentalists quake at the very idea. The notion is not at all far-fetched from an engineering standpoint and might yet be used to power city-sized space dreadnoughts of the next century if we utterly fail to perfect more efficient methods of converting matter into energy. Incidentally, the intermittent explosion rocket drive was tested by Orion people, using conventional explosives in scale models. Wernher von Braun was evidently unimpressed with the project until he saw films of a model in flight.

This kind of experiment goes back at least as far as Goddard, who tested solid-propellant repeater rockets before turning to his beloved, persnickety, high-impulse liquid fuels. No engineer doubts there'll be lots of glitches between a small model using conventional explosives, and a megaton-sized version cruising through space by means of nuke blasts. But it probably will work, and God knows it doesn't have a whole slew of moving parts. Structurally, in fact, it may be a more robust solution for space dreadnoughts than are some other solutions. It seems more elegant to draw electrical power from the sun to move your space dreadnought, for instance—until we realize that the solar cell arrays would be many square kilometers in area. Any hefty acceleration with those gossamer elements in place would require quintupling the craft's mass to keep the arrays from buckling during maneuvers. The added mass would be concentrated in the solar array structure and its interface with the rest of the craft.

On the other hand, there's something to be said for any system that draws its power from an inexhaustible source—and the Orion system falls short in that department since it must carry its nukes with it. The mass driver is something else again. It can use a nearby star for power, though it must be supplied with some mass to drive. Lucky for dwellers of this particular star system: we can always filch a few megatons of mass from the asteroid belt.

The mass driver unit is fairly simple in principle. It uses magnetic coils to hurl small masses away at high speed, producing thrust against the coils. Gerard O'Neill has demonstrated working models of the mass driver. In space, a mass driver could be powered by a solar array or a closed-cycle reactor, and its power consumption would not be prohibitively high. The thrust of the device is modest—too low for planetary liftoff as currently described. Its use in an atmosphere would be limited, power source aside, by aerodynamic shock waves generated by the mass accelerated to hypersonic velocity within the acceleration coils.

For fuel mass, O'Neill suggests munching bits from a handy asteroid—though almost any available mass would do. The mass need not be magnetic since it can be accelerated in metal containers, then allowed to continue while the metal "buckets" are decelerated for re-use.

In case you're not already ahead of me, notice that the mass driver offers a solution to the problem of "space junk" that already litters orbital pathways. The mass-driver craft can schlep around until it locates some hardware nobody values anymore, dice and compact it into slugs, feed it into the mass driver buckets, and hurl the compacted slugs away during its next maneuver. Of course, the craft's computer will have to keep tabs on whatever is in line with the ejected masses, since the slugs will be potentially as destructive as meteorites as they flee the scene. Imagine being whacked by a ten-kilogram hunk of compacted aluminum garbage moving at escape velocity!

Solar plasma, the stream of ionized particles radiated by stars, has been suggested as a "solar wind" to be tapped by vast gossamer sails attached to a space vehicle—with the pressure of light radiation adding to the gentle "wind." Carl Wiley, writing as "Russell Saunders," outlined the space windjammer proposal in 1951. His sail was envisioned as a parachute-like arrangement of approximately hemispherical shape, made of lithium, many square kilometers in area. Wiley argued that, while such a craft could hardly survive any environment but space, it could be made to revolve with its sail as it circles a planetary mass. By presenting a profile view of the sail as it swings toward the sun, and the full circular view as it swings away again, the craft could gradually build up enough velocity to escape the planet entirely. Even granting this scheme a sail quickly deflated or rearranged into windsock proportions, it seems unlikely that a starsailer could move very effectively into a solar wind in the same way that a boat tacks upwind. The interstallar yachtsman has an advantage, though: he can predict the sources of his winds. He cannot be sure they won't vary in intensity, though; which leads to scenarios of craft becalmed between several stars until one star burns out, or becomes a nova.

It takes a very broad brush to paint a military operation of such scale that solar sails and mass drivers would be popular as power plants. These prime movers are very cost-effective, but they need a lot of time to traverse a lot of space. By the time we have military missions beyond Pluto, we may also have devices which convert matter completely into photons, yielding a photon light drive. In the meantime, nuclear reactors can provide enough heat to vaporize fuel mass for high-thrust power plants in space. So far as we know, the ultimate space drive would use impinging streams of matter and antimatter in a thrust chamber. This is perhaps the most distant of far-out power plants, and presumes that we can learn to make antimatter do as we say. Until recently, there was grave doubt that any particle of antimatter could be stable within our continuum. That doubt seems to be fading quickly, according to reports from Geneva. Antiprotons have been maintained in circular paths for over eighty hours. The demonstration required a nearly perfect vacuum, since any contact between antimatter and normal matter means instant apocalypse for both particles. And as the particles are mutually annihilated, they are converted totally into energy. We aren't talking about your workaday one or two percent conversion typical of nuclear weapons, understand: total means *total*. A vehicle using an antimatter drive would be able to squander energy in classic military fashion!

The power plants we've discussed so far all lend themselves to aircraft and spacecraft. Different performance standards apply to land- and water-based vehicles, which must operate quietly, without lethal effluents, and slowly at least during docking stages. Turbines can be quiet, but they produce strong infrared signatures and they use a lot of fuel, limiting their range somewhat. When you cannot be quick, you are wise to be inconspicuous. This suggests that electric motors might power wheeled transports in the near future, drawing power from lightweight storage batteries or fuel cells. The fuel cell oxidizes fuel to obtain current, but the process generates far less waste heat than a turbine does. The fuel cell also permits fast refueling—with a hydride, or perhaps hydrogen—which gives the fuel cell a strong advantage over conventional batteries. However, remember that the fuel cell "burns" fuel. No fair powering a moonrover or a submarine by fuel cells without an oxidizer supply on board.

When weight is not a crucial consideration, the designer can opt for heavier power plants that have special advantages. The flywheel is one method of storing energy without generating much heat as that energy is tapped. A flywheel can be linked to a turbine or other drive unit to provide a hybrid engine. For brief periods when a minimal infrared signature is crucial, the vehicle could operate entirely off the flywheel. Fuel cells and electric motors could replace the turbine in this hybrid system. Very large cargo vehicles might employ reactors; but the waste heat of a turbine, reactor, or other heat engine is always a disadvantage when heatseeking missiles are lurking near. It's likely that military cargo vehicles will evolve toward sophisticated hybrid power plants that employ heat engines in low-vulnerability areas, switching to flywheel, beamed power, or other stored-energy systems producing little heat when danger is near. As weapons become more sophisticated, there may be literally almost no place far from danger—which implies development of hybrid power plants using low-emission fuel cells and flywheels for wheeled vehicles.

MATERIALS

Perhaps the most direct way to improve a vehicle's overall performance is to increase its payload fraction, *i.e.*, the proportion of the system's gross weight that's devoted to payload. If a given craft can be built with lighter materials, or using more energetic material for fuel, that craft can carry more cargo and/or can carry it farther, faster.

Many solids, including metals, are crystalline masses. Entire journals are devoted to the study of crystal growth because, among other things, the alignment and size of crystals in a material profoundly affect that material's strength. Superalloys in turbine blades have complex crystalline structures, being composed of such combinations as cobalt, chromium, tungsten, tantalum, carbon, and refractory metal carbides. These materials may lead to hyperalloys capable of sustaining the thermal shock of a nuke at close range.

As we've already noted, graphite-coated steel objects have shown some capacity to survive a nuke at close quarters. There may be no alloy quite as good as the old standby, graphite, especially when we note that graphite is both far cheaper and lighter in weight. Superalloys aren't the easiest things to machine, either. Anybody who's paid to have superalloy parts machined risked cardiac arrest when he saw the bill. Graphite is a cinch to machine; hell, it even lubricates itself.

More conventional alloys of steel, aluminum, and titanium may be around for a long time, with tempering and alloying processes doubling the present tensile strengths. When we begin processing materials in space, it may be possible to grow endless crystals which can be spun into filament bundles. A metal or quartz cable of such stuff may have tensile strength in excess of a million pounds per square inch. For that matter, we might grow doped crystals in special shapes to exacting tolerances, which could lead to turbine blades and lenses vastly superior to anything we have today. Until fairly recently, quartz cable had a built-in limitation at the point where the cable was attached to other structural

members. Steel cable terminals can simply be swaged—
squeezed—over a steel cable, but quartz can't take the
shear forces; you can cut through quartz cable with a
pocketknife. This problem is being solved by adhesive
potting of the quartz cable end into specially formed
metal terminals. Your correspondent was crushed to
find himself a few months behind the guy who applied
for the first patents in this area. The breakthrough takes
on more importance when we consider the advantages
of cheap dielectric cable with high flexibility and extremely high tensile strength at a fraction of the weight
of comparable steel cable. Very large structures of the
future are likely to employ quartz cable tension members with abrasion-resistant coatings.

Vehicles are bound to make more use of composite
materials as processing gets more sophisticated. Fiber-
glass is a composite of glass fibers in a resin matrix; but
sandwich materials are composites too. A wide variety
of materials can be formed into honeycomb structures
to gain great stiffness-to-weight characteristics. An air-
breathing hypersonic craft might employ molybdenum
honeycomb facing a hyperalloy inner skin forming an
exhaust duct. The honeycomb could be cooled by duct-
ing relatively cool gas through it. On the other side of
the honeycomb might be the craft's outer skin; say, a
composite of graphite and high-temperature polymer.
Advanced sandwich composites are already in use, and
show dramatic savings in vehicle weight. The possible
combinations in advanced sandwich composites are almost infinite, with various layers tailored to a given
chemical, structural, or electrical characteristic. Seven-
teen years ago, an experimental car bumper used a
composite of stainless steel meshes between layers of
glass and polymer to combine lightness with high impact resistance. A racing car under test that year had a
dry weight of just 540 lb., thanks to a chassis built up
from sandwich composite with a paper honeycomb core.
The writer can vouch for the superior impact and abra-
sion resistance of this superlight stuff, which was all
that separated his rump from macadam when the little

car's rear suspension went gaga during a test drive. The vehicle skated out of a corner and spun for a hundred meters on its chassis pan before coming to rest. The polymer surface of the pan was scratched up a bit, yet there was no structural damage whatever. But we considered installing a porta-potty for the next driver . . .

Today, some aircraft use aluminum mesh in skins of epoxy and graphite fiber. The next composite might be titanium mesh between layers of boron fiber in a silicone polymer matrix. The chief limitation of composites seems to be the adhesives that bond the various materials together. It may be a long time before we develop a glue that won't char, peel, or embrittle when subjected to temperature variations of hypersonic aircraft. The problem partly explains the metallurgists' interest in welding dissimilar metals. If we can find suitable combinations of inert atmosphere, alloying, and electrical welding techniques, we can simply (translation: not so simply) lay a metal honeycomb against dissimilar metal surfaces and zap them all into a single piece.

Several fibers are competing for primacy in the search for better composites; among them boron, graphite, acetal homopolymer, and aramid polymers. Boron may get the nod for structures that need to be superlight without a very high temperature requirement, but graphite looks like the best bet in elevated temperature regimes. Sandia Laboratories has ginned up a system to test graphite specimens for short-term high temperature phenomena including fatigue, creep, and stress-rupture. The specimens are tested at very high heating rates. It's easy to use the report of this test rig as a springboard for guessing games. Will it test only graphite? Very high heating rates might mean they're testing leading edges intended to survive vertical re-entry at orbital speeds. Then again, there's a problem with the heat generated when an antitank projectile piles into a piece of Soviet armor. Do we have materials that can punch through before melting into vapor? And let's not forget armor intended to stand up for a reasonable time against a power laser. For several reasons, and outstand-

ing heat conductivity is only one of them, graphite
looks good to this guesser. If the Sandia system isn't
looking into antilaser armor, something like it almost
certainly will be—and soon.

Before leaving the topic of materials, let's pause to
note research into jet fuels. A gallon of JP-4 stores
roughly 110,000 Btu. Some new fuels pack an additional 65,000 Btu into a gallon. Even if the new fuels
are slightly heavier, the fuel tank can be smaller. The
result is extended range. It seems reasonable to guess
that JP-50, when it comes along, will double the energy
storage of JP-4.

VEHICLE CONFIGURATIONS

Now that we're in an age of microminiaturization, we
have a new problem in defining a vehicle. We might all
agree that a vehicle carries something, but start wran-
gling over just how small the "something" might be. An
incendiary bullet carries a tiny blazing chemical payload; but does that make the bullet a vehicle? In the
strictest sense, probably yes. But a bullet is obviously
not a limiting case—leaving that potential pun unspent—
when very potent things of almost *no* mass can be
carried by vehicles of insect size.

Payloads of very small vehicles could be stored information, or might be a few micrograms of botulism or
plutonium, perhaps even earmarked for a specific human target. Ruling out live bats and insects as carriers,
since they are normally pretty slapdash in choosing the
right target among possibly hundreds of opportunities,
we could develop extremely small rotary-winged craft
and smarten them with really stupendous amounts of
programming without exceeding a few milligrams of
total mass. A swarm of these inconspicuous mites would
be expensive to produce, but just may be the ultimate
use for "clean room" technology in which the U.S. has a
temporary lead.

The mites would be limited in range and top speed,
so that a hypersonic carrier vehicle might be needed to
bring them within range of the target like a greyhound

with plague fleas. The carrier would then slow to disgorge its electromechanical parasites. One immediately sees visions of filters to stop them; and special antifilter mites to punch holes in the filters; and sensors to detect antifilter mite action; and so on.

It's hard to say just how small the mites could be after a hundred years of development. One likely generalization is that the smaller the payload, the longer the delay before the payload's effect will be felt. Take the examples of plutonium or botulism: a human victim of either payload can continue performing his duties for a longer time—call it mean time before failure—if he is victimized by a tinier chunk of poison. Some canny theorists will be chortling, about now, at the vision of a billion mites slowly building a grapefruit-sized mass of plutonium in some enemy bunker. That's one option, for sure. But the blast, once critical mass is reached, would be ludicrously small when compared with other nuke mechanisms.

The best use of mites might be as spies, storing data while hunkered down in an inconspicuous corner of the enemy's war room, scaring the bejeezus out of the local spiders. Or would the enemy's spiders, too, be creatures of the clean room? Pick your own scenario . . .

There is no very compelling reason why mites couldn't actually resemble tiny flies, with gimbaled ornithopter wings to permit hovering or fairly rapid motion in any direction. There may be a severe limitation to their absolute top speed in air, depending on the power plant. Partly because of square/cube law problems, a mite could be seriously impeded by high winds or rain. A device weighing a few milligrams or less would have the devil's own time beating into a strong headwind. Perhaps a piezoelectrically driven vibrator could power the tiny craft; that might be simpler than a turbine and tougher to detect. Whatever powers the mite, it would probably not result in cruise speeds over a hundred miles an hour unless an antimatter drive is somehow shoehorned into the chassis. Even with this velocity limitation, though, the mites could probably maneuver

much more quickly than their organic counterparts—
which brings up a second dichotomy in vehicles.

Information storage is constantly making inroads into
the need for human pilots, as the Soviets proved in
their unmanned lunar missions. A military vehicle that
must carry life-support equipment for anything as deli-
cate as live meat, is at a distinct disadvantage versus a
similar craft that can turn and stop at hundreds of g's.
Given a human cargo, vehicle life-support systems may
develop to a point where bloodstreams are temporarily
thickened, passengers are quick-frozen and (presuma-
bly) harmlessly thawed, or some kind of null-inertia
package is maintained to keep the passenger comfortable under five-hundred-gravity angular acceleration.
During the trip, it's a good bet that the vehicle would
be under computer guidance, unless the mission is
amenable to very limited acceleration. It also seems
likely that women can survive slightly higher acceleration than men—an old s.f. idea with experimental veri-
fication from the people at Brooks AFB. Women's
primacy in this area may be marginal, but it's evidently
true that Wonder Woman can ride a hotter ship than
Superman. It's also true that your pocket calculator can
take a jouncier ride than either of them. In short, there
will be increasing pressure to depersonalize military
missions, because a person is a tactical millstone in the
system.

Possibly the most personalized form of vehicle, and
one of the more complex per cubic centimeter, would
be one that the soldier wears. Individualized battle
armor, grown massive enough to require servomechanical
muscles, could be classed as a vehicle for the wearer.
The future for massive man-amplifying battle dress
doesn't look very bright, though. If the whole system
stands ten meters tall it will present an easier target;
and if it is merely very dense, it will pose new problems of traction and maneuverability. Just to focus on
one engineering facet of the scaled-up bogus android, if
the user hurls a grenade with his accustomed arm-swing
using an arm extension fifteen feet long, the end of that

extension will be moving at roughly Mach 1. Feedback sensors would require tricky adjustment for movement past the trans-sonic region, and every arm-wave could become a thunderclap! The user will have to do some fiendishly intricate rethinking when he is part of this system—but then, so does a racing driver. Man-amplified battle armor may pass through a certain vogue, just as moats and tanks have done. The power source for this kind of vehicle might be a turbine, until heat-seeking missiles force a change to fuel cells or, for lagniappe, a set of flywheels mounted in different parts of the chassis. The rationale for several prime movers is much the same as for the multi-engined aircraft: you can limp home on a leg and a prayer. Aside from the redundancy feature, mechanical power transmission can be more efficient when the prime mover is near the part it moves. Standing ready for use, a multiflywheel battle dress might even sound formidable, with the slightly varying tones of several million-plus RPM flywheels keening in the wind.

For certain applications including street fighting, there may be a place for the lowly skateboard. It's a fact that the Soviets have bought pallet loads of the sidewalk surfers, ostensibly to see if they're a useful alternative to mass transit. It's also true that enthusiasts in the U.S. are playing with motorized versions which, taking the craze only a step further, could take a regimental combat team through a city in triple time. But if two of those guys ever collide at top speed while carrying explosives, the result may be one monumental street pizza.

No matter how cheap, dependable, and powerful, a military vehicle must be designed with an eye cocked toward enemy weapons. Nuclear warheads already fit into missiles the size of a stovepipe, and orbital laser-firing satellites are only a few years away. A vehicle that lacks both speed and maneuverability will become an easier target with each passing year. By the end of this century, conventional tanks and very large surface ships would be metaphors of the Maginot Line, expensive fiascos for the users.

The conventional tank, despite its popularity with the Soviets, seems destined for the junk pile. Its great weight limits its speed and maneuverability, and several countries already have antitank missile systems that can be carried by one or two men. Some of these little bolides penetrate all known tank armor and have ranges of several kilometers. Faced with sophisticated multistage tank killer missiles, the tank designers have come up with layered armor skirts to disperse the fury of a high-velocity projectile before it reaches the tank's vitals. Not to be outdone, projectile designers have toyed with ultrahigh-velocity projectiles that are boosted almost at the point of impact. It may also be possible to develop alloy projectile tips that won't melt or vaporize until they've punched through the tank's skirt layers. Soon, the tanks may employ antimissile missiles of their own, aimed for very short-range kills against incoming antitank projectiles. This counterpunch system would just about *have* to be automated; no human crew could react fast enough. The actual mechanism by which the counterpunch would deflect or destroy the incoming projectile could be a shaped concussion wave, or a shotgun-like screen of pellets, or both. And it's barely possible that a tank's counterpunch could be a laser that picks off the projectile, though there might not be time to readjust the laser beam for continued impingement on the projectile as it streaks or jitters toward the tank.

Given the huge costs of manufacturing and maintaining a tank, and the piddling costs of supplying infantry with tank-killing hardware, the future of the earthbound battle tank looks bleak. It's wishful thinking to design tanks light enough to be ACV's. Race cars like the Chaparral and the formidable Brabham F1, using suction for more traction, are highly maneuverable on smooth terrain. Still, they'd be no match for homing projectiles; and with no heavy armor or cargo capacity for a counterpunch system, they'd almost surely be gallant losers.

All this is not to suggest that the tank's missions will be discarded in the future, but those missions will probably be performed by very different craft. We'll take up those vehicles under the guise of scout craft.

More vulnerable than the tank, an aircraft carrier drawing 50,000 tons on the ocean surface is just too easy to find, too sluggish to escape, and too tempting for a nuclear strike. It's more sensible to build many smaller vessels, each capable of handling a few aircraft—a point U.S. strategists are already arguing. Ideally the aircraft would take off and land vertically, as the Hawker Harrier does. Following this strategy, carriers could be spread over many square kilometers of ocean reducing vulnerability of a squadron of aircraft.

A pocket aircraft carrier might draw a few hundred tons while cruising on the surface. Under battle conditions the carrier could become an ACV, its reactor propelling it several hundred kilometers per hour with hovering capability and high maneuverability. Its shape would have to be clean aerodynamically, perhaps with variable-geometry catamaran hulls.

Undersea craft are harder to locate. Radar won't reveal a submerged craft, and sonar—a relatively short-range detection system unless the sea floor is dotted with sensor networks—must deal with the vagaries of ocean currents, and temperature and pressure gradients as well as pelagic animals. There may be a military niche for large submersibles for many years to come, perhaps as mother ships and, as savant Frank Herbert predicted a long time ago, cargo vessels.

A submerged mother ship would be an ideal base for a fleet of small hunter-killer or standoff missile subs. These small craft could run at periscope depth for a thousand miles on fuel cells, possibly doubling their range with jettisonable external hydride tanks. A small sub built largely of composites would not be too heavy to double as an ACV in calm weather, switching from ducted propellers to ducted fans for this high-speed cruise mode. From this, it is only a step to a canard swing-wing craft, with schnorkel and communication gear mounted on the vertical fin. The sub packs a pair of long-range missiles on her flanks just inside the ACV skirt. The filament-wound crew pod could detach for emergency flotation. High-speed ACV cruise mode might limit its range to a few hundred kilometers. The swing wings are strictly for a supersonic dash at low altitude, using ducted fan and perhaps small auxiliary jets buried in the aft hull, drawing air from the fan plenum.

Heavy seas might rule out the ACV mode, but if necessary the little sub can broach vertically like a Poseidon before leveling off into its dash mode. With a gross weight of some thirty tons it would require some additional thrust for the first few seconds of flight—perhaps a rocket using hydride fuel and liquid oxygen. The oxygen tank might be replenished during undersea loitering periods. Since the sub would pull a lot of g's when re-entering the water in heavy seas, the nose of the craft would be built up with boron fibers and polymer as a composite honeycomb wound with filaments. The idea of a flying submersible may stick in a few craws, until we reflect that the SUBROC is an unmanned flying submersible in development for over a decade.

On land, military cargo vehicles will feature bigger, wider, low-profile tires in an effort to gain all-terrain capability. Tires could be permanently inflated by supple closed-cell foams under little or no pressure. If the cargo mass is distributed over enough square meters of tire "footprint," the vehicle could challenge tracked craft in snow, or churn through swamps with equal aplomb. The vehicle itself will probably have a wide squat profile (tires may be as high as the cargo section) and for more maneuverability, the vehicle can be hinged in the middle. All-wheel drive, of course, is *de rigeur*.

It's a popular notion that drive motors should be in the wheels, but this adds to the unsprung portion of the vehicle's weight. For optimal handling over rough terrain, the vehicle must have a minimal unsprung weight fraction—which means the motors should be part of the sprung mass, and not in the wheels which, being between the springing subsystem and the ground, are unsprung weight.

Relatively little serious development has been done on heavy torque transmission via flexible bellows. When designers realize how easily a pressurized bellows can be inspected, they may begin using this means to transmit torque to the wheels of cargo vehicles.

The suspension of many future wheeled vehicles may depart radically from current high-performance practice. Most high-performance vehicle suspensions now involve wishbone-shaped upper and lower arms, connecting the wheel's bearing block to the chassis. A rugged alternative would be sets of rollers mounted fore and aft of the bearing block, sliding vertically in chassis-mounted tracks. The tracks could be curved, and even adjustable and slaved to sensors so that, regardless of surface roughness or vehicle attitude above that surface, the wheels would be oriented to gain maximum adhesion. Turbines, flywheels, fuel cells and reactors are all good power plant candidates for wheeled vehicles.

The bodies of these vehicles will probably be segments of smooth-faced composite, and don't be surprised if two or three segment shapes are enough to form the whole shell. This is cost-effectiveness with a vengeance; one mold produces all doors and hatches, another all wheel and hardware skirts, and so on. On the other hand, let's not forget chitin.

Chitin is a family of chemical substances that make up much of the exoskeletons of arthropods, including insects, spiders and crabs. The stuff can be flexible or inflexible and chemically it is pretty inert. If biochemists and vehicle designers get together, we may one day see vehicles that can literally grow their skins and repair their own prangs. As arthropods grow larger, they often have to discard their exoskeletons and grow new ones; but who's betting the biochemists won't find ways to teach beetles some new tricks about body armor?

Some cargo—including standoff missiles, supplies, and airborne laser weapons—will be carried by airborne transports. In this sense a bomber is a transport vehicle. Here again, advanced composite structures will find wide use, since a lighter vehicle means a higher payload fraction. Vertical takeoff and landing (VTOL), or at least very short takeoff and landing (VSTOL), will greatly expand the tactical use of these transports which will have variable-geometry surfaces including leading and trailing edges, not only on wings but on the lifting body. Consider a VSTOL transport. With its triple-delta wings fully extended for maximum lift at takeoff, long aerodynamic "fences" along the wings front-to-rear guide the airflow and the lower fences form part of the landing gear fairings. Wing extensions telescope rather than swing as the craft approaches multimach speed, and for suborbital flight the hydrogen-fluorine rocket will supplant turbines at around thirty kilometer altitude. In its stubby double-delta configuration the craft can skip-glide in the upper atmosphere for extended range, its thick graphite composite leading surfaces aglow as they slowly wear away during re-entry. During periodic maintenance, some of this surface can be replaced in the field as a polymer-rich putty.

As reactors become more compact and MHD more sophisticated, the rocket propellant tanks can give way to cargo space although, from the outside, the VSTOL skip-glide transport might seem little changed. Conversion from VSTOL to VTOL could be helped by a special application of the mass driver principle. In this case the aircraft, with ferrous metal filaments in its composite skin, is the mass repelled by a grid that would rise like scaffolding around the landing pad. This magnetic balancing act would be reversed for vertical landing—but it would take a lot of site preparation which might, in turn, lead to inflatable grid elements rising around the landing site.

Once an antimatter drive is developed, cargo transports might become little more than streamlined boxes with gimbaled nozzles near their corners. Such a craft could dispense with lifting surfaces, but would still need heat-resistant skin for hypersonic flight in the atmosphere. But do we have to look far ahead for cargo vehicles that travel a long way? Maybe we should also look back a ways.

For long-range transport in the lower atmosphere, the dirigible may have a future that far outstrips its past. Though certainly too vulnerable for deployment near enemy gunners, modern helium-filled cargo dirigibles can be very cost-effective in safe zones. Cargo can be lifted quietly and quickly to unimproved dump areas, and with a wide variety of power plants. The classic cigar shape will probably be lost in the shuffle to gain more aerodynamic efficiency, if a recent man-carrying model is any guide. Writer John McPhee called the shape a deltoid pumpkin seed, though its designers prefer the generic term, *aerobody*. So: expect somebody to use buxom, spade-nosed aerobodies to route cargo, but don't expect the things to fly very far when perforated like a collander from small-arms fire. The aerobody seems to be a good bet for poorer nations engaged in border clashes where the fighting is localized and well-defined. But wait a minute: what if the gasbags were made of thin, self-healing chitin? Maybe the aerobody is tougher than we think.

Among the most fascinating military craft are those designed for scouting forays: surveillance, pinpoint bombing sorties, troop support, and courier duty being only a few of their duties. The Germans briefly rescued Mussolini with a slow but superb scout craft, the Fieseler Storch. Our SR-71 does its scouting at Mach 3, while the close-support A-10 can loiter at a tiny fraction of that speed. Now in development in the U.S., Britain, and Germany is a family of remotely piloted scout craft that may be the next generation of scout ships, combining the best features of the Storch and the SR-71.

The general shape of the scout ship is that of a football flattened on the bottom, permitting high-speed atmospheric travel and crabwise evasive action while providing a broad base for the exhaust gases of its internal ACV fans. The ship is MHD powered, drawing inlet air from around the underlip of the shell just outboard of the ACV skirt. The skirt petals determine the direction of deflected exhaust for omnidirectional maneuvers, though auxiliary jets may do the job better than skirt petals.

The scout uses thick graphite composite skin and sports small optical viewing ports for complete peripheral video rather than having a single viewing bubble up front. The multiple videos offer redundancy in case of damage; they permit a stiffer structure; and they allow the occupant, if any, maximum protection by remoting him from the ports.

The question of piloting is moot at the moment. Grumman, Shorts, and Dornier are all developing pilotless observation craft for long-range operations, but a scout craft of the future would probably have a life-support option for at least one occupant. The design has an ovoid hatch near its trailing edge. For manned missions, an occupant pod slides into the well-protected middle of the ship, and could pop out again for emergency ejection. For unmanned missions the occupant pod might be replaced by extra fuel, supplies, or weapons. Some version of this design might inherit the missions of the battle tank, but with much-improved speed and maneuverability.

Well, we've specified high maneuverability and a graphite composite skin. Given supersonic speed and automatic evasion programs, it might be the one hope of outrunning an orbital laser weapon!

Of course the scout doesn't exceed the speed of light. What it might do, though, is survive a brief zap long enough to begin a set of evasive actions. Let's say the enemy has an orbital laser platform (OLP) fairly near in space, not directly overhead but in line-of-sight, four hundred miles from the scout which is cruising innocently along at low altitude at a speed of Mach 1. The laser is adjusted perfectly and fires.

What does it hit? A thick polished carapace of graphite composite, its skin filaments aligned to conduct the laser's heat away from the pencil-wide target point. Sensors in the scout's skin instantly set the craft to dodging in a complex pattern, at lateral accelerations of about 10 g's. At this point the occupant is going to wish he had stayed home, but he should be able to survive these maneuvers.

Meanwhile the OLP optics or radar sense the change of the scout's course—but this takes a little time, roughly two millisec, because the OLP is four hundred miles away. Reaiming the laser might take only ten millisec, though it might take considerably longer. Then the OLP fires again, the new laser burst taking another two millisec to reach the target.

But that's fourteen thousandths of a second! And the scout is moving roughly one foot per millisec, and is now angling to one side. Its change of direction is made at well over three hundred feet per sec, over four feet of angular shift before the second ("corrected") laser shot arrives. The scout's generally elliptical shell is about twenty feet in length by about ten in width. Chances are good that the next laser shot would miss entirely, and in any case it would probably not hit the same spot, by now a glowing scar an inch or so deep on the scout's shell.

Discounting luck on either side, the survival of the jittering scout ship might depend on whether it could dodge under a cloud or into a steep valley. It might, however, foil the laser even in open country by redirecting a portion of its exhaust in a column directly toward the enemy OLP. The destructive effect of a laser beam depends on high concentration of energy against a small area. If the laser beam spreads, that concentration is lost; and beam spread is just what you must expect if the laser beam must travel very far through fog, cloud, or plasma. If the scout ship could hide under a tall, chemically seeded column of its own exhaust for a few moments, it would have a second line of defense. And we must not forget that the laser's own heat energy, impinging on the target, creates more local plasma which helps to further spread and attenuate the laser beam.

One method of assuring the OLP more hits on a scout ship would be to gang several lasers, covering all the possible moves that the scout might make. The next question would be whether all that fire-power was worth the trouble. The combination of high-temperature composites, MHD power, small size, and maneuverability might make a scout ship the same problem to an OLP that a rabbit is to a hawk. All the same, the hawk has the initial advantage. The rabbit is right to tremble.

An unmanned scout ship, capable of much higher rates of angular acceleration, would be still more vexing to an OLP. If the OLP were known to have a limited supply of stored energy, a squadron of unmanned scouts could turn a tide of battle by exhausting the OLP in futile potshots. It remains to be seen whether the jittering scout craft will be able to dodge, intercept, or just plain outrun a locally-fired weapon held by some hidden infantryman. But given a compact reactor or an antimatter drive, the scout ship could become a submersible. In that event the scout craft could escape enemy fire by plunging into any ocean, lake, or river that's handy. The broad utility of such a craft might make obsolete most other designs.

But what of vehicles intended to fight in space? As colonies and mining outposts spread throughout our solar system, there may be military value in capturing or destroying far-flung settlements—which means there'll be military value in intercepting such missions. The popular notion of space war today seems to follow the Dykstra images of movies and TV, where great whopping trillion-ton battleships direct fleets of parasite fighters. The mother ship with its own little fleet makes a lot of sense, but in sheer mass the parasites may account for much of the system, and battle craft in space may have meter-thick carapaces to withstand laser fire and nuke near-misses.

Let's consider a battle craft of reasonable size and a human crew, intended to absorb laser and projectile weapons as well as some hard radiation. We'll give it reactor-powered rockets, fed with pellets of some solid fuel which is exhausted as vapor.

To begin with, the best shape for the battle craft might be an elongated torus; a tall, stretched-out dough-nut. In the long hole down the middle we install the crew of two—if that many—weapons, communication gear, life support equipment, and all the other stuff that's most vulnerable to enemy weapons. This central cavity is then domed over at both ends, with airlocks at one end and weapon pods at the other. The crew stays in the very center where protection is maximized. The fuel pellets, composing most of the craft's mass, occupy the main cavity of the torus, surrounding the vulnera-ble crew like so many tons of gravel. Why solid pellets? Because they'd be easier than fluids to recover in space after battle damage to the fuel tanks. The rocket en-gines are gimbaled on short arms around the waist of the torus, where they can impart spin, forward or angu-lar momentum, or thrust reversal. The whole craft would look like a squat cylinder twenty meters long by fifteen wide, with circular indentations at each end where the inner cavity closures meet the torus curvatures.

The battle craft doesn't seem very large but it could easily gross over 5,000 tons, fully fueled. If combat accelerations are to reach 5 g's with full tanks, the engines must produce far more thrust than anything available today. Do we go ahead and design engines producing 25,000 tons of thrust, or do we accept far less acceleration in hopes the enemy can't do any better? Or do we redesign the cylindrical crew section so that it can eject itself from the fuel torus for combat maneu-vers? This trick—separating the crew and weapons pod as a fighting unit while the fuel supply loiters off at a distance—greatly improves the battle craft's performance. But it also means the crew pod must link up again very soon with the torus to replenish its on-board fuel supply. And if the enemy zaps the fuel torus hard enough while the crew is absent, it may mean a long trajectory home in cryogenic sleep.

Presuming that a fleet of the toroidal battle craft sets out on an interplanetary mission, the fleet might start out as a group of parasite ships attached to a mothers' ship. It's anybody's guess how the mother ship will be laid out, so let's make a guess for critics to lambaste.

Our mother ship would be a pair of fat discs, each duplicating the other's repair functions in case one is damaged. The discs would be separated by three compression girders and kept in tension by a long central cable. To get a mental picture of the layout, take two biscuits and run a yard-long thread through the center of each. Then make three columns from soda straws, each a yard long, and poke the straw ends into the biscuits near their edges. Now the biscuits are facing each other, a yard apart, pulled toward each other by the central thread and held apart by the straw columns. If you think of the biscuits as being a hundred meters in diameter with rocket engines poking away from the ends, you have a rough idea of the mother ship.

Clearly, the mother ship is two modules, upwards of a mile apart but linked by structural tension and compression members. The small battle craft might be attached to the compression girders for their long ride to battle, but if the mother ship must maneuver, their masses might pose unacceptable loads on the girders. Better by far if the parasites nestle in between the girders to grapple onto the tension cable. In this way, a fleet could embark from planetary orbit as a single system, separating into sortie elements near the end of the trip.

Since the total mass of all the battle craft is about equal to that of the unencumbered mother ship, the big ship can maneuver itself much more easily when the kids get off mama's back. The tactical advantages are that the system is redundant with fuel and repair elements; a nuke strike in space might destroy one end of the system without affecting the rest; and all elements become more flexible in their operational modes just when they need to be. Even if mother ships someday become as massive as moons, my guess is that they'll be made up of redundant elements and separated by lots of open space. Any hopelessly damaged elements can be discarded, or maybe kept and munched up for fuel mass.

Having discussed vehicles that operate on land, sea, air, and in space, we find one avenue left: within the earth. Certainly a burrowing vehicle lacks the maneuverability and speed of some others—until the burrow is complete. But under all that dirt, one is relatively safe from damn-all. Mining vehicles already exist that cut and convey ten tons of coal a minute, using extended-life storage batteries for power. One such machine, only 23 inches high, features a supine driver and low-profile, high traction tires. Perhaps a future military "mole" will use seismic sensors to find the easiest path through rocky depths, chewing a long burrow to be traversed later at high speed by offensive or defensive vehicles, troop transports, and supply conduits. Disposal of the displaced dirt could be managed by detonating a nuke to create a cavern big enough to accept the tailings of the mole. The present plans to route ICBM's by rail so that enemies won't know where to aim their first strike, may shift to underground routing as the subterranean conduit network expands.

AN ALTERNATIVE TO VEHICLES?

A vehicle of any kind is, as we've asserted, essentially a means to carry something somewhere. So it's possible that the vehicle, *as a category*, might be obsolete one day. The matter transmitter is a concept that, translated into hardware, could obsolete almost any vehicle. True, most conceptual schemes for matter transmitters posit a receiving station—which implies that some vehicle must first haul the receiving station from Point A to Point B. But what if the transmitter needed no receiving station? A device that could transmit people and supplies at light speed to a predetermined point without reception hardware would instantly replace vehicles for anything but pleasure jaunts. The system would also raise mirthful hell with secrecy, and with any armor that could be penetrated by the transmitter beam. If the beam operated in the electromagnetic spectrum, vehicles might still be useful deep down under water, beneath the earth's surface, or inside some vast Faraday cage.

But until the omnipotent matter transmitter comes along, vehicle design will be one of the most pervasive factors in military strategy and tactics.

REFERENCES

Air Force Times, 12 June 1978

Aviation Week & Space Technology, January 1976, p. 111

Biss, Visvaldis, "Phase Analysis of Standard and Molybdenum-Modified Mar-M509 Superalloys," *J. Testing & Evaluation*, May 1977

Bova, Ben, "Magnetohydrodynamics," *Analog*, May 1965

Clarke, Arthur, *Report on Planet Three and Other Speculations* (N.Y.: Signet Books, 1973)

Committee on Advanced Energy Storage Systems, *Criteria for Energy Storage Research & Development* (Washington, D.C., N.A.S., 1976)

Compressed Air, April 1978

Fairchild Republic Co., Data release on A-10, 1978

Ing, Dean, "Mayan Magnum," *Road & Track*, May 1968

Marion, R.H., "A Short-Time, High Temperature Mechanical Testing Facility," *J. Testing & Evaluation*, January 1978

McPhee, John, *The Curve of Binding Energy* (N.Y.: Farrar, Straus & Giroux, 1974)

O'Neill, Gerard, *The High Frontier* (N.Y.: Bantam Books, 1978)

Owen, J. I. H. (ed.), *Brassey's Infantry Weapons of the World* (N.Y.: Bonanza Books, 1975)

Pretty, R. T. & D. H. R. Archer (eds.), *Jane's Weapon Systems* (London: Jane's Yearbooks, 1974)

Raloff, Janet, "U.S.-Soviet Energy Pact," *Science Digest*, February 1976

Rosa, Richard, "How to Design a Flying Saucer," *Analog*, May 1965.

Saunders, Russell, "Clipper Ships of Space," *Astounding*, May 1951

Singer, Charles *et al*, *A History of Technology, Vol. I* (N.Y.: Oxford University Press, 1954)

VITAL SIGNS

Before July, it promised to be an off-year. Not an election year, nor especially a war year—either of which seems to enrich bail-bondsmen. Early in the summer I was ready to remember it as the year I bought the off-road Porsche and they started serving couscous Maroc at Original Joe's. But it was in mid-July when I learned that the Hunter had been misnamed, and that made it everybody's bad year.

It had been one of those muggy days in Oakland with no breeze off the bay to cool a sweaty brow. And I sweat easily since, as a doctor friend keeps telling me, I carry maybe fifty pounds too many. I'm six-two, one-eighty-eight centimeters if you insist, and I tell him I need the extra weight as well as height in my business, but that's bullshit and we both know it. It's my hobbies, not my business, that make me seem a not-so-jolly fat man. My principal pastimes are good food and black-smithy, both just about extinct. My business is becoming extinct, too. My name's Harve Rackham, and I'm a bounty hunter.

I had rousted a check-kiting, bail-jumping, small-time scuffler from an Alameda poolroom and delivered him, meek as mice, to the authorities after only a day's legwork. I suppose it was too hot for him to bother running for it. Wouldn't've done him much good any-

how; for a hundred yards, until my breath gives out, I
can sprint with the best of 'em.

I took my cut from the bail-bondsman and squeezed
into my Porsche. Through the Berkeley tunnel and out
into Contra Costa County it was cooler, without the
Bay Area haze. Before taking the cutoff toward home I
stopped in Antioch. Actually I stopped twice, first to
pick up a four-quart butter churn the antique shop had
been promising me for weeks and then for ground
horsemeat. Spot keeps fit enough on the cheap farina
mix, but he loves his horsemeat. It was the least I could
do for the best damn' watchcat in California.

Later, some prettyboy TV newsman tried to get me
to say I'd had a premonition by then. No way: I'd read a
piece in the *Examiner* about a meteorite off the central
coast, but what could that possibly have to do with me?
I didn't even have a mobile phone in the Porsche, so I
had no idea the Feebies had a job for me until I got
home to my playback unit. The FBI purely hates to
subcontract a job, anyway. Especially to me. I don't fit
their image.

My place is only a short drive from Antioch, a white
two-story frame farmhouse built in 1903 in the shadow
of Mount Diablo. When I bought it, I couldn't just stop
the restoration at the roof; by the time I'd furnished it
in genuine 1910 I'd also become a zealot for the black-
smith shop out back. By now I had most of my money
tied up in functional antiques like my Model C folding
Brownie camera, my hurricane lamps with polished reading reflectors, swage sets for the smithy, even Cumber-
land coal for the forge and a cannonball tuyere. I had
no one else to spend my money on but before I got
Spot, I worried lot. While I was tracking down bail-
jumpers, some thief might've done a black-bag job on
the place. With Spot around, the swagman would have
to run more than seventy miles an hour.

If I'd had more than five acres, I couldn't've paid for
the cyclone fence. And if I'd had less, there wouldn't've
been room for Spot to run. The fence doesn't keep Spot
in; it keeps sensible folks out. Anybody who ignores the

CHEETAH ON PATROL signs will have a hard time ignoring Spot, who won't take any food or any shit from any stranger. I'm a one-cat man, and Spot is a one-man cat.

I saw him caper along the fence as he heard the guttural whoosh of the Porsche fans. I levered the car into boost mode, which brings its skirts down for vastly greater air-cushion effect. Just for the hell of it, I jumped the fence.

An off-road Porsche is built to take a Baja run, with reversible pitch auxiliary fans that can suck the car down for high cornering force on its wheels, or support it on an air cushion for brief spurts. But I'd seen Feero on film, tricking his own Baja Porsche into bouncing on its air cushion so it'd clear an eight-foot obstacle. You can't know how much fun it was for me to learn that unless you weigh as much as I do.

Of course, Spot smelled the horsemeat and I had to toss him a sample before he'd quit pestering me. After we sniffed each other around the ears—don't ask me why, but Spot regards that as a kind of backslap—I went to the basement and checked Spot's automatic feeder. My office is in the basement, too, along with all my other contemporary stuff. From ground level up, it's *fin-de-siècle* time at my place, but the basement is all business.

My phone playback had only two messages. The first didn't matter, because the last was from Dana Martin in Stockton. "We have an eighty-eight fugitive and we need a beard," her voice stroked me; softly annealed on the surface, straw-tempered iron beneath. "My SAC insists you're our man. What can I say?" She could've said, whatever her Special Agent in Charge thought in Sacramento, she hated the sight of me. She didn't need to: ours was an old estrangement. "I can come to your place if you'll chain that saber-toothed animal. And if you don't call back by five p.m. Friday, forget it. I wish they'd pay me like they'll pay you, Rackham." Click.

My minicomputer terminal told me it was four-forty-six. I dialed a Stockton number, wondering why the

FBI needed a disguising ploy to hunt a fugitive fleeing from prosecution. It could mean he'd be one of the shoot-first types who can spot a Feebie around a corner. I can get close to those types but I'm too easy to target. The hell of it was, I needed the money. Nobody pays like the Feebies for the kind of work I do.

Miz Martin was out mailing blueprints but was expected shortly. I left word that I'd rassle the sabertooth if she wanted a souffle at my place, and hung up chuckling at the young architect's confusion over my message. Time was, brick agents didn't have to hold down cover jobs. Dana did architectural drafting when she wasn't on assignment for her area SAC, who's in Sacramento.

I took a fresh block of ice from the basement freezer and put it in my honest-to-God icebox upstairs. I had nearly a dozen fertile eggs and plenty of cream, and worked up a sweat all over again playing with my new butter churn until I'd collected a quarter-pound of the frothy cream-yellow stuff. It smelled too good to use for cooking, which meant it was just right. After firing up the wood stove, I went outside for coolth and companionship.

I'd nearly decided La Martin wouldn't show and was playing "fetch" with my best friend when, far down the graveltop road, I heard a government car. When you hear the hum of electrics under the thump of a diesel, it's either a conservation nut or a government man. Or woman, which Dana Martin most assuredly is.

Spot sulked but obeyed, stalking pipe-legged into the smithy as I remoted the automatic gate. Dana decanted herself from the sedan with the elegance of a debutante, careless in her self-assurance, and stared at my belt buckle. "It's a wonder your heart can take it," she sniffed. Dana could well afford to twit me for my shape. She's a petite blonde with the face of a littlest angel and a mind like a meat cleaver. One of those exquisite-bodied little charmers you want to protect when it's the other guy who needs protection.

I knew she worked hard to keep in shape and had a

fastidious turn of mind so, "We can't all have your tapeworm," I said.

I thought she was going to climb back into the car, but she only hauled a briefcase from it. "Spare me your ripostes," she said; "people are dying while you wax clever. You have an hour to decide about this job."

Another slur, I thought; when had I ever turned down Feebie money? I let "no comment" be mine, waved her to my kitchen, poked at the fire in the stove. Adjusting the damper is an art, and art tends to draw off irritation like a poultice. I started separating the eggs, giving Dana the cheese to grate.

She could've shredded Parmesan on her attitude. "I can brief you," she began, "only after you establish an oral commitment. My personal advice is, don't. It needs an agile man."

"Hand me the butter," I said.

She did, shrugging. "All I can tell you beforehand, is that the fugitive isn't human."

"Spoken like a true believer, Dana. As soon as somebody breaks enough laws, you redefine him as an unperson."

Relishing it: "I'm being literal, Rackham. He's a big, nocturnal animal that's killed several people. The Bureau can't capture him for political reasons; you'll be working alone for the most part; and it is absolutely necessary to take him alive."

"Pass the flour. But he won't be anxious to take *me* alive; is that it?"

"In a nutshell. And he is much more important than you are. If you screw it up, you may rate a nasty adjective or two in history books—and I've said too much already," she muttered.

I stirred my supper and my thoughts, adding cayenne to both. Obviously in Bureau files, my dealings with animals hadn't gone unnoticed. They knew I'd turned a dozen gopher snakes loose to eliminate the varmints under my lawn. They knew about my ferret that kept rats away. They knew Spot. I'd taken a Kodiak once, and they knew that, too. But true enough, I was

slower now. I postulated a Cape Buffalo, escaped while
some South Africans were presenting it to a zoo worth
its weight in krugerrands to antsy politicians. "I think
I'll give this one a 'bye," I sighed and, as afterthought;
"but what was the fee for taking it *a la* Frank Buck?"

"Who the devil is Frank Buck?"

"Never mind. How much?"

"A hundred thousand," she said, unwilling.

I nearly dropped the dry mustard. For that, I could
find Spot a consort and dine on escargot every night.
"I'm in," I said quickly. "Nobody lives forever."

While the souffle baked, Dana revealed how far afield
my guess had gone. I fed her flimsy disc into my office
computer downstairs and let her do the rest. The display showed a map of Central California, with a line
arching in from offshore. She pointed to the line with a
light pencil. "That's the path of the so-called meteorite
last Saturday night. Point Reyes radar gave us this
data." Now the display magicked out a ream of figures.
"Initial velocity was over fifteen thousand meters per
second at roughly a hundred klicks altitude, too straight
and too fast for a ballistic trajectory."

"Would you mind putting that into good old feet and
miles? I'm from the old school, in case you hadn't
noticed," I grinned.

"You're a goddamn dinosaur," she agreed. "Okay: we
picked up an apparent meteorite coming in at roughly a
forty-five degree angle, apparent mass um, fifty tons or
so, hitting the atmosphere at a speed of about—fifty
thousand feet per second. Accounting for drag, it
should've still impacted offshore within a few seconds,
sending out a seismometer blip, not to mention a local
tsunami. It didn't.

"It decelerated at a steady hundred and forty g's and
described a neat arc that must've brought it horizontal
near sea-level."

I whistled. "Hundred and forty's way above human
tolerance."

"The operative word is 'steady.' It came in so hot it

made the air glow, and it was smart—I mean, it didn't behave as though purely subject to outside forces. That kind of momentum change took a lot of energy under precise control, they tell me. Well, about eleven seconds after deceleration began it had disappeared, too low on the horizon for coverage, and loafing along at sub-mach speed just off the water."

"Russians," I guessed.

"They know about it, but it wasn't them. Don't they wish? It wasn't anybody human. The vehicle came in over the Sonoma coast and hedge-hopped as far as Lake Berryessa northwest of Sacramento. That's where the UFO hotline folks got their last report and wouldn't you know it, witnesses claimed the usual round shape and funny lights."

I sprinted for the stairs, Spot-footed across the kitchen floor, snuck a look into the oven. "Just in time," I called, as Dana emerged from below.

She glanced at the golden trifle I held in my pot-holder, then inhaled, smiling in spite of herself. "You may have your uses at that."

"Getting up here so fast without jolting the souffle?"

"No, cooking anything that smells this good," she said, and preceded me to the dining room. "I don't think you have the chance of a cardiac case on this hunt, and I said as much to Scott King."

She told me why over dinner. The scrambled interceptors from Travis and Beale found nothing, but a Moffett patrol craft full of sensor equipment sniffed over the area and found traces of titanium dioxide in the atmosphere. Silicon and nox, too, but those could be explained away.

You couldn't explain away the creature trapped by college students near the lake on Sunday evening. Dana passed me a photo, and my first shock was one of recognition. The short spotted fur and erect short ears of the quadruped, the heavy shoulders and bone-crunching muzzle, all reminded me of a dappled bear cub. It could have been a terrestrial animal wearing a woven metallic harness but for its eyes, small and lowset near the muzzle. It looked dead, and it was.

"The pictures were taken after it escaped from a cage on the Cal campus at Davis and electrocuted itself, biting through an autoclave power line. It was evidently a pet," Dana said, indicating studs on the harness, "since it couldn't reach behind to unlock this webbing, and it wasn't very bright. But it didn't need to be, Harve. It was the size of a Saint Bernard. Guess its weight."

I studied the burly, brawny lines of the thing. "Two hundred."

"Three. That's in kilos," Dana said. "Nearly seven hundred pounds. If it hadn't got mired in mud near a student beer-bust, I don't know how they'd have taken it. It went through lassos as if they were cheese, using this."

Another photo. Above each forepaw, which seemed to have thumbs on each side, was an ivorylike blade, something like a dewclaw. One was much larger than the other, like the asymmetry of a fiddler crab. It didn't seem capable of nipping; slashing, maybe. I rolled down my sleeves; it wouldn't help if Dana Martin saw the hairs standing on my forearms. "So how'd they get it to the Ag people at Cal-Davis?"

"Some bright lad made a lasso from a tow cable. While the animal was snarling and screeching and biting the cable, they towed it out of the mud with a camper. It promptly chased one nincompoop into the camper and the guy got out through the sliding glass plate upfront—but he lost both legs above the ankle; it seems the creature ate them.

"The Yolo County Sheriff actually drove the camper to Davis with that thing fighting its way through the cab in the middle of the night." Dana smiled wistfully. "Wish I could've seen him drive into that empty water purification tank, it was a good move. The animal couldn't climb out, the Sheriff pulled the ladder up, and a few hours later we were brought into it and clamped the lid down tight."

"Extraterrestrial contact," I breathed, testing the sound of a phrase that had always sounded absurd to me. The remains of my souffle were lost in the metallic taste of my excitement—okay, maybe "excitement" wasn't quite the right word. "If that's the kind of pets they keep, what must *they* be like?"

"Think of Shere Khan out there," Dana jerked a thumb toward a window, "and ask what *you*'re like."

Why waste time explaining the difference between a pet and a friend? "Maybe they're a race of bounty hunters," I cracked lamely.

"The best guess is that the animal's owner is hunting, all right. Here's what we have on the big one," she said, selecting another glossy. "Four men and a woman weren't as lucky as the fellow who lost his feet."

I gazed at an eight-by-ten of a plaster cast, dirt-flecked, that stood next to a meter stick on a table. Something really big, with a paw like a beclawed rhino, had left pugmarks a foot deep. It might have been a species similar to the dead pet, I thought, and said so. "Where'd this cast come from?"

"Near the place where the beer-bust was busted. They're taking more casts now at the Sacramento State University campus. If the hunter's on all-fours, it may weigh only a few tons."

"Davis campus; Sac State—fill it in, will you?"

It made a kind of sense. Once inside a chilled-steel cage, the captive pet had quieted down for ethologists at Davis. They used tongs to fumble a little plastic puck from a clip on the harness, and sent it to Sacramento State for analysis, thinking it might be some kind of an owner tag. It turned out to be a bug, an AM/FM signal generator—and they hadn't kept it shielded. The owner must have monitored the transmitter and followed it to Sacramento. More guesswork: its vehicle had traveled in the American River to a point near the Sac State labs where the plastic puck was kept.

And late Tuesday evening, something big as a two-car garage had left a depression on the sand of an island in the river, and something mad as hell itself had come up over the levee and along a concrete path to the lab.

A professor, a research assistant, a top-clearance physicist brought in from nearby Aerojet, and an FBI field agent had seen the hunter come through a pumice block wall into the lab with them, but most of the information they had was secure.

Permanently.

Dana Martin didn't offer photos to prove they'd been dismembered, but I took her word for it. "So your hunter got its signal generator back," I prompted, "and split."

"No, no, and yes. It's *your* hunter, and our man had left the transmitter wrapped in foil in the next room, where we found it. But yes, the hunter's gone again."

"To Davis?"

"We doubt it. Up the river a few klicks, there's an area where a huge gold dredge used to spit its tailings out. A fly-fisher led us to remains in the trailings near the riverbank yesterday. A mighty nimrod type who'd told his wife he was going to sight in his nice new rifle at the river. That's a misdemeanor, but he got capital punishment. His rifle had been fired before something bent its barrel into a vee and—get this—embedded the muzzle in the man's side like you'd bait a hook."

"That's hard to believe. Whatever could do that, could handle a gorilla like an organ grinder's monkey."

"Dead right, Rackham—and it's loose in the dredge tailings."

Well, she'd warned me. I knew the tailings area from my own fishing trips. They stretch for miles on both sides of the American River, vast high cairns of smooth stones coughed up by a barge that had once worked in from the river. The barge had chewed a path ahead of it, making its own lake, digesting only the gold as it wandered back and forth near the river. Seen from the air, the tailings made snaky patterns curling back to the river again.

This savage rape of good soil had been committed

long ago and to date the area was useless. It was like a maze of gravel piles, most of the gravel starting at grapefruit size and progressing to some like oval steamer trunks. A few trees had found purchase there; weeds; a whole specialized ecology of small animals in the steep slopes. The more I thought about it, the more it seemed like perfect turf for some monstrous predator.

I took a long breath, crossed my arms, rubbed them briskly and stared across the table at Dana Martin. "You haven't given me much to go on," I accused.

"There's more on the recording," she said softly.

I guessed from her tone: "All bad."

Shrug: "Some bad. Some useful."

I let her lead me downstairs. She had an audiotape salvaged from the lab wreckage, and played me the last few minutes of it.

A reedy male expounded on the alien signal generator. "We might take it apart undamaged," he ended, sounding wistful and worried.

"The Bureau can't let you chance it," said another male, equally worried.

A third man, evidently the Aerojet physicist, doubted the wisdom of reproducing the ar-eff signals since what looked like junk on a scope might be salient data on an alien receiver. He offered the use of Aerojet's X-ray inspection equipment. A young woman—the research assistant—thought that was a good idea at first. "But I don't know," she said, and you could almost hear her smile: "it looks kinda neat the way it is."

The woman's sudden voice shift stressed her non sequitur. It sounded idiotic. I tossed a questing frown at Dana and positively gaped as the recording continued.

The Feebie again: "I suppose I could ask Scott King to let you disassemble it. Hell, it's harmless," he drawled easily in a sudden about-face. King, as I knew, was his—and Dana Martin's—SAC in the region.

The reedy older voice was chuckling now. "That's more like it; aren't we worrying over trifles?"

The physicist laughed outright. "My sentiments exactly." Under his on-mike mirth I could hear the others joining in.

And then the speaker overloaded its bass response in a thunderous crash. Several voices shouted as the second slam was followed by clatters of glass and stone. Clear, then: "Scotty, whatthehell—", ending in a scream; three screams. From somewhere came a furious clicking, then an almost subsonic growling *whuffff*. Abrupt silence. Posterity had been spared the rest.

I glowered at Dana Martin. "What's good about that?"

"Forewarning. Our man wasn't the sort to vacillate, and the professor was known as a sourball. It's barely possible that they all were being gassed somehow, to hallucinate during the attack."

"Maybe," I said. "That would explain why your man thought he saw Scotty King coming through the wall. Ah,—look, Dana, this just about tears it. You need a covey of hoverchoppers to find this, this hunter of yours. I get a picture of something that could simply stroll up to me while I grinned at it, and nothing short of a submarine net could stop it. Won't I even have a brick agent to help?"

"Every hovercraft we can spare is quartering the Berryessa region. And so are a lot of chartered craft," she said softly, "carrying consular people from Britain, France, the Soviets, and the United Chinese Republics. *They know*, Rackham, and they intend to be on hand from the first moment of friendly contact."

"Some friendly contact," I snorted. I realized now that the air activity over Lake Berryessa was a deliberate decoy. "Surely we have the power to ground the rest of these guys . . ."

"The instant our government makes contact, we are committed by treaty to sharing that confrontation with the rest of the nuclear club," Dana said wearily. "It's an agreement the Soviets thought up last year, of which we have been forcibly reminded in the past days."

I showed her my palms.

"*You're not government*," she hissed. "We're a laissez faire democracy; we can't help it if a private U.S. citizen does the first honors. Could we help it if he should dynamite the spacecraft in perfectly understandable panic?"

"Destroy a diamond-mine of information? Are you nuts?" For the first time my voice was getting out of hand.

"Perfectly sane. We've got a kit for you to record the experience if you can get into the craft—maybe remove anything that looks portable, and hide it. We don't want you to totally wreck the vehicle, just make it a hangar queen until another civilian friend has studied the power plants and weaponry, and then he might blow it to confetti."

I was beginning to see the plan. Even if it worked it was lousy politics. I told her that.

"This country," she said, "has an edge in communications and power plants at the moment. We'd a whole lot rather keep that edge, and learn a few things to fatten it, then take a chance that everybody—including Libya—might get into an equal technological footing with us overnight. *Now* will you drop the matter?"

"I may as well. Am I supposed to ask the damn' hunter for some thermite so I can burn his ailerons a little?"

"We've sunk a cache of sixty per cent dynamite in the river shallows for you—common stuff you could buy commercially. We've marked it here on a USGS map. Best of all, you'll have a weapon."

I brightened, but only for a moment. It was a gimmicked Smith & Wesson automatic, a bit like a Belgian Browning. Dana took it from her briefcase with reverence and explained why the special magazine carried only seven fat rounds. I could almost get my pinkie in the muzzle: sixty calibre at least. It was strictly a short-range item rigged with soluble slugs. Working with the dead pet and guessing lot, Cal's veterinary science wizards had rendered some of its tissues for tallow and molded slugs full of drugs. They might stop the hunter.

On the other hand, they might not.

If I couldn't make friends with it I would be permitted to shoot for what, in my wisdom, I might consider noncritical spots on its body.

Finally, *if* I hadn't been marmaladed and *if* I had it stunned, I was to punch a guarded stud on the surveillance kit which looked like an amateur's microvid unit with a digital watch embedded in its side. At that point I could expect some other co-opted civilian to "happen" onto me with his Hoverover.

I wondered out loud how much money the other guy was getting for his part in this, and Dana reminded me that it was none of my damned business. Nor should I worry too much about what would happen after the beast was trussed up in a steel net and taken away. It would be cared for, and in a few days the Feebies would "discover" what the meddling civilians had done, and the rest of the world could pay it homage and raise all the hell they liked about prior agreements which, so far as anyone might prove, would not have been violated. It was sharp practice. It stank. It paid one hundred thousand dollars.

I collected the pitifully small assortment of data and equipment, making it a small pile. "And with this, you expect me to set out?"

"I really expect you to *crap* out," she said sweetly, "in which case you can expect to be iced down for awhile. We can do it, you know."

I knew. I also knew she had the extra pleasure of having told me not to commit myself. There was one more item. "What if I find more than one hunter?"

"We only need to bag one. For reasons I'm not too clear on, we don't think there's more. Something about desperation tactics, I gather." She frowned across the stuff at me. "What's so funny—or are you just trembling?"

I shook my head, waved her toward the stairs. "Go home, Dana. I was just thinking: it's our tactics that smack of desperation."

She swayed up the stairs, carrying her empty case, talking as she went. It was no consolation to hear that nobody would be watching me. The little foil-wrapped AM/FM bug would be my only bait, and of course they'd be monitoring that; but it was essential that I dangle the bait only in some remote location. Lovely.

Spot ambled out as he heard my automatic gate energize, chose to frisk alongside Dana Martin's sedan as she drove away. I called him back, closed the gate, and felt Spot's raspy tongue on the back of my hand. I shouted at him and he paced away with injured dignity, his ears back at half-mast. How could I explain it to him? I knew he was enjoying the salt taste of sweat that ran down my arm in defiance of the breeze off Mount Diablo. It might have been worse: some guys get migraines. I'd known one—a good one, too, in my business—who'd developed spastic colon. All I do is sweat, without apologizing. You can't explain fear to a cheetah . . .

I spent the next hour selecting my own kit. In any dangerous business, a man's brains and his equipment are of roughly equal quality. Nobody has yet worked out a handier field ration than "gorp," the dry mix of nuts, fruit bits and carob I kept—but I tossed in a few slabs of pemmican, too. Water, spare socks, a McPhee paperback, and my usual stock of pills, including the lecithin and choline.

I considered my own handguns for a long time, hefting the Colt Python in a personal debate, then locked the cabinet again and came away emptyhanded. In extremis, my own Colt would've been too great a temptation—and I already had a weapon. Whether it would work was something else again.

When the Porsche was loaded I spent another hour in my office. The maps refreshed my memory, corrected it in a few cases. A new bridge over the American River connected Sacramento's northeast suburb of Orangevale with Highway Fifty, cutting through the dredge tailings. Gooseflesh returned as I imagined the scene at that moment. Dark as a hunter's thoughts, not enough moon to help, the innocent romantic gleam of riffles on water between the tailings to the south and the low cliffs on the north side. More tailings on the other side too, upriver near Orangevale. This night— and maybe others—it would be approximately as quiet, as inviting, as a cobra pit. I pitied anyone in that area, but not enough to strike out for it in the dark. I needed a full day of reconnaissance before setting out my bait, and a good night's sleep wouldn't hurt.

Usually, sleep is no problem. That night it was a special knack. And while I slept, a pair of youthful lovers lay on a blanket near the river, too near the Sac State campus, and very nearly died.

Saturday morning traffic was light on the cutoff to Interstate Five. I refueled just south of Sacramento, then drove across to the El Dorado Freeway and fought the temptation to follow it all the way to Lake Tahoe. A part of my mind kept telling me I should've brought Spot along for his nose and ears, but I liked him too much to risk him.

I left the freeway east of the city and cruised slowly toward the river, renewing auld acquaintance as I spotted the river parkway. Nice: hiking and bridle trails paralleled the drive, flowing in and out of trees that flanked the river. I didn't wonder why the area was deserted until I saw the road crew lounging near their barricade. The flagman detoured me to a road that led me to a shopping center. I checked a map, took an arterial across the river, spotted more barricades and flagmen barring access to the drive along the north bank of the river as well.

That flagman's khakis had been creased; and who irons work khakis these days? Also, he'd been too pale for a guy who did that every day. I found a grocery store and called Stockton from there, cursing.

Dana Martin answered on the first ring, bright and bubbly as nearbeer and twice as full of false promise.

"Hi, you ol' dumplin'," she cascaded past, after my first three words. I stammered and fell silent. "I won't be able to make it today, but you have Wanda's address; she's really dynamite. Why don't you call on her, shug, say around noonish, give or take an hour? Would you mind just terribly?"

I'd worked with Dana enough to know that the vaguer she sounded, the exacter she meant. Wanda at twelve on the dot, then—except that I didn't know the lady or her address. "Uh, yeah, sure; noonish more or less. But I've mislaid her address. You got her phone number?"

Slow, saccharine: "She hasn't got a phone, honeybuns. Must you have a map for such a dynamite lady?"

Map. Dynamite. Ahhh, shee-it, but I was dull. "Right; I must have it somewhere. The things I do for love," I sighed.

Dana cooed that she had just oodles of work to do, and hung up before I could object that the whole god-damn river area was crawling with fuzz in false clothing.

I went back to the Porsche and studied my map. The explosive cache was fairly near a dead-end road, only a few miles downriver. I found the road led me past a few expensive homes to a turnaround in sight of the river. No barricades or khakiclads that I could see, but the damned dredge had committed some of its ancient crimes nearby. I guessed there were so many dead-end roads near the river it would take an army to patrol them all. It was nearly two hours before noon and it occurred to me that the time might best be spent checking available routes to and from the tailings areas.

Shortly before noon I hauled ass from a bumpy road near Folsom and headed for my tryst with Wanda. I'd marked several routes on the map, where I could get very near tailings or sandbars from Sacto to Folsom. It was the sort of data the Feebies couldn't have given me, since they didn't really know what the Porsche could do.

At eleven fifty-three I realized I was going to be late if I kept to the boulevards. I checked my route, turned

right, zipped on squalling tires to a dead end, and
shifted to air cushion mode. A moment later the Porsche
was whooshing over the lawn of some wealthy citizen,
scattering dandelion puffs but leaving no tracks as it
took me downslope and over a low decorative fence.

Using the air cushion there's always the danger of
overspeeding the Porsche's primary turbo, but I kept
well below redline as I turned downriver just above the
ripples. In air cushion mode, the legendary quick response of a Porsche is merely a myth. The car comes
about like a big windjammer and tends to wander with
sidewinds, so I had my hands full. But I navigated five
miles of river in four minutes flat.

Triangulating between bridges, eyeballing the map, I
estimated that the cache of dynamite was at the foot of a
bush-capped stone outcrop that loomed over the river.
I slowed, eased onto a sandbar, let the car settle and
left the turbo idling. At exactly noon by my watch, I
stood over a swirl of bubbly river slime as long and
broad as my kitchen. It had sticks and crud in it, and
reminded me of the biggest pizza in town, which made
my belly rumble. Junk food has its points too.

I was thirty feet from the Porsche, and past my
grumbling gut and the turbo whistle I could hear the
burbling hiss of the river. Nothing else. It was high
noon on a sandbar on a hot Saturday in the edge of
Sacrabloodymento, perfect for a meal and a snooze, and
there I stood feeling properly unnerved, waiting for a
woman to tell, or bring, or ask me something. I put one
hand to my jacket, feeling the automatic in my waistband
for cold-steel comfort, and to nobody at all I shook my
head in disgust and said, "Wanda."

"Mister Rackham," said the voice above me, and I
damned near jumped into the river. He was decked out
in waders and an old fishing vest of exactly the right
shades to blend with the terrain. He had a short spinning rig, and behind the nonglint sunglasses he was
grinning. He'd sat inside those bushes atop that jumble
of rocks and watched me from above the whole time,

getting his jollies. I'd busted my hump to be punctual but judging from this guy's demeanor, fifteen minutes one way or the other wouldn't've mattered. No wonder people learn to scoff at government orders!

He'd done nothing for my mood, or my confidence. I cleared my throat. "Would you mind telling me—" I trailed off.

"I'm Agent Wanda. And there can't be two car-and-mercenary combos like you, *any*where." He didn't climb down but made a longish cast into the river; began to reel in. "New developments," he said casually. "Fortunately all the white noise around us should raise hob with any shotgun mikes across the water."

I waited until he'd reeled in, changed his spinner for another lure, and flashed me the I.D. in his lure wallet as though by accident. Wanda explained that while the decoy action at Lake Berryessa still seemed to be working on the foreign nationals, some of that cover might be wearing thin. The night before, a lovestruck couple had been thoroughly engaged—even connected, one might infer—near the river when something, surely not boredom, added a religious touch to their experience. According to the girl it seemed to be a great guardian angel, suddenly transformed into a moving rock of ages wielding a terrible swift sword.

Agent Wanda broke off to tell me the girl was a devout fundamentalist, evidently a newcomer to the oldest sport, who'd been overcome by her sense of the rightness and safety of it all—until a huge boulder nearby became a winged angel, gave a mighty chuff, flashed a scimitar in the faint moonlight, and glided into the river like a stone again to sink from sight. It left pugmarks. It probably weighed five tons.

To the girl it had been a powerful visitation. To her boyfriend, who also got a set of confused images of the thing, it had been a derailment. But the girl was the niece of the Sacramento County Sheriff who had—and here fisherman Wanda drawled acid—not been told of the security blanket. The girl trusted her uncle, called

him in hysterics. He knew an explosion had taken its
toll at a campus lab, and had heard from Yolo County
where his counterpart had delivered a wild woolly package to another campus, and like any good lawman he
put some things together. By now, elements of the city,
county, state and United States were gradually with-
drawing the cordon of bozos he had deputized and
strung along the river. It was quick action, but far too
obvious to suit the feds. Worse still, the campus radio
station at Sac State had already got an exclusive from
the young man.

School media, Wanda told me, have their own news
stringers and an alternative network in National Public
Radio. When KERS-FM ran its little hair-raiser on
Saturday morning, it scooped the whole country including the FBI. The Feebies had only managed by minutes to quash a follow-up story which, in its usual ballsy
aggressive way, NPR's network headquarters in Washington had accepted from Sacramento. It described a
huge version of the dead specimen, complete with silvery harness and flaming sword. As a dogdays item for
summer consumption, it had almost been aired coast-to-
coast over NPR. It would have blown the government's
cover from hell to lunch. As it was, KERS had already
aired too much of the truth in Sacramento but with TV,
Wanda sighed, fortunately almost nobody listens to NPR.

I resolved, in the future, to pay more attention to
National Public Radio; it was my kind of network. Meanwhile, the national government was drawing off the
protective net along the river, to avoid tipping our hand
to other governments—while casually allowing hundreds
of nature lovers to wander into harm's way. When
officialdom up and down the line conspires to endanger
a thousand people, I reasoned, it must be balancing
them against a whole lot more. Millions, maybe. It was
a minimax ploy: risk a little, save a lot. I began to feel
small, like the lure on the end of Wanda's monofilament line: hurled into deep water and very, very
expendable.

I watched Wanda cast again, the line taking a detour into the deepest part of the channel. "I expect my explosives are under all that crap," I said, jerking a palm toward the slowly wheeling green pizza in the lee of the stone outcrop.

"Sure is. Looks natural, doesn't it? Just grab the edge and pull it in when you need it. It's anchored on a swivel to a weighted canvas bag. And you know what's in the bag."

I stared at the spinning pizza, and damned if it wasn't a work of plastic camouflage. Real debris, polyurethane slime and bubbles, gyrating in an eddy. I said, "Never know what's real along the river, I guess."

"That's the point," Wanda replied, pulling against a snag almost below him. "The hunter was in plain sight last night, not ten meters from those kids, and the girl claims she never felt so safe. Even thought she saw an approving angel for a few seconds."

"Like your man thought he saw his SAC coming through that wall on the campus?"

"Could be," he nodded. "We thought you should know that, and the part about your quarry being at home in the water."

He frowned at the river; his rod bent double until he gave it slack. I touched my sidearm for luck as his line moved sideways, then began a stately upstream progression. "Jesus, I must have a salmon," he said, his face betraying a genuine angler's excitement.

With the bright July sun and the clear sierra water, I saw a dark sinuous shape far below the surface and grinned. I knew what it was; it wasn't salmon time, and salmon don't move with the inexorable pace of a finned log moving upstream. "No, you have a problem," I said. "And so do I, if a gaggle of Soviet tourists come snooping around here in copters."

"Just keep it in mind," said Wanda, scrambling up, reluctantly letting more line out. "Play it safe and don't have a higher profile than necessary." Then, plaintively, as I turned to go: "What the hell do I have here?"

"Sturgeon."

Pause as the upstream movement paused. Then, "How do I land it?"

I nodded toward the plastic pizza. "Try some sixty per cent dynamite. Or wait him out. Some of 'em get to be over ten feet long; don't worry, they're domestic."

He called to me as I trudged to my Porsche: "Domestic, *schmomestic*; what's that got to do with it?"

I called back: "I mean it's not a Soviet sturgeon. At least you needn't worry about catching an alien."

When I drove away he was still crouching there, a perfect metaphor of the decent little guy in a big government, jerking on his rod and muttering helplessly. I kept the Porsche inches off the water en route downriver as far as the county park and thrilled a bunch of sporty car freaks as I hovered to the perimeter road, trying to let the good feeling last. It wouldn't; all the Feebie had to do was cut his line and he'd be free of his problem. All I had to do was unwrap an alien transmitter and my problem would come to me in a hurry. Maybe.

For sure, I wasn't about to do it in full view of a dozen picnickers. I hadn't yet seen a piece of ground that looked right for me, and I'd covered a lot of river. To regain the low profile I drove twenty miles back upriver on the freeway without being tailed, and to exercise my sense of the symbolic I demolished a pizza in Folsom. Thus fortified, I found a secondhand store in the restored Gay Nineties section of Folsom and bought somebody's maltreated casting rig with an automatic rewind. Wanda had been right to use fishing as a cover activity. I was beginning to grow paranoid at the idea of foreign nationals watching me—and drawing sensible conclusions.

I drove from Folsom to a bluff that overlooked the river and let my paranoia have its head as I studied the scene. Somewhere, evidently downriver, lay my quarry. I'd assumed it was nocturnal simply because it hadn't shown in daylight. But for an instant, just before I caught a glimpse of that sturgeon, I'd realized the hunting beast might have been on the other end of Wanda's line. Truly nocturnal? Not proven . . .

I'd also assumed, without thinking it out, that the hunter was strictly a land animal. Scratch another assumption; it apparently could stroll underwater like a hippo. Gills? Scuba?

The report about the sword led me to a still more worrisome train of thought. A saber was hardly the weapon I'd expect from an intelligent alien. What other, more potent, weapons did it carry? Its harness might hold anything from laser weapons to poison gas—unless, like the smaller animal, it too was a pet. Yet there had been no evidence of modern weapons against humans. The fact was, I hadn't the foggiest idea what range of weapons I might run up against.

Finally there was the encounter with the lovers, sacrificial lambs who weren't slaughtered after all. Why? They could hardly have been more vulnerable. Maybe because they were mating; maybe, for that matter, because they *were* vulnerable. All I could conclude was that the hunter did discriminate.

One thing sure: he knew how to keep a low profile with his own vehicle. So where do you hide a fifty-ton spacecraft? Surely not where it can be spotted from the air. The likeliest place seemed to be in the river itself, but I could think of a dozen reasons why that might not be smart. And if the Feebies couldn't track it by satellite from Berryessa to Sacramento, the hunter was either damned smart, or goddamn lucky.

I decided to make some luck on my own by being halfway smart, and eased the Porsche down to the river. It takes less fuel to hover on the water if you're not in a big hurry, and I cruised downstream slowly enough to wave at anglers. Mainly, I was looking for a likely place to spend the night.

A glint from the bluffs told me someone was up there among the trees in heavy cover. Birdwatcher, maybe. From the British Embassy, maybe. I swept across to a banana-shaped island in plain sight and parked, then unlimbered my spinning rig and tried a few casts. I never glanced toward the bluffs and I still don't know if it was perfidious Albion or paranoia that motivated me. But while sitting on a grassy hummock I realized that I couldn't choose a better stakeout than one of these islands.

It required a special effort for me to scrunch through the sand at the water's edge. If I'd weighed five tons it should slow me a lot more. Even a torpedo doesn't move through water very fast; if I chose an island with extensive shallows and a commanding view, I'd have plenty of warning. Well, that was the theory . . .

By the time I'd found my island, the sun was nearing trees that softened the line of bluffs to the west, and dark shadows crept along the river to make navigation chancy. It's no joke if the Porsche's front skirts nose into white water, especially if the turbo intake swallows much of it. I floated upslope past clumps of brush and cut power as my Porsche nosed into tall weeds at the low crest. I stretched my legs, taking the fishing equipment along for protective coloration, and confirmed my earlier decision. It was the best site available.

The island was maybe two hundred yards long; half that in width. Tailings stretched away along both sides of the river. Sand and gravel flanked the island on all sides and the Porsche squatted some twenty feet above the waterline. The nearest shallows were thirty yards from me and, accounting for the lousy traction, I figured Spot might cover the distance in four or five seconds. Surely, surely the hunter would be slower: In that time I could jump the Porsche to safety and put several rounds into a pursuer.

Then I bounced my hand off my forehead and made a quick calculation. If I hoped to be ready for damnall at any second, I absolutely *must not* let the turbo cool down. It takes roughly twelve seconds before the Porsche can go from dead cold to operational temperature, but if I kept it idling I'd be okay. Fuel consumption at idle: ten quarts an hour. I sighed and trudged back to the car, and went back to Folsom and refueled. Oh, all right: and had Oysters Hangtown with too much garlic and synthetic bacon. Hell; a guy's gotta eat.

I cruised back to the island again by way of the tailings. I'd been half afraid the air cushion wouldn't work along those steep piles of river-rounded stone. Now I was all the way afraid, because it only half worked. You can't depend on ground effect pressure when the "ground" is full of holes and long slopes. It was like roller-coasting over an open cell sponge; controlling it was a now-you-have-it, now-you-don't feeling. As sport it could be great fun. As serious pursuit it could be suicide.

Back among the tall weeds atop the island, I let the Porsche idle as I walked the perimeter again, casting with my pitiful used rig now and then for the sake of form. How any trout could be so naive as to hit my rusty spinner I will never know; I played the poor bastard until he finally threw the hook. Ordinarily I would've taken him home for an Almondine. But they spoil fast, and I wasn't planning on any fires, and if Providence was watching maybe it would give me a good-guy point. God knows I hadn't amassed many.

There were no pugmarks or prints in the sand but mine, and the tic tac toeprints of waterbirds. I returned to the Porsche and unwrapped the foil shielding from the rounded gray disc that had already cost too many lives. It was smaller than a hockey puck, featureless but for a mounting nipple. It didn't rattle, hum, or shine in the lengthening shadows, but it had been manufactured by some nonhuman intelligence, and it damned well gave me indigestion. I knew it was broadcasting as it lay in my hand even if I couldn't detect it: calling like unto like, alien to alien, a message of—what? Distress? Vengeance? Or simply a call to the hunt? I imagined the hunter, responding to the call by cruising upriver in its own interstellar Porsche, as it were, and got busy with an idea that seemed primitive even to me, while the light was still good enough to work by.

I cut a pocket from my jacket, a little bag of aramon fiber that held the alien transmitter easily. Then, using a fishhook as a needle, I sewed the bag shut and tied it, judging the monofilament line to be twenty pound test. Finally I jammed the rod into the crotch of a low shrub, took the bag, and walked down the gentle slope kicking potential snags out of the way. I laid the bag in the open, hidden by weeds fifteen yards from the water's edge, and eyeballed my field of fire from the Porsche that whined softly to me from above. It was ready to jump. So was I.

A light overcast began to shoulder the sun over the horizon, softening the shadows, making the transition to darkness imperceptible. I retreated to the car, grumbling. I knew there were special gadgets that Dana Martin's puppeteers could have offered me. Night-vision glasses, mass-detector bugs to spread around, constant two-way tightband TV between yours truly and the feds—the list became a scroll in my head. The trouble was, it *was* all special, the kind of equipment that isn't available to private citizens. The microvid was standard hardware for any TV stringer and its "mayday" module could be removed in an instant. If I wound up as a morgue statistic surrounded by superspy gadgetry, my government connection would be obvious. I didn't know how Dana's SAC would explain the alien hockey puck, but I knew they'd have a scenario for it. They always do.

I cursed myself for retreating down that mental trail, practically assuming failure, which could become a self-fulfilling prophecy. Night birds called in the distance, and told me the whispering whine of my turbo was loud only in my imagination. I released the folding floptop on the Porsche and let it settle noiselessly behind me, something I should have done earlier. I might be more vulnerable sitting in the open, but my eyes and ears were less restricted. My panoramic rearview commanded the upriver sweep, the big-bore automatic was in my hand, and the Porsche's tanks were full—well, nearly full. What was I worried about?

I was worried about that standing ripple a stone's throw off; hadn't it moved? I was spooked by the occasional splash and plop of feeding trout; were they really trout? I was antsy as hell over the idea that I might spend the next eight hours this way, nervous as a frog on a hot skillet, strumming my own nerves like a first-timer on a fruitless stakeout.

Recalling other vigils, days and nights of boredom relieved only by paperbacks and the passing human zoo with its infinitely varied specimens, I began to relax. The trout became just trout, the ripple merely a ripple, the faint billiard-crack of stones across the channel to my left, only a foraging raccoon. Soon afterward, another series of dislodged stones drew my interest. I decided my 'coon was a deer, and split my attention between the tailings and the innocent channel to my right. I'd been foxed once or twice by scufflers who melted away while I was concentrating on a spider or a housecat.

A third muffled cascade of stones, directly across on my left, no more than fifty yards away across the narrow channel. With it came a faint odor, something like a wet dog, more like tobacco. I hoped to see a deer and that's what I saw, the biggest damn' buck I'd ever seen in those parts. It relieved me tremendously as it picked its way down toward the water. Though they're actually pretty stupid, deer know enough to stay well clear of predators. The buck that moved to the shoreline hadn't got that big by carelessness, I figured, which meant that the alien hunter almost certainly couldn't be nearby.

Well, I said "almost." In the back of my mind I'd been hoping to see something like that big buck; some evidence that the locale was safe for the likes of me. He picked his way along the shore, staring across in my general direction. As part of the dark mass of the Porsche among the scrub and weeds, I moved nothing but my eyes, happy to have him for a sentry on my left, and alert for anything that might be moving through the channel to my right.

It took the animal perhaps a minute to disappear up a ravine in the tailings—but long before that I began to feel a creeping dread. It came on with a rush as I strained to see the path of the buck along the water's edge. Where the "buck" had made his stately promenade there was a new trail that gleamed wet in the overcast's reflection from the city, and instead of dainty hoofprints I saw deep pugmarks in the patches of sand. They seemed the size of dinner plates. I had wanted to see something safe, and I had seen it, and somewhere up in the tailings a fresh rumble told me the alien hunter was not far off.

I let the adrenal chill come, balled my fists and shuddered hard. If I couldn't trust my eyes or instincts, whatthehell *could* I trust? My ears; the hallucination had been visual, my eldritch buck larger than life, the clatter of stones a danger sign I had chosen to misinterpret.

I knew that my hunter—and the deadly semantics of that phrase implied "the one who hunted me"—would make another approach. I didn't know when or how. Damning the soft whistle of the turbo, I fought an urge to put my foot to the floor, idly wondering what my traitor eyes would offer next as a talisman of safety. I'd made some new decisions in the past minutes: one, that the first thing I saw coming toward me would get seven rounds of heavy artillery as fast as I could pull the trigger.

I waited. I heard a swirl of water to my right, thought hard of trout, expected a shark-sized rainbow to present itself. Nothing. Nothing visual, at least—but in the distance was an almost inaudible hollow slurp as if someone had pulled a fencepost from muck. I opened my mouth wide, taking long silent breaths to fuel the thump between my lungs, and made ready to hit the rewind stud that would reel in the transmitting bait a few feet. I was leaning slightly over the doorsill, the spinning rig in one hand, the Smith & Wesson in the other, staring toward the dim outlines of weeds near my lure. I saw nothing move.

I could hear a distant labored breathing, could feel an errant breeze fan the cold sweat on my forehead, yet the stillness seemed complete. A cool and faintly amused corner of my mind began to tease me for my terror at nothing.

The truth telegraphed itself to the tip of my spinning rod; the gentlest of tugs, the strike of a hatchery fingerling, and in a silent thunderclap of certainty I realized that despite the breeze I had not seen the high grass move either, was hallucinating the visual tableau. To see nothing was to see safety. Not only that: I felt safe, so safe I was smiling. So safe there was no danger in squeezing a trigger.

I fired straight along the fishing line. Yes, goddammit; blindly, since my surest instinct told me it was harmless fun.

When firing single rounds at night, you're wise to fire blindly anyway. I mean, blink as you squeeze; the muzzle flash blinds anyone who's looking toward it and by timing your blinks, you can maintain your night vision to some extent. In this case, I heard a hell of a lot, thought it all hilariously silly, but still I saw nothing move until after my second blink and the round I sent with it.

The second round hit something important because my vision and my sense of vulnerability returned in a flicker. Straight ahead of me, a great dark silvery-banded shape rolled aside with a mewling growl and crunch of brush, and I knew it would be on me in seconds. I floored the accelerator, hit the reel rewind stud, let the Porsche have its head for an instant holding the steering wheel steady with my knee.

Subjectively it seemed that the car took forever to gain momentum, pushing downslope through that rank tobacconist's odor. I dropped the automatic in my lap to steer one-handed, desperately hoping to recover the tiny transmitter.

As my Porsche whooshed to the water's edge I saw the hunter's bulk from the tail of my eye, its snuffling growl louder than its passage through the brush. I was twenty feet out from the shore when it reached the water and surged into the shallows after me. Only the downward slope of the channel saved me in that moment as the hunter submerged. A flash of something ivory-white, scimitar-curved, and the Porsche's body panel drummed just behind the left front wheel skirt. Then I scooted for the far shore.

I turned upstream at the water's edge, grasping the spinning rig, unwilling to admit that the spring-loaded rewind mechanism had reeled in nothing but bare line. The hunter had taken my lure; now I had no bait but myself. At the moment, I seemed to be enough.

Furious at my own panic, I spun the Porsche slowly so that it backed across the shallows. Apparently I could outrun the hunter, but it wasn't giving up yet. A monstrous bow wave paced me now, a huge mass just below the water. It was within range of my handgun but you can't expect a slug to penetrate anything after passing through a foot of water. I took my bearings again, seeing a sandbar behind me, and hovered toward it.

I saw massive humped shoulders cleave the bow wave, grabbed for my weapon, fired two more rounds that could not have missed, marveled at the hunter's change of pace as it retreated into deeper water. There was nothing for me to shoot at now, no indication of the hunter's line of travel. I angled out across the channel, knowing my pursuer was far too heavy to float and hoping "deep" was deep enough. Every instant I had the feeling that something would lash up through the Porsche's bellypan until I heard the heavy snort from fifty yards downstream. I'd been afraid the damned thing could breathe underwater, but apparently it had to surface for breath just like any mammal. Chalk up one for my side.

Moving far across the sandbar, I settled the car and let it idle, waiting for the next charge, straining to hear anything that might approach. Under the whirl of possibilities in my head lay the realization that the hunter had lost or abandoned its habit of fooling me; since my second shot, my vision and hearing had agreed during its attacks. All the same, I didn't entirely believe my senses when the hunter splashed ashore a hundred yards downriver, bowling over a copse of saplings to disappear into the darkness.

The overcast was my ally, since it reflected the city's glow enough to reveal the terrain. I wondered where the hunter was going, then decided I might follow its wet trail if I had the guts. And since I didn't, that was when I thought of backtracking its spoor.

I traversed the river, guided my car up a tailings slope, cut power to a whisper. Standing to gaze over the windshield I could see where the "deer" had moved over the tailings, leaving a dull dark gleam of moist trail on the stones. In a few minutes the stones would be dry. I spotted more damp stones just below the crest of the tailings ravine and followed.

Hardly half a mile downstream the tail petered out, the stones absorbing or losing their surface moisture. But the trail led me toward a bend in the river, and I could see a set of monster pugmarks emerging from the shallows.

I guessed I'd find more pugmarks directly across the river, but I didn't want to bet my life on it. The hunter could be anywhere, on either side of the river. I estimated that the brute couldn't travel more than thirty miles an hour over such terrain, and knew it had been within fifteen minutes of me when I unwrapped the transmitter. A seven-mile stretch? No, wait: I'd heard its original approach over a period of a minute or two, so it had been moving slowly, cautiously. My hunter had probably been holed up within a couple of miles of me—perhaps in its own vehicle somewhere deep in the river.

The Porsche was not responding well and, climbing out with my weapon ready, I inspected the car for damage. There was only one battle scar on it, but that one was a beaut: a clean slice down through the plastic shell, starting as a puncture the size of a pick-ax tip. It allowed the air cushion skirt to flap a bit behind the wheel well, and it told me that the stories about the hunter's sword hadn't been hogwash.

I tested my footing carefully, moved off from my idling machine, then squatted below the hillock crest so I could hear something besides the turbo. Again there came the lulling murmur of the river, a rustle of leaves applauding a fidget of breeze. No clatter of stones, no sign of stealthy approach. I wondered if I had been outdistanced. Or outsmarted.

A subtle movement in the tailings across the river drew my attention. I wasn't sure, but thought I'd caught sight of stones sliding toward the river. Why hadn't I heard it? Perhaps because it was two hundred yards away, or perhaps because it suggested safety. I obeyed the hackles on my neck and slipped back to the Porsche.

As I was oozing over the doorsill I saw above the rockslide and watched a small tree topple on the dim skyline. An instant later came the snap of tortured green wood; I judged that the hunter was more hurried than cautious. Its wet trail would be fresh. I applied half throttle down the slope, passed across the river near enough to spot telltale moisture climbing the tailings, and gunned the turbo.

Twice I felt the car's flexible skirts brush protruding stones as I moved up the adjoining pile of tailings. I was trying to see everything at once: clear escape routes, dark sinister masses of trees poking up through the stones, my alien adversary making its rush over treacherous footing. When the Porsche dipped into the vast depression I nearly lost control, fought it away from the steep downward glide toward a hidden pool. I wasn't quite quick enough and my vehicle slapped the water hard before shuddering across the surface. I tried to accelerate, felt the vibration through my butt and knew I'd drawn water into the air cushion fans. I'd bent or lost a fan blade—the last thing I needed now. Traveling on wheels was out of the question in this terrain; walking wasn't much better, and if I tried to move upslope again the unbalanced fan might come apart like a grenade.

I brought the Porsche to a stop hovering over water, checking my position. I'd found a big water pocket, one of those places where a rockslide shuts off a small valley in the tailings and, over the years, becomes a dead lake. The tarn was fifty yards or so long, thirty yards wide; the water came up within fifteen yards of the crest. That was a hell of a lot higher than the river, I thought. The stones around the water's edge were darker for a foot or so above the water—whether from old stain or fresh inundation, I couldn't tell. Yet.

I felt horribly vulnerable, trapped there at the bottom of a sloping stone pit, knowing I couldn't be far from an alien hunter. The fan warning light glowed, an angry ruby eye on the dashboard. I let the car settle until its skirts flung a gentle spray in all directions, trying to stay afloat with minimum fan speed. If the fans quit, my Porsche would sink—and if I tried to rush upslope I would blow that fan, sure as hell. Nor could I keep hovering all night. Idle, yes; hover, no.

My own machine was making so much racket, I couldn't immediately identify the commotion coming from somewhere beyond my trap. Then, briefly, came a hard white swath of light through treetops that were just visible over the lip of the pit. A hovering 'copter—and a big one, judging from the *whock-whock* of its main rotors—was passing downriver with a searchlight.

The big machine lent momentum to the hunter: the huge beast came tearing over the lip of my pit in a sudden avalanche of stones large and small, twisting to lie flat, watching back toward a new enemy that shouted its way downriver.

The hunter was simply awesome, a quadruped the size of a shortlegged polar bear with the big flat head of an outsize badger. Around its vast middle, crossing over the piledriving shoulders, ran broad belts that could have been woven metal. They held purses big as saddlebags on the hunter's flanks. The beast's weight was so tremendous that the stones beneath it shifted like sand when it moved suddenly; so powerful that it had plowed a furrow through the tailings crest in its haste to find shelter. But with such a mass it couldn't travel in this terrain fast unless it made a big noise and a furrow to match. It hadn't, until now. Once again I revised my estimate of its den, or vehicle. The hunter couldn't have started toward me from any great distance.

I had a clear field of fire as the searchlight swept my horizon again, but the hunter was fifty yards away; too far to risk wasting a single round. It was intent on the big 'copter and hadn't seen me yet. I gunned the Porsche directly across the water, intending to make one irrevocable pass before angling upslope on my damaged fans toward the river. There should be time for me to empty the Smith & Wesson.

There should have been, but there wasn't.

Alerted by the scream of the turbo and the squall of galled fan bearings, the hunter rolled onto its back, sliding down in my direction, forepaws stretched wide. I saw a great ivory blade slide from one waving forepaw, a retractable dewclaw as long as my forearm, curved and tapered. The hunter scrambled onto its hind legs, off-balance on the shifting stones but ready for battle.

I wrenched the wheel hard, trying to change direction. Crabbing sideways, the Porsche slid directly toward certain destruction as the hunter hurled a stone the size of my head. I was already struggling upright, trying to jump, when the stone penetrated body panels and cannoned into the chassis.

I think it was the edge of my rollbar that caught me along the left breast as the Porsche shuddered to a stop under the staggering impact. That was when the forward fan disintegrated and I fell backward into the pool. Blinding pain in my left shoulder made me gasp. I shipped stagnant water, also lost my grip on the weapon in my right hand, but surfaced a few yards from the great beast. It was at the pool's edge as I raised the Smith & Wesson, but the convulsion of my spluttering cough made me duck instead of firing.

The hunter had another stone now, could have pulped me with it, but poised motionless over me; immeasurably powerful, looming too near to miss if it chose to try. I jerked a glance toward the Porsche, which had slowly spun on its aft fan cushion toward deeper water before settling into the stuff. My car began to sink, nose tilted down, and the hunter emitted a series of loud grinding clicks as it watched my car settle. It didn't seem to like my car sinking any better than I did.

Since I'd originally intended to simply immobilize the brute, why didn't I fire again? Probably because it would've been suicide. The hunter held one very deliberate forepaw out, its palm vertical, then lobbed the stone behind me. It was clearly a threat, not an attack; another stone, easily the size of a basketball, was tossed and caught for my edification. When the dewclawed paw waved me nearer, I came. There was really no choice. The effort to swim made my shoulder hurt all the way down to my belly, and the grating of bone ends told me I had a bad fracture.

The damned shoulder hurt more every second and, standing in the shallows now, I eased my left hand into my belt to help support my useless left arm. No good. Without releasing the drenched Smith & Wesson which might or might not fire when wet, I ripped a button from my shirt and let the gap become a sling. Not much better, but some. The hunter towered so near I was blanketed by the rank bull durham odor; could actually feel the heat of its body on my face.

Again the hunter slowly extended both forepaws, digits extended, palms vertical. There was enough cloud reflection for me to see a pair of flat opposable thumbs on each paw, giving the beast manipulation skills without impeding the ripping function of those terrible middle digits.

I stuck the pistol in my belt and held up my right hand, and not all of my trembling was from pain. But I'd got it right: my enemy had signaled me to wait. I was willing enough. Just how much depended on that mutual agreement, I couldn't have imagined at that moment; I figured it was only my life.

Still moving with care and deliberation, the hunter retracted the swordlike dewclaw and fumbled in a saddlebag, bringing forth a wadded oval the thickness of a throw rug. It glowed a dim scarlet as it unfolded and became rigid, two feet across and not as flimsy as it had looked. Around the flat plate were narrow detents like a segmented border. I squinted at it, then at the bulk of the hunter.

The glow improved my vision considerably; I could see three smallish lumps through the bristly scant fur of the hunter's abdomen, and a greatly distended one, the thickness and length of my thigh, ending in a pouch near the hind legs. I took it to be a rearward-oriented sex organ. In a way, I was right.

The hunter sat back with a soft grunt, still looming over me, watching with big eyes set behind sphincter-like lids. I didn't make a move, discounting the sway when I yielded to a wave of pain.

The hunter propped the glowing plate against one hind leg and ran its right "hand"—obviously too adroit to be merely a paw—along the edge of the plate. I saw a slow rerun of myself squinting into my own face, looking away, trying not to fall over. It made me look like a helpless, waterlogged fat man.

Then the display showed a static view of me, overlaid by others, as a series of heavy clicks came from the plate. The picture became a cartoonish outline of me. After more manipulation by the hunter, the cartoon jerkily folded into a sitting position. The hunter looked at me, thumbed the margin of the plate again. The cartoon sat down again. So did I.

The hunter placed its left "hand" to its chest and made a big production of letting its eyelids iris shut.

"What the hell does that mean," I said.

Instantly the eyes were open, the dewclaw extended and waving away in what I took to be a slashing negation.

I knew one sign: "wait." I raised my empty hand, palm out, and thought hard. Humans have a lot of agreed-upon gestures that seem to be based on natural outcomes of our bodies and their maintenance. But we're omnivores. Pure predators, carnivorous like the great cats, have different gestural signs. I didn't *know* the hunter was in either category but you've got to start somewhere.

I cudgeled my memory for what I'd read of the ethologists, people like Tinbergen and van Iersel and Lopez, whose books had helped me live with a cheetah. The slashing motion was probably a mimed move of hostility, a rejection. Maybe it was hunterese for "no."

To test the notion, I made an obvious and slow gesture of reaching for the automatic in my belt. The eyes irised, the dewclaw slashed the air again as easily as it could have slashed me. I started to say something, suddenly suspected that the hunter didn't want me to talk. I remembered something about speech interfering with gestural language, then pointed to the weapon with my finger and made a throwing-away gesture of my own.

Distinctly and slowly in the red glow, the hunter folded its left hand to its breast and closed its eyes in a long blink. I brought my good hand to my breastbone and blinked in return. It made sense: if an intelligent predator closes its eyes and withdraws its natural weapon from sight, that compound gesture should be the opposite of hostility. Unless I was hopelessly—maybe fatally—wrong, I had signs for "no" and "yes" in addition to "wait."

The hunter's next attempt with the display took longer, with several evidently botched inputs. It seemed to breathe through a single sphinctered nostril in its muzzle, and the snuffling growl of its breath was irregular. I began to wonder if any of those drugged bullets was having an effect; tried not to cough as I watched. My chest hurt, too—not with the spectacular throb of my collarbone but enough to make me short of breath.

The dimness of the display suggested that the hunter could see infrared, including the heat signatures of prey, better than I could. That display was now showing a cartoon of the hunter and of me, gesturing, while clouds of little dots migrated from each head to the other. Germs? Were we infecting each other?

The hunter pointed a thumb at the display. Sign: "yes." Then the display, under the hunter's guidance, stopped the gestures and the dots flowing from my side. The next cartoon was pellucid and coldblooded, as the figure of the hunter slashed out at the me-figure. The human part of the display disintegrated into a shapeless mass of dots. The hunter tapped the display plate and signed, "no."

If the hunter wanted those dots to pass between us, they must mean something useful. If not germs, then what? If I stopped gesturing, the dots stopped. Uh-huh! The dots were communications; messages. There was an assumption built into the display sequence: it assumed that our brains were in our heads. For all I'd known, the hunter's brain might've been in its keester.

So I was being warned to cooperate, to talk or I'd be dead meat. I signed "yes" twice and coughed once, tasting salt in my mouth.

The display went blank, then showed the hunter sketch without me. Not alone, because from its bulging pouch a small hunter's head protruded, biting on the prominent sex organ of the big beast. Not until then did I harbor a terrible surmise. I pointed from the display to the hunter, and I was close enough that I could point specifically at the big swollen organ.

She lifted the long dribbling teat from her pouch, and she signed, "yes."

She. Oh sweet shit. The hunter was a huntress, a female with a suckling babe, and I'd mistaken the lone functioning teat for a male organ. But she had no suckling babe, as she indicated by patting the empty pouch. No, and she wouldn't ever have it again. The little one had been an infant, not a pet. It hadn't been entirely our fault but I felt we, the human race, stumblebums of the known universe, had killed it. Or let it kill itself, which was almost as bad.

My fear of the revenge she might take—and a pang of empathy for a mourning mother of any species—conspired to make me groan. That brought on a cough, and I ducked my head trying to control the spasm because it hurt so goddamn much to cough. I wasn't very successful. Luckily.

When I looked up again, the huntress was staring at me, her head cocked sideways in a pose that was almost human. Then she spread the short fur away from her belly with both hands and I saw a thick ooze of fluid that matted the fur there. When she pointed at the weapon in my belt, then at the puncture wound, I knew at least one slug had penetrated her flesh. But it might have been from the guy she'd met with the new rifle. Not likely: she had specifically indicated my weapon. When she ducked her head and grunted, I cocked my own head, waiting. She repeated the charade, complete with the series of coughing grunts and ducked head, as if imitating me.

By God, she *was* imitating me. It didn't take a Konrad Lorenz to know when an animal is in pain, and she was generating a sign for "hurt" that was based on my own behavior.

I signed "yes." Staring at the woven belt that bandoliered over her shoulders, I saw that another slug had been deflected by a flat package with detent studs— pushbuttons for a big thumb. The studs were mashed, probably deformed by the slug's impact, and while I may never know for sure, I suspect that little package had been responsible for the hallucinations before I put it out of commission.

The huntress was punching in a new display. Images

fled across the screen until she had the one she wanted, a high-resolution moving image. Somehow I knew instantly it was a family photo, my huntress lounging on a sort of inflated couch while another of her species, slightly smaller and with no pouch, stood beside her leaning on a truly monstrous dewclaw like a diplomat on his umbrella. Proud father? I think so. He—it—was looking toward the infant that suckled in her protective custody.

The huntress pointed at her breast, then at the image to assure me that the image was indeed of her.

I gave a "yes," managing to avoid another cough which could have been misinterpreted. I was beginning to feel cold; on hindsight I suppose it was mild shock. If I fainted, I'd stop communicating. The huntress had made it very clear what would happen if I stopped communicating.

From a saddlebag she drew the little transmitter she'd stolen back from me, still in the sewn-up pocket. She developed a cartoon of the disc, gestured to show it represented the real one, adjusted the display. The disc image floated across the display to the now-still-shot of the infant. She stared at me, unmoving.

Of course I understood. I signed "yes."

She patted her empty pouch, held both hands out, drew them toward her. In any language, a bereft mother was imploring me for the return of her baby.

I signed "no," then gritted my teeth against the fit of coughing that overtook me, and this time I knew the salt taste was blood in my throat. When I looked up, I knew the cough had saved my life; the dewclaw was an inch from my belly, and she was dribbling something like dark saliva from her fanged mouth while she insisted "yes," and "yes" again.

I ducked my head and formally grunted. I was hurt, I was sorry. I pointed to the image of the infant hunter, made the negative sign again, again the sign for my pain. Anguish can be mental, too; we seemed to agree on that.

She withdrew the threatening scythe, wiped her

mouth, changed the display again. Now it was an image of the infant with an image of me. Expectant stare.

I denied it, pointing off in the distance. She quickly multiplied the image of me, made them more slender. Other men had her baby? I agreed.

She showed another swarm of dots moving between her baby and the men's images, waited for my answer.

Negative. Her baby wasn't communicating with us. I don't know why I told the truth, but I did. Eventually she'd get around to the crucial question. If I lied she might take me hostage. If I told the truth she might mince me. She sat for a long moment, swaying, staring at me and, if the dark runnel meant what I think it did, sobbing. I also think she was as nearly unconscious as I was.

At last she fumbled the display into a single outline of her baby, then—with evident reluctance—made an adjustment. The image collapsed into shapeless fragments.

I started to make the "pain" sign, but it developed into the real thing before I could recover. Then I signed "yes." Her baby was dead.

She tucked her muzzle into forearms crossed high, soft grinding clicks emanating from—I think—some head cavity, swayed and snuffled. Not a message to me or anyone else. A deeply private agony at her loss.

My next cough brought enough blood that I had to spit, and I put one hand out blindly as I bowed to the pain. I felt a vast enveloping alien hand cover my own, astonishingly hot to the touch, and looked up to find her bending near me. Her tobaccolike exhalation wasn't unpleasant. What scared me was the sense of numbness as I tried to get my breath. I slumped there as she withdrew her big consoling hand, watched dully as she pointed to the image of the infant's remains.

She motioned that she wanted the body. I thought if I stood up, I could breathe. I signed "yes" and "no" alternately, then tried an open-handed shrug as I struggled to my feet. It helped, but even as I was making the sign for her to wait, she kept insisting. Yes, yes, give me my baby. The big dewclaw came out. I couldn't blame her.

But the way I could get her baby back was by calling a mayday, and my microvid with its transmitter was in the sunken Porsche. As I turned, intending to gesture into the pool, I saw that the Porsche hadn't completely sunk after all, was floating still. Maybe I could find the microvid. I stumbled backward as the huntress lurched up to stop me, signing negation with murderous slashes.

She came as far as the shallows, erect, signing for me to wait as I kicked hard in the best one-armed side-stroke I could manage. I was giddy, short of breath, felt I wasn't going to make it; felt the grating in my collar-bone, told myself I *had* to, and did.

My next problem was getting into the car and, as my feet sank, they touched something smooth below the car. My mind whirled, rejecting the idea that the bottom was only two feet down. But a faint booming vibra-tion told me the bottom was hollow. Then I knew where the huntress kept her vehicle. My Porsche had settled squarely atop an alien ship, hidden beneath the surface of that stagnant pool.

I got the door open, sloshed inside, managed to find the microvid with my feet and brought it up from the floorboards with my good hand, coughing a little blood and a lot of water. The car's running lights worked even if the headlights were under water, and I found the mayday button before I aimed the gadget toward the huntress. She had staggered back to shore, dimly lit by the glow of the Porsche's rear safety lights, and was gesturing furiously.

As near as I could tell, she was waving me off with great backhanded armsweeps. She pointed down into the pool, made an arc with her dewclaw that ended in a vertical stab. I could barely see her but thought I understood; it wouldn't be healthy for me to stay there when she lifted off. I agreed and signed it, hoping her night vision could cope with my message, showing her my microvid and signing for her to wait.

The last I saw of her, the huntress was slowly advancing into the depths of the pool. She was signing, "No! Clear out."

I wanted to leave, but couldn't make my muscles obey. I was cold, freezing cold; bone-shivering, mind-numbing cold, and when I collapsed I lost the microvid over the side.

Not far out from the Porsche, a huge bubble broke the surface, a scent of moldy cavendish that must have come from an alien airlock. *They aren't really all that different from us,* I thought, and *I wish I could've told somebody that and ohjesus I can feel a vibration through the chassis. Here we go . . .*

Olfactory messages have got to be more basic than sight or sound. By the smell of starch and disinfectant, I could tell I was in a hospital long before I could make sense of the muttered conversation, or recognize that the buttercup yellow smear was featureless ceiling. In any case, I didn't feel like getting up right then.

Just outside my private room in the hall, a soft authoritative female voice insisted that she would not be pressured into administering stimulants at this time, exclamation point. Rackham had bled a lot internally from his punctured lung, and the ten-centimeter incision she'd made to reposition that rib was a further shock to his system, and for God's sake give the man a chance.

Other voices, one female, argued in the name of the national interest. If the good doctor watched newscasts, she knew Harvey Rackham was in a unique position vis-a-vis the human race.

The doctor replied that Rackham's position was flat on his arse, with a figure-eight strap holding his clavicle together and a pleurovac tube through his chest wall. If Miz Martin was so anxious to get stimulants into Rackham, she could do it herself by an old-fashioned method. Evidently the doctor had Dana Martin pegged; that was the first time I ever knew that caffeine can be administered as a coffee enema.

A vaguely familiar male cadence reminded the doctor that Rackham was a robust sort, and surely there was no real risk if his vital signs were good.

The doctor corrected him. Vital signs were only good considering Rackham's condition when the chopper brought him in. His heartrate and respiration were high, blood pressure still depressed. If he carried twenty less kilos of meat on him—at least she didn't say "flab" —he'd be recovering better. But the man was her patient, and she'd work with what she had, and if security agencies wanted to use Rackham up they'd have to do it after changing physicians. Then she left. I liked her, and I hadn't even seen her.

Dana Martin's trim little bod popped into view before I could close my eyes; she saw I was awake. "Harve, you've given us some anxious hours," she scolded cutely.

I'd heard some of that anxiety, I said, and flooded her with questions like the time of which day, how long would I be down, where was the alien, did they know it was a female.

"Hold on; one thing at a time, fella." Scott King stepped near, smiling, welcoming me back as if he meant it. Scotty, Dana's area SAC, was an ex-linebacker with brains. I'd met him years before; not a bad sort, but one who went by the book. And sometimes the book got switched on him. From his cautious manner I gathered he was thumbing through some new pages as he introduced me to Señor Hernan Ybarra, one of the non-permanent members of the U.N. Security Council. Ybarra, a somber little man in a pearl-gray summer suit that must have cost a fortune, showed me a dolorous smile but was barely civil to the two Feebies, managing to convey that there was nothing personal about it. He just didn't approve of the things they did for a living.

I put my free hand out, took Ybarra's. I said, "Security Council? Glad to meet a man with real clout."

The eyes lidded past a moment's wry amusement. "A relative term," he assured me. "Our charter is to investigate, conciliate, recommend adjustments, and—" one corner of his mouth tried to rebel at the last phrase, "—enforce settlements."

"What's wrong with enforcement, *per se?* I've been in the business myself."

With softly accented exactness: "It is an egregious arrogance to speak of *our* enforcing a Sacramento settlement."

"The clout is with the hunting people," Dana chimed in, patting my hand, not letting it go. Her sex-appeal pumps were on overdrive, which meant she was on the defensive.

I let her think I was fooled. "Hunting people? You've found more, then?"

"They found us," King corrected me, "while we were draining that sinkhole in the middle of the night. Smart move, immobilizing that shuttle craft by parking on it. We owe you one."

I thought about that. "The huntress didn't lift off, then," I said, looking at King for confirmation.

A one-beat hesitation. "No. Paramedics realized you were lodged on top of something when they found you. The most important thing, right now, is whether you had any peaceful contact with the female hunter before you zapped each other."

"Is anybody taping us now?"

Ybarra and King both indicated their lapel units with cables snaking into coat pockets. "Rest assured," King said laconically.

I told them I'd managed a couple of lucky hits with the medicated slugs. When I mentioned that the visual hallucinations and the shallow whatthehell feeling stopping after I hit a piece of the huntress's equipment, a sharp glance passed between Ybarra and King.

"So: it would seem not to be an organic talent," Ybarra mused with relief. "Go on."

I gave a quick synopsis. The hovercraft that passed downriver—chartered by Chinese, Ybarra told me—, the way I'd managed to get myself walloped when falling from my Porsche, my sloppy sign language with

the huntress, my despairing retreat to the half-sunken
car to find my microvid.

"So you made no recording until you were safely
distant," Ybarra muttered sadly, sounding like a man
trying to avoid placing blame. "But still you were making sign language?"

"Mostly the huntress was doing that. She wanted me
the hell out of there. I wanted to, believe me."

King, in hissing insistence: "*But where is the microvid
unit?*"

"You'll find it in the pool somewhere," I said. The
shrug hurt.

King shook his head. "No we won't. Maybe the hunting people will." At my glance he went on: "Pumping
out the pool must have given them a fix. They came
straight down like a meteorite and shooed us away
before dawn this morning. No point in face-to-face negotiation; anybody that close, acts like he's on laughing
gas. But they've been studying us a while, it seems."

"How'd they tell you that?"

"Clever system they have," Ybarra put in; "a computer-
developed animation display that anyone can receive on
VHF television. The hunting people make it clear that
they view us as pugnacious little boys. The question
before them, as we understand it, is whether we are
truly malign children."

"You can ask the huntress. She's reasonable."

"That is what we cannot do," Ybarra said. "They
acknowledge that the female came here mentally
unbalanced."

Scotty King broke in, waving his hand as if dispos-
ing of a familiar mosquito: "Spoiled young base com-
mander's wife; serious family argument. She takes their
kid, steals a jeep, rushes off into cannibal country. Kid
wanders off; distraught mother searches. Soap opera
stuff, Harve. The point is, they admit she was nuts."

"With her baby dead from cannibal incompetence," I
added, spinning out the analogy. "Who *wouldn't* be half
crazy? By the way, what base do they command?"

King looked at Ybarra, who answered. "Lunar farside; the Soviets believe their site is just beyond the libration limit in the Cordillera chain. The hunting people are exceedingly tough organisms and could probably use lunar mass to hide a fast final approach before soft-landing there."

"You don't have to tell me how tough they are," I said, "or that we reacted like savages—me included."

"It is absolutely vital," Ybarra said quietly, "that we show the hunting people some sign that we attempted a friendly interchange. If we cannot, our behavior is uniformly bad in their view. Some recording of your sign talk is vital," he said again.

"Find the microvid. Or bring me face to face with the huntress, since she didn't lift off after all." I brightened momentarily, trying to be clever. "The vital signs are hers, after all."

Silence. Stolid glances, as Dana withdrew her hand.

"You may as well tell him," Ybarra husked.

"I wouldn't," Dana warned. She knew me pretty well.

Scotty King: "It took a half-hour to find you after your mayday, Harve; and two hours more to pump the water down to airlock level. The female had turned on some equipment but she never tried to lift off. There were no vital signs when we reached her."

Dana Martin cut through the bullshit. "She's dead, Rackham. We don't know exactly why, but we learned that much before their second ship came barreling in."

I made fists, somehow pleased at the fresh stabbing twinge through my left shoulder. "So I killed her. No wonder you're afraid of a global housecleaning."

King: "Not much doubt they could do it."

"And they might exercise that option," Ybarra added, "without a recording to verify your story."

Dana Martin sought my gaze and my hand. "Now you see our position, and yours," she said, all the stops out on her Wurlitzer of charm.

I pulled my hand away. "Better than you do," I

growled. "You people have taped this little debriefing.
And the flexible display the huntress used seemed to
have videotape capability, or it couldn't have developed
an animation of me on the spot. She was taping, too,
out there on the rockpile."

King, staccato: "Where is her recording?"

"Ask the hunting people." My voice began to rise
despite my better judgment. "But don't ask anything
more from *me*, goddamn you! Take your effing debrief
tape and run it for the hunting people. Or don't. Just
get out and leave me alone."

Scott King cleared his throat and came to attention.
"We are prepared, of course, to offer you a very, very
attractive retainer on behalf of the State Department—"

"So you can pull more strings, hide more dynamite,
slip me another weapon? Get laid, Scotty! I've had a
gutful of your bloody mismanagement. My briefings
were totally inadequate; your motives were short-sighted;
the whole operation was half-assed, venal and corrupt."

Dana abandoned the cutesypie role; now she only
looked small and cold and hard. "How about your own
motives and venality?"

"Why d'you think I'm shouting," I shouted.

King became stiffly proper. "Let me get this straight
for the record. You won't lift a hand for the human race
because you're afraid to face the hunting people again."

"Don't you understand *any*thing, asshole? I'm not
afraid: I'm *ashamed!* That grief-stricken predator showed
more respect for life processes than all of us put together. In the most basic, vital way—the huntress was
my friend. You might say yes when your friend says no,
but once you've agreed to defer a selfish act you've
committed a friendly one."

Ybarra had his mouth ready. "Don't interrupt," I
barked. "The first agreement we made was to hold
back, to confer; to wait. I know a cheetah named Spot
who wouldn't waste a second thought on me if he
thought I'd had anything to do with killing one of his
kits. He'd just put me through Johnny Rubeck's machine. And I wouldn't blame him."

Ybarra's face revealed nothing, but King's was flushed. "You're inhuman," he said.

"Jesus, I hope so," I said, and jerked my thumb toward the door.

Well, I've had a few hours to think about it, mostly alone. What hurts a lot more than my collarbone is the suspicion that the huntress waited for me to clear out before she would move her ship. Okay, so she'd wasted some lives in her single-minded desperation to recover her child. In their ignorance those killed had been asking for it. Me? I was begging for it! It was no fur off her nose if I died too, and she was lapsing into a coma because I'd shot her full of drugs that may have poisoned her, and other humans had used her own baby's tissues to fashion weapons against her. And there she sat, for no better reason than an uncommon decency, waiting. And it killed her.

It's bad enough to get killed by enmity; it's worse to get it through friendship. In my friend's place, I know what I'd have done, and I don't like thinking about that either. When you're weak, waiting is smart. When you're strong, it's compassion. Compassion can kill you.

As soon as I get out of here I'm going into my smithy in the shadow of Mount Diablo and pound plowshares for a few weeks, and talk to Spot, and mull it over.

If I get out of here. Nobody seems very anxious to stick to the hospital routines; they're all watching the newscasts, essentially doing what I'm doing.

What the hunting people are doing.

Waiting.

the Sun to a paroxysm of fury. All will die. There can be no escape—except, possibly, for a very few. *This is their story.* 656 pp. • 65630-9 • $4.50 _____

KILLER STATION—Earth's first space station *Pleiades* is a scientific boon—until one brief moment of sabotage changes it into a terrible Sword of Damocles. 55996-6 • 384 pp. • $3.50 _____

THE MESSIAH STONE—"An unusual thriller . . . not only in subject matter, but in the fact that the author claims that the basic idea behind the book is real! [THE MESSIAH STONE] concerns the possession of a stone; the person who controls the stone rules the world. The last such person is rumored to be Adolf Hitler. . . . Harrowing adventure and nonstop action."—*Science Fiction Review.* 65562-0 • 416 pp. • $3.95 _____

ZOBOA—It started with the hijacking of four atomic bombs, and ended with the Space Shuttle atop a pillar of fire. . . . "From the marvelous, cinematic opening pages, Caidin sweeps the reader along in a raucous, exciting thriller."—*Publishers Weekly* 65588-4 • 448 pp. • $3.50 _____

To order these Baen Books, check each title selected and return with a check or money order for the combined cover price. Send to Baen Books, 260 Fifth Avenue, New York, N.Y. 10001.

Distributed by Simon & Schuster
1230 Avenue of the Americas • New York, N.Y. 10020

TRAVIS SHELTON
LIKES BAEN BOOKS
BECAUSE THEY TASTE GOOD

Recently we received this letter from Travis Shelton of Dayton, Texas:

> *I have come to associate Baen Books with Del Monte. Now what is that supposed to mean? Well, if you're in a strange store with a lot of different labels, you pick Del Monte because the product will be consistent and will not disappoint.*
>
> *Something I have noticed about Baen Books is that the stories are always fast-paced, exciting, action-filled and seem to be published because of content instead of who wrote the book. I now find myself glancing to see who published the book instead of reading the back or intro. If it's a Baen Book it's going to be good and exciting and will capture your spare reading moments.*
>
> *Another discovery I have recently made is that I don't have any Baen Books in my unread stacks—and I read four to seven books a week, so that in itself is a meaningful statistic.*

Why do *you* like Baen Books? Drop us a letter like Travis did. The person who best tells us what we're doing right—and where we could do better—will receive a Baen Books gift certificate worth $100. Entries must be received by December 31, 1987. Send to Baen Books, 260 Fifth Avenue, New York, N.Y. 10001. And ask for our free catalog!